DEADLY RECKONING

A KATE REID NOVEL
BOOK 8

ROBIN MAHLE

HARP HOUSE PUBLISHING, LLC.

Published by HARP House Publishing

March, 2018 (1st edition)

1

The old Datsun pickup blew through the narrow lane that snaked between the tall trees. Scattered leaves on the ground whirled in the truck's wake as they'd fallen from the branches that were arched over the road.

They were the bitter remains of a cold December and as January arrived, it did nothing but prolong the dormant landscape. And in Crown Pointe, Kentucky, the small town that once thrived on a booming mining industry, bitter spirits were all that remained. This was especially true for Tommy Conroy, who was behind the wheel, and Joanne Waverly, a young couple trapped in a dying town.

With shaky hands, Joanne counted the money again, laying out each bill on her legs that were clothed in ripped jeans. "We should've got more." She pushed back her long blonde hair that needed to be washed.

"They ran out of pop. What were we supposed to do? What we should've done was get there earlier." Tommy kept his foot on the gas as he glanced at the money.

To some people in this town, mostly forgotten by the rest of the country, pop was a hot commodity. Once a month when the food stamps arrived, or EBT cards were reloaded, the grocery chain stores marked down their cases of pop. Those with stamps who were lucky enough to arrive before the stock disappeared cleaned out the inventory. The idea then was to sell off the cases to the smaller mom and pop grocery stores for cheaper than wholesale. The end result was a roughly 50 cents on the dollar return in cold hard cash. And voila, cash for food stamps. That was how they got the money to buy the drugs. It was mainly opioids but heroin was a fine substitute and was becoming cheaper than the pills anyway.

"It's gonna have to be enough." Tommy continued driving toward the hills. "Besides, we're almost there, so just keep your shit together. You're getting agitated and your nose is running."

Joanne used the back of her hand to wipe her nose, darting an angry glare at Tommy. "Yeah? Maybe you should drive faster in this piece of shit truck of yours."

"You wanna walk?" he shot back.

She peered through the passenger window. "Just hurry is all."

He turned onto the unpaved path that led to the cabin near the edge of town. "We're here, all right?" The small pickup rolled to a stop behind an old Chevy Caprice. He grabbed the gear shift and put it in park before cutting the engine. "You just let me do the talking. I can already see you ain't right. And we got no one else to go to right now."

"Fine." Joanne opened the door in a huff and stepped out.

He walked around the pickup, pulling up his sagging jeans and adjusting his grey hoodie. "I'll tell you what, why don't you just sit tight here? I'll go inside. Better that way. We don't know these people and it's best if they don't see both of us."

"Fine. I'll wait. It's cold as shit out here anyway." She stepped back into the truck and watched Tommy approach the front door. Through glassy eyes, she noticed the door open but the person inside was nothing more than a silhouette. Tommy disappeared beyond the threshold.

Joanne picked at her fingernails, fidgeted with the radio, and wiped her nose until it turned red. The eternity of his exit was unbearable until finally she spotted him again. With a smile on his face, he made his way toward the car. Relief was coming for her and just in the nick of time.

Joanne pulled up from her slumped position with anticipation. As he drew near, though, her brow furrowed. A man unfamiliar to her followed Tommy. She raised her chin at him as if to bring to his attention that he wasn't alone. What frightened her most of all was the look on the man's face. Had Tommy cheated him somehow?

Tommy picked up on her gesture and turned around. From inside the truck, Joanne spotted the man raise a bat overhead. And just as quickly as the bat appeared, it crashed down against the side of Tommy's skull. The thwack echoed in her ears. "No!" She braced herself against the passenger door.

The force of the blow knocked Tommy to the ground and he disappeared from her view. The man now headed straight for her. She scrambled to crawl into the driver's seat. The key was still in the ignition, an act that just might save her life. But in her panicked state, she fumbled with the gearshift. Shaking and screaming, she tried to start the engine. Joanne peered through the windshield, hoping Tommy might rise up, but he hadn't. If she wanted to live, she had to leave him behind.

At last, the engine turned and rumbled. With her hand on the gear shift, she thrust the small pickup into reverse, grinding the gears. Next to her, the window shattered. The bat was now inches from her face, painted with Tommy's blood. Another scream ripped from her throat, and then she was silenced.

~

THE FBI's BEHAVIORAL ANALYSIS UNIT (BAU) AT QUANTICO was where Senior Unit Agent Nick Scarborough finished his presentation and turned off the projector. "Duncan, would you mind turning on the lights?" He squinted for a moment when the conference room illuminated. "Thanks. There is one other thing I'd like to mention before wrapping up. I'd like to offer my congratulations to Agent Kate Reid, who has completed her training hours and is now officially part of the BAU team." He nodded to her.

Several months had passed since she had been offered the apprenticeship with Agent Noah Quinn, the BAU's lead profiler. In that time, she completed additional training that was required for all new BAU agents. But that was finished now. She was here and she was one of them. Nevertheless, the question of her acceptance weighed heavily on her mind. The fact that she lived with Nick Scarborough didn't help matters. Nepotism rumors ran through the ranks. Quinn, her new supervisor, had made her feel welcomed but she believed the other team members still reserved judgment. Perhaps watching her work a case would sway them but to date, nothing had come down the pike except for consultations with a few FBI field offices. It wasn't like the Washington Field Office where she previously worked. It was smaller and much more hands-on, and Kate missed that. She also missed Dwight and Alicia, her former partners. Dwight was now SSA Jameson, the WFO's resident BAU agent, and Agent Alicia Vasquez was essentially second-in-command, as Kate had been until her departure last summer. They were still in need of a third agent but hadn't found the right fit as of yet, at least according to Dwight. Since she left, he'd told her it would be difficult to fill her shoes, but she didn't think so.

"Good job, Reid. Congrats." SSA Cameron Fisher, a New Yorker and perpetual toothpick chewer, was the first to offer a pat on the back. "Welcome aboard." Fisher worked with the field coordinators for the National Center for the Analysis of Violent Crime (NCAVC). A few years older than team leader, Nick Scarborough, the wiry man in his mid-forties stood just shy of six feet. With a pointed chin, ridiculously high cheekbones, and a thick head of graying hair, he was damn good at his job. But then, it took the best of the best to be a part of this team.

Agent Eva Duncan was still a bit of an enigma to Kate. Athletic with long, thick caramel hair and skin to match, she was on the downhill slide to forty, beating Kate to it by about five years, and Kate was a hair's breadth taller. She handled a variety of tasks, from providing expert testimony to assisting field agents with crime analyses. Duncan was the go-to agent and someone Kate should get to know better.

Finally, there was Agent Levi Walsh. And right away, Kate saw something special in him. He had kind eyes, deep blue, that somehow still held wonder in them. The man had seen too much sun, leaving a mild leathery look that would worsen in his later years, though he was just around forty now. The former military man from Alabama was rough around the edges, but there was something attractive about him Kate couldn't exactly place. He was the team's investigative analyst who offered suggestions and guidance to local law enforcement regarding threat response. In other words, in the case of their unit, if a predator was on the loose, Walsh would use Quinn's profile and provide the local police with critical response tactics to protect the public and help track down the unsub.

Kate stood to learn a great deal from all of them and waited for the chance. But her heart lay in profiling, and that was Agent Quinn's job. The younger, baby-faced man, much too refined for her taste, was smart and ambitious. There were things she'd already picked up from him. Things she couldn't quite tell yet if they would be to her advantage or his.

As the others offered their best wishes, it was Quinn who closed out the meeting. "We are very glad to have you here, Reid. It's about time I got some help around here." He smiled as the team broke up and the room cleared. "One second, Reid. You have a minute?"

Kate stopped in her tracks. "Sure."

Quinn waited for her to enter his office and closed the door behind him. "Have a seat." He returned to his desk. "So, now that it's official, I wanted to talk to you about something."

She pulled out a chair and dropped into it. "I'm all ears."

"I was thinking about conducting a study that would broaden our understanding of the mind of a sociopath."

"Okay." It wasn't unusual for a profiler to publish a paper in his field, but Kate couldn't figure out why he was telling her this unless he wanted her to do the leg work.

"I bring this up because I'd like to get your input on a case you were personally involved with."

And now she understood. He wanted to pick her brain about Hendrickson. Kate tucked her brunette hair behind her ear. "Look, I get the curiosity factor, but I've worked exceptionally hard at putting the past behind me. I'm sure you can understand that."

"I do. Absolutely. And I wouldn't want to rehash what you went through."

She crossed her slender legs and folded her hands in her lap. "Good."

"As I understand it, Scarborough asked something similar of you a while ago when you were at the Academy."

Kate measured his persistence with some restraint. "He did. But it was a brief lecture he was giving and I answered a few questions. Which, in hindsight, I wasn't ready for at the time."

"This wouldn't take place in front of any group. This would simply be me asking you questions that could offer further acumen."

"I don't know," Kate began. "To be honest, the fact that this is coming up now when we've been working together for some months is a bit of a surprise."

Quinn appeared mildly guilty, insomuch as he was capable. "The completion of your hours was required before we could do this on the books, so to speak. But hey, I understand and I certainly don't want to put you in a position that makes you at all uncomfortable. I would like to ask that perhaps down the road you might reconsider making such a contribution."

She held his gaze. "I'll consider it. In my own time."

HANDLE'S BAR WAS THE FAVORITE HANGOUT OF THE WFO team. It was also the place Kate met Noah Quinn for the first time, not realizing who he was and humoring him at the behest of Agent Alicia Vasquez. The fact that he'd hit on her way back then was something she still teased him about on occasion. His face turned a light shade of pink at the mere mention of it.

But tonight, Kate was here not as part of the WFO team, but to see her friends who had taken the reins and just wrapped up an investigation—the first one without her. So they were going to celebrate.

"There you are!" Alicia Vasquez stood from the booth. "I

thought maybe you guys got too big for your britches and decided to ditch us." She embraced Kate.

"Never. Just got caught up in traffic." Kate squeezed Alicia as though she hadn't seen her in years when it had only been a few months. "Dwight." Her heart soared at the sight of her friend. She missed him so much. Missed both of them. But she and Dwight shared a special bond and it had been difficult being away from him.

"Hello, gorgeous." Dwight kissed her cheek and turned to Nick. "Good to see you too, brother." A firm handshake followed but not without a pat on the back between the men who also shared a strong bond.

"Feels like old home week," Nick slipped into the booth after Kate. "So, you just closed out a case, I hear."

"You heard correctly." Dwight raised a hand to get the waitress' attention. "What are you drinking?"

"Coke is fine," Nick replied.

"Right." Dwight was only one of two people who knew of Nick's struggle to control his drinking. "Kate, what are you having?"

"A glass of red will do for me, thanks."

"Got it. A Coke and a house red," he said to the waitress. On her departure, he continued. "You're all official-like, now, eh?"

Kate smiled. "That's what they tell me. Guess I'll have to wait till I get that paycheck to know for sure."

Dwight rested his hand on hers as it lay on the table. "I couldn't be prouder of you, Kate."

"Same here, my friend." Alicia held up her glass for a toast. "Here's to getting the gang back together again."

"Congratulations to both of you on your investigation," Nick said. "Couldn't have been easy when you're down a man. Cheers."

"I have a few promising candidates on tap, but this one over here," Dwight glanced at Alicia, "she came through. Her work was invaluable. I couldn't have done it without her."

"Thanks, boss. So, Kate, how's Quinn? Treating you right, I hope?"

"So far so good," Kate replied.

"You ever give him shit about him hitting on you here?"

"Nah." Kate felt compelled to issue the white lie in order to shield Nick.

He eyed her as if he already knew better but dismissed it with a sip of his Coke.

"He did ask me something today, actually," Kate continued. "Something that I thought was a little odd. He asked if I could help him with a study he wanted to conduct. But that it would involve picking my brain about Hendrickson."

"Are you serious?" Concern masked Nick's face. "What did you say?"

"Well, I said it wasn't something I wanted to relive and asked if I could take a pass—for now."

"And was he okay with that?" Dwight asked.

"Seemed to be. Didn't say anything to me after that. Still, you know I've been working around him for several months now and he's never said one word about Hendrickson. Now all of a sudden he's got an interest?"

"Maybe he's just looking to get published. It would do a lot for his career," Nick replied.

"Maybe. Still, kind of a shitty thing to ask someone." Alicia eyed Kate. "And to be honest, it's not like he couldn't find out most things just by reading your file. I mean, come on. The Academy conducts enough psych tests before passing you anyway. There's probably a few hidden gems in there he could expose."

"Thanks, Alicia. I appreciate that." Kate's reply came off a little more sarcastic than she intended.

"I didn't mean..."

"No. It's okay. I'm not bothered by it. Really. Hendrickson is nothing if not an interesting case study. I, of all people, recognize that. But it's just not something I prefer to recall if I don't have to."

The group seemed to shake off the topic, and as the evening wore on, the old team rehashed old stories until the time had come to call it a night.

Nick tossed back the rest of his third soda. "You about ready to head home?"

"Probably should," Kate replied. "I'm sure we all have an early start tomorrow. It was so great seeing you guys. It's been too long. Let's make sure that doesn't happen again."

"Just try to keep us away." Dwight readied himself to leave.

The four of them walked outside, leaving together as they all had so many times before from this bar, only they wouldn't see each other again for a while. It was just the way of things, no matter how good their intentions were.

The valet brought around Nick's car. "Here you go, sir."

"Thank you." He turned to the others. "Thanks again for setting this up. And congratulations to you both. Goodnight."

As they drove away in Nick's luxury SUV, he glanced at Kate from behind the wheel. "That was a lot of fun. It was really good seeing those two again. I miss them."

Kate held her hands near the vent and waited for the air to warm them. "It was fun. I never doubted those two could handle anything that came their way." She noticed he became quiet. "You okay? You really do miss them, don' t you?"

"Oh, it's not that. I mean, I do miss them, but I was just thinking about what Quinn asked you today."

"Already forgotten. It's no big deal. I told him no and he backed off. No pressure."

"I know. It's just that I hope with you there, working for him, he doesn't try to sway you. Honestly, you've got enough on your plate trying to learn the ropes without any added pressure."

"He won't. I've established the boundaries. I don't think he's the type to push beyond them." That remained to be seen. He'd hinted around at things while they were working the Copeland case a few months ago, but she tried to put that in the back of her mind. "Besides, he reminded me that you once did the same thing."

"I did?"

"Yeah. When I first moved here. When I entered the Academy. Remember you asked me to present the Hendrickson case with you?"

He nodded. "Well, yeah. I remember, but how did he know that?"

"I don't know. Must've been in my records somewhere."

Nick peered at the road ahead. "Right."

2

The beefy aroma of reheated meatloaf wafted through the station house. Although, it only mildly camouflaged the musty odor that usually inhabited the space. The Crown Pointe Police Station was housed in a fifty-year-old building in need of some repair, like most of the buildings in this town.

The interior walls were adorned with seventies-style wood paneling, painted white only recently to help conceal their outdated appearance. That was done by the kids from the local high school who wanted to do some good in the community. Despite what many believed, there were still citizens of Crown Pointe who wanted to improve their town.

But for the deputies, which numbered only two, their days consisted mostly of answering calls related to drug overdoses, a few petty thefts, and rising domestic violence. Right now, however, it was lunchtime.

"Peggy makes a hell of a meatloaf." Deputy Shane Lazaro nosed the Tupperware dish with delight as he walked back to his desk. The twenty-three-year-old with kind brown eyes and a goofy smile hailed from Missouri. He moved to Crown Pointe with his wife after her father passed, her mother too frail to be on her own. Now he was a cop in the small town. "You want some? Plenty here."

"No thanks. Got a ham and cheese sandwich waiting for me in the fridge," Deputy Eric Slocum replied. "Guess I could take a break and eat some lunch."

"That there is what they call Pavlov's dog, my friend," Lazaro added.

"Whatever you say." Eric Slocum, a few years older than Lazaro, was born and raised in Crown Pointe and had once been a high school football hero. He hiked up his brown uniform pants and made his way to the break room, but not before the front door burst open. He swung back around.

"Where's Chief Tate?" A woman, harried and panic-stricken, entered the station. Her eyes darted back and forth, her stance wide as if ready to lunge.

"Mrs. Waverly, what's wrong?" Slocum approached her and gently placed his hands on her shoulders. "Calm down and tell us what happened."

Lazaro was already on his feet and waited for whatever it was the woman he knew well had to say.

"It's Joanne. She hasn't been home in two days and I just got a call from Tommy's mother. He hasn't been home either. You have to find them."

"Mrs. Waverly, now I know you understand that Joanne has been prone to going missing on occasion. And she usually turns up after a few days. Don't you think this could be the same thing?" Slocum asked.

"Normally, I'd be inclined to agree with you, Eric, but I don't believe that is the case this time."

"And why is that?" Lazaro asked.

"Because I called Karen and you know how close those two girls are. Like peas in a pod. She said Joanne usually swings by after the checks come out. You know, to do whatever it is those two girls do."

The deputies eyed one another, knowing exactly what it was they did.

"Look, I know how this sounds, but I'm telling you, this is different. Please, I need you both to believe me."

"Okay," Slocum began. "Come sit down over here and tell me everything you know. From the last time you saw Joanne to right now." He led her to his desk.

"I need to see the chief. Please, can't you get him? He'll know what to do," Mrs. Waverly said.

"Let's get a statement from you first. I believe Chief is on a call just now anyway."

She sat down but continued to shake her head. "You know what, no. I'm sorry, Eric. I need to see the chief. This can't wait. I have a God-awful, terrible feeling about this. Please. Now you have to help me find Joanne." Mrs. Waverly stood again and headed toward Chief Tate's office.

"Ma'am." Lazaro followed her. "Ma'am, just hold tight."

"No, I will not." Her voice raised. "Chief Tate?" She knocked on the door. "Can I speak to you please? It's urgent."

"He's on a call. Please come back and sit down." Lazaro took her arm.

"I will not." She ripped it away. "And don't you dare touch me again, you hear me?"

"I'm sorry, ma'am. I didn't mean anything by it." But before he could continue, the chief opened his door.

"What's with the hollering? I had to cut my very important conversation short thanks to all the racket." A towering beanpole of a man, Chief Tate emerged from his office. His middle-aged eyes narrowed with concern.

"I'm sorry, Chief. Mrs. Waverly is here because of her daughter," Lazaro said.

"I see." He peered down at her. "What's going on here, Kim? You looking for Joanne?"

"Yes, sir, I am. I'm sorry for the ruckus, but like I was telling Eric over here, she's been gone too long and it just isn't like her. And her friend Karen said she didn't come by when she was supposed to and I'm just at my wit's end trying to figure out where she's gone."

"Okay. Okay, now. Just calm down and come into my office and tell me everything." The chief led her inside and eyed his men to follow. He returned to his desk, placing his hands atop it, and laced his fingers. "Go ahead and start from the beginning. You say Joanne hasn't been home in a few days?"

"That's right." She briefly scrutinized the deputies, implying they'd been dismissive of her concerns. "Well, you know, the checks came the other day."

The chief nodded.

"And she left with Tommy first thing and hasn't been back since."

"And you say you called Karen Biggs and she hadn't seen her either."

"No, sir. And that's what caused my hackles to raise. That's just real unusual. And then I hear from Tommy's momma and she says he hasn't been home either. So now I'm getting real concerned."

"Course you are." The chief leaned back in his chair. "But you know how Joanne can get sometimes. She's no stranger to the kickers. And with the price going up so high, it's getting harder to find, and so it's entirely possible she and Tommy went out farther to go and get 'em."

"Chief Tate—Henry—I know you think Joanne is some dirt bag drug addict. And maybe you're right. But she's still my daughter. I love her and I think something real bad's happened to her."

"Kim, I do not think for one second Joanne is a dirt bag anything. She's just a young woman who's been struggling. You know how much I care about the people of this community. And how hard it's been trying to stop this epidemic. People around here need my help. And I do not judge. That is something only the Lord Almighty has the right to do. So Eric and Shane will take a drive around town and talk to some people. See if anyone's spotted her or Tommy in the last couple days." He eyed his deputies. "You two think you can get on that this afternoon?"

"Yes, sir, we can," Lazaro replied. "I'm very sorry, Mrs. Waverly. I meant no offense and neither did Deputy Slocum."

"Then it's settled." The chief peered back at Mrs. Waverly. "They'll take a look around and get back with me today. I'll call you if we find anything. I promise." He stood from his desk.

"Thank you, Henry. I sincerely appreciate it." She raised from the chair and turned toward the deputies. "I'm sorry if I was out of line. But I'm sure you can understand my position. If it were your daughter..."

"We understand, Mrs. Waverly," Slocum replied.

They waited for her to leave before the chief spoke again. "You know the drill. Check the usual spots. Ask around. I'm sure we'll find her holed up in Devil's Den, but just do what you can."

"Ten-four, Chief." Slocum patted Lazaro on the back. "Come on, let's go see what we can dig up." He headed out but stopped short and turned back to the chief. "I suspect if we find her, we'll find Tommy Conroy too. If that's the case, should we call up his ma?"

"Well, I guess that depends on what you find. Why don't you just touch base with me first. We'll go from there."

~

Woodbridge, Virginia was where Kate had called home for the past few years after leaving San Diego amid tragedy. With arms wrapped around her for warmth, she leaned against her SUV parked alongside the curb in front of a church near Nick's bayside apartment, a place she now shared with him.

The evening temperature was dropping and her breath was visible in the air. She spotted Nick emerge from the church and walk down the stone steps toward her. "Hey. How was the meeting?"

He shrugged. "Fine. More of the same."

His indifference to the AA meetings was a point of concern. "You don't feel like you're getting much out of them anymore?"

"I suppose I do. It's just... hard. Hard listening to people who were really bad off. And those who still seem to struggle." He kissed her cheek. "I'm ready to get out of here."

"Say no more." She entered the driver's side and waited for him to close the passenger door before pressing the ignition. "I'm still proud of you."

"Don't be. I'm just doing what I should've done a long time ago." He paused for a moment. "But thanks anyway."

Kate pulled away and headed back toward their apartment. "I know it hasn't been easy. I also know you're doing this mostly for me. But I think you should get to the point where you feel like it's more for you, and that it's doing you good."

"I said I'd get help with my drinking and that's what I'm doing." He peered through the passenger window.

"Okay." A change in topic was needed if she wanted to avoid confrontation. "It's nice out tonight. Cold, but clear."

"Uh-huh."

Kate left it alone after that. Nick had been going to AA meetings since she came onboard at the BAU. And while he'd stopped drinking, he also stopped doing much of anything else except work. She figured it would just be a matter of time and he'd come back around. He always did.

"Quinn hasn't said anything to you about me, has he? About the meetings?" Nick asked.

"Of course not. I haven't told anyone. You asked me not to and it's no one's business anyway."

"Yeah. Thanks."

She eyed him again before pulling into the parking garage of their apartment building. "Is there something you're not telling me? You seem really on edge."

He opened his door. "I'm just tired. I don't mean to snap at you."

They were quiet until reaching the apartment. Nick unlocked the door and closed it behind Kate as she entered.

"You hungry?" Kate walked into the kitchen. "I haven't eaten dinner yet. I could whip up something for us."

"Yeah, sure. I could eat. Look, I'm sorry if I seem upset. I'm not."

"You sure about that?" She pulled out a pan from the bottom cabinet and filled it with water.

"Not about the meetings. I know it's what's best. I guess it's the job. The team. I just get the feeling they're keeping me at arm's length. Like they still don't trust me," he said.

"Have you talked to Unit Chief Cole about this? He was their boss before you. He might be able to offer some insight."

"I don't want to run to him with every little concern I have. It just feels different. Not like what we had at the WFO."

Kate nodded. "I miss them. Our old team. But this was what we wanted, right? Moving up and moving on?"

Nick dropped onto the barstool at the counter. "I guess so."

THE LIVING ROOM OF LYNN AND JOHN FLOYD WAS reminiscent of the time Ronald Reagan was entering his second presidential term. Burgundy couches and walnut tables, complete with glass inserts. Its glory days, however, much like those of the former president, were long gone. Well-worn, with throws covering the bulk of the couches' surfaces and ring marks adorning the tables. But it was where they called home. It used to be a home filled with love and laughter—and prosperity. But those days were gone too. Prosperity was no longer a word tossed around in reference to a place like Crown Pointe.

John Floyd had been a miner, a foreman for many years until the industry dried up. Now he was well past his prime, walked with a limp and had a tricky back. Lynn had been a manager at the Big Bear diner. Now she had diabetes and bad feet. Neither held such positions of high regard anymore.

As they sat on the sofa counting the pills Lynn began, "Looks like we might need to make another trip. I guess it's my turn. Better get it set up for tomorrow."

"It's best. You're going to have to find another clinic, though. Last I heard, the center shut down. DEA came in and busted the doc."

"Damn it. We're running out of places to go, John."

"I know that. But we'll cross that bridge when we get there. Besides, I hope we'll be done with all this soon."

"We set out to make a difference and that's exactly what I aim to do. Don't go second-guessing this now. What's done is done. She deserved better. We both know that." Lynn stood. "I'll head out in the morning. Be back before supper. I'm off to bed now. Fixin' to be a long day tomorrow."

LYNN FLOYD HELD ON TO THE GRAB BAR AND STEPPED ON THE bus. As she made her way down the aisle, a young man in uniform stood up to give her his seat. "That's very kind of you, young man, but I'm not so old you need to step aside. Go on and sit down. I'll be just fine. And thank you for your service."

"Yes, ma'am." He returned to his seat.

She found a place to sit near the back, which was fine. It was closer to the bathroom. The long journey and weak bladder was an arduous combination, so this spot would suit her.

The driver closed the door and the bus pulled away from the terminal. Lynn had made this trip before. So had John. The job was to get to the clinic, get the prescription, which was easier than getting Sudafed at the CVS, then go back home. Easy as pie. But John was right. They, being the Feds, were cracking down, which was a good thing, but not for the Floyds. This was what they needed to do to survive. If this source dried up, they'd have to turn to something worse. And Lynn didn't like the idea of trying to score heroin. That was tantamount to walking into the belly of the beast and she wasn't interested in doing that. But as the old saying went, "Needs must when the devil drives."

She was awakened hours later by a passenger who sat down next to her, and had to remind herself she was on the bus to Florida.

"I'm so sorry to wake you," the woman said.

"It's all right. Can you tell me where we are?"

"Tallahassee."

"Oh. Well then, I should thank you. I'll be getting off at the next stop." Lynn prepared for her departure, making another trip to the bathroom, but this time, to freshen up her brunette hair that was now mashed down on one side thanks to her having fallen asleep. Upon brief observation, she picked at the gray sprigs that had appeared in larger numbers. "Nothing a bottle of color from the drug store can't fix."

The bus slowed and the time had come for her to do her job. And that was to appear in pain and wait for the doctor to issue her prescription. She hadn't seen this one before, but he was all too willing to put pen to paper and scratch out a three-month supply of OxyContin. And why not? He was paid a hefty sum by the insurers, the drug companies, and anyone else looking to make a buck off the suffering of human beings. It would've been fine if she was really in pain. But these doctors didn't care. They didn't order x-rays or do exams. She'd be in and out inside of fifteen minutes, script in hand, and heading off to the clinic's in-house pharmacy.

That was exactly how it went down. "Thank you very much, ma'am. You have yourself a nice day." Lynn placed the bottles of Oxy in her purse and left the clinic. Outside, the sun was shining bright on this winter's day in Florida, although she wished to have spent the day doing something—anything else. But she wasn't doing this for her. This wasn't even for John. This was for their daughter.

The next few hours, Lynn couldn't sleep, which was fine. It would've meant a rough night had she fallen asleep again. It was already pushing 6pm, and by the time she got back home, it'd be almost eight.

The journey had come to an end. Lynn walked off the bus, through the terminal, and back to her car. It was the only car they owned, but John didn't drive anymore. He was on disability now. Not that he suffered all that much. The occasional hitch in his stride, throwing out his back. The disability was just another way to bring in some money. Most everybody was on some sort of government aid around here. How else were they going to survive without decent jobs?

On her return home in the darkening skies, she opened the front door and found John in front of the television. "I'm back." She set down her purse on the nearby kitchen table and retrieved the bottles.

"You get 'em?" His voice carried into the kitchen.

"I got 'em." She walked into the living room where he anxiously looked on. "Three months' worth, just like we talked about."

"Good. You did good, sweetheart." He reached for her hand. "Remember why we're doing this. I know it ain't easy."

Lynn revealed a tempered smile and took hold of a photograph sitting on a side table. "I know who we're doing this for." She peered at the picture of their daughter in her cheerleading uniform when she was happy, healthy, and beautiful. But that all had changed.

"I'll never forget neither."

3

The northern part of Crown Pointe had once been a thriving area. In fact, in the late 1990s and early 2000s, an apartment building sprouted up with the help of Federal aid dollars and a non-profit, which had since left town. The building had been cheaply built and was already in disrepair. Several units were vacant and the people who did live there were all Section 8, a subsidized government housing program.

But the law in this town had come to know the building as Hotel Oxy where the drug was bought, sold, and consumed at alarming rates. It was the logical first stop in their search for Joanne Waverly at the behest of her mother.

"She's probably here along with Tommy." Slocum stepped out of the driver's seat. "Let's go take a look."

"Right behind you." Lazaro followed as the two made their way along the sidewalk. "You ever feel like getting out of here?"

"What? You mean get out of Crown Pointe?" Slocum asked.

"Yeah."

"No. I was born here. I know damn near everyone. I ain't going anywhere."

Lazaro shook his head. "Even with this shit? All the drugs?"

"Yeah. Even with all the drugs. I'm not deserting these people. They need us. They need our help."

"I reckon so," Lazaro added.

They arrived at the manager's office. Slocum walked inside and waited for his partner to join him. Both were slightly taken aback by the odor. They knew the manager well and had become as accustomed as one could to the man's lack of personal hygiene.

"Afternoon, deputies. What can I do for you?" The manager sat at his desk and peeked out from behind his woefully outdated computer.

"Afternoon, Travis. We're looking for Joanne Waverly. You seen her 'round lately?" Slocum asked.

The manager cast his eyes upward at the ceiling and appeared to be staring at a water stain. "No. No, sir. I don't believe I have."

"What About Tommy Conroy? Any signs of him?" Lazaro added.

The man shook his head again. "No, sir. Although they don't come here too often from what I can tell. Why? They in trouble or something?"

"Or something. Just looking for them is all," Slocum replied.

"Well, you know the usual suspects are always lingering around, but I ain't seen those two in some time."

"Okay then. We appreciate your help." Slocum turned but stopped short. "Do me a favor and give us a call at the station if you do catch sight of them."

"Will do. You both have a good day now."

As they left the office, Slocum began, "Let's just take a walk around. They might've slipped in without ol' Travis spotting them."

Lazaro nodded. "Sure. Whatever you say, boss."

An unassuming man appeared troubled as he walked inside the police station. With his gray wool Stetson in hand, he continued in but didn't see anyone. "Pardon? Chief Tate, you available?" The man's soft voice didn't match his tall, rotund appearance, but it did carry well enough inside the small station as the chief emerged from his office.

"Charlie? What are you doing here? Everything all right with the missus?" The chief offered his hand.

"Yes, sir. She's doing fine. Save for the fact that our Andy's gone missing."

"What's that now?" The chief's hackles raised.

"He didn't come home last night, and of course, the wife's nervous something's happened."

"Come on into my office, Charlie. Tell me exactly what's going on." The chief ushered the distraught father to the chair. "When was the last time you heard from Andy?"

"Oh, I'd say around four o'clock yesterday. He came home from school, just like usual. Maggie was home already. Her shift at the store was over. I was still working at the courthouse, though."

"How's that going for you, by the way?"

"Oh, real good. They keep me busy. It's nice to be busy again, that's for sure."

"Glad to hear. So, where did Andy go after he came home from school? To a friend's?" the chief asked.

"Maggie says he was heading for the corner store for a pop 'cause we just ran out. Kid drinks way too much of it. Anyways, he never did come back."

Chief Tate knitted his brow. "And you're just now coming to me?"

"Well, I did think Maggie was overreacting. I came home from work and we made some calls to his friends. The thing is, it seems Andy's been slipping through our fingers more often than not lately, and I just figured this was one of those times. He's sixteen years old. You remember when you were sixteen, Chief?"

"Yes, sir, I do. But those were different times. You know we've got our hands full in this town now."

"I am aware of the problem. I didn't reckon Andy was mixed up in any of that."

"I'm sure he's not. I'll tell you what, I'll call out to the boys. They're running around anyways, and I'll ask them to take a drive and see if they can spot him. Or maybe have them talk to Grif there at the store and see if Andy ever showed up there yesterday." The chief stood. "I'm sure he'll turn up soon in any case."

"I know you're right." The man stood only inches shorter than Tate. "I appreciate you taking the time, Chief."

"Not at all, Charlie. You and Maggie take care and I'll be in touch soon, you hear?"

"Yes, sir." He tipped his head. "Evening."

Chief Tate watched Charlie get into his Ford pickup. Thoughts swirled in his head. Two missing kids in as many days. Maybe three, if Tommy Conroy doesn't turn up. Something was amiss. He hoped to God there wasn't a bad batch going around. These kids didn't have two pennies to rub together, so whatever money they could scrounge usually bought the cheapest version of the drugs. It was generally laced with Fentanyl and was some kind of dangerous combination. "Son of a bitch." He pressed the button on his radio. In a department this size, the chief wore multiple hats. Dispatcher was but one. "Slocum, you copy? Over."

"At your service. Go ahead, Chief."

"Where you boys at?"

"Just leaving Hotel Oxy."

He closed his eyes. "I wish you would stop calling it that."

"Sorry, Chief."

"I just had a visit from Charlie Walcott. Says his son Andy didn't come home after a visit to the store for a pop yesterday afternoon. I'm gonna need you two to check out the corner store."

"Another missing kid?" Slocum asked.

"That's right. I take it that means you didn't have any luck locating Joanne Waverly?"

"No, sir. Not yet."

"Damn. All right. How many more places you need to check out?"

"Still need to hit Devil's Den," Slocum replied. "Not sure what to do after that. Guess I'm hoping we'll find her there."

"From your mouth to God's ear. All right, then. Keep looking and find out if Griffin saw Andy Walcott yesterday afternoon."

"Ten-four." Slocum placed the radio back in its cradle, but before he had a chance to speak, Lazaro turned to him.

"Another one?"

"Guess so."

"Chief think they're related?"

"You heard him, same as me. He just said go talk to Griffin. So that's what we'll do." Slocum turned around the patrol car and headed south toward the corner store. "Hell, maybe we'll get lucky and he'll have seen Joanne Waverly too."

"You think so?" Lazaro asked.

Slocum glared at him. "No. I do not."

ON THE EDGE OF TOWN, SURROUNDED BY TOWERING SWEET Birch and the Kentucky Coffee tree, a clearing appeared. Trailers dotted the open area and were in various stages of disrepair. Most were uninhabitable, but still home to those desperate enough, which were not in short supply here. This was Devil's Den, named for the nearby single mine shaft that had been abandoned almost thirty years ago after it collapsed and killed five miners.

"Pull up behind this one. It's empty." Dawn Murphy was twenty-five and had recently been let go from her job at the local elementary school. She'd been a server in the cafeteria for two years, and in those two years, attendance at the school had dropped by nearly a quarter. The kids were aging out and going into the middle school and no one was moving into Crown Pointe. The dwindling population meant they no longer needed Dawn even though she'd been an exemplary employee. Now she was lucky to get twenty hours a week at the local grocery store.

"You sure no one's there?"

Dawn's companion, which was all she could ever see him being, was Steven Schiller. He was thirty, divorced, and never got around to visiting his two kids who lived in the next town over. "I'm sure. Just pull in here."

"All right. All right." Steven rolled to a stop just behind the tin awning that had partially collapsed. Behind the trailer were two lawn chairs. They weren't the only ones who frequented this particular location. Just the only ones today.

Dawn stepped out into the crisp air. A few dead leaves crunched underfoot as she walked atop the dried soil. It hadn't rained in the past couple of weeks. January usually brought with it a few inches of rain, but it was slow in coming this year. She sat down on one of the lawn chairs and grew concerned it wouldn't hold her weight. Considering she scarcely broke the 90-pound mark, that suggested the chair was definitely worse for wear.

Steven soon joined her.

"Well?" she asked.

"Oh, right. Here." He handed her the can of pop. "I put two, twenty mils in there. Ground 'em up. They been sitting for a couple of hours. Should be ready to go."

"Twenty mils was all you could get?"

Steven nodded. "Yeah. Som' bitch wouldn't give me the eighties I wanted. Best I could do."

Dawn tossed back the can of Coke and leaned into the chair, waiting for the high, but got a wild hair and turned to Steven. "Hey, you wanna go into the shaft?"

"What? Now?"

"Why not? Come on. It'll be fun. I haven't been inside in years."

"I guess so. I mean, shit, what else we got to do?" he replied.

She pushed off the chair and helped Steven up.

The abandoned mineshaft was about the distance of two football-fields away and boarded up. But people always took down the boards and went inside as far as they could untill they hit the collapsed section. It was like a rite of passage for the kids in town.

"I see it. Just ahead." Dawn began to jog closer. "Come on, slowpoke."

"Christ, Dawn. This ain't no damn race. Besides, I'm just starting to feel good. I don't want to run off my high."

"You ain't gonna run it off with this little bit of distance." She reached the entrance and ducked under one of the boards. "Holy shit. It's cold in here."

He stopped short of the entrance. "I didn't bring no jacket. I don't want to freeze my balls off in there."

"Stop being such a baby, Steven. Just get in and maybe I'll show you something nice."

He hunched over and followed her in. "Finally, something worth my time."

Only a few feet in and the light faded. The air grew damp and the ground was soft and black.

"Man, it's just like I remember," Dawn said. "See, you ain't originally from around here, but this was the place to be. Us kids would play around in here. They used to have some tracks but they pulled up what was left after the collapse. Now it's just a hole for another few feet." She turned to face him, and in a creepy voice added, "A deep, dark hole."

Steven moved next to her and reached for her crotch. "You mean like the one you got?" He smiled.

"Don't be so disgusting." She slapped his hand.

"What? You said you was gonna show me something."

Dawn continued inside, and the darker it became, the more she used her hands to guide her along.

"Don't be going too far now, you hear? Place is still a damn death trap," Steven said.

"Jesus!" Dawn pulled away her hand from the earthen walls. "What the hell?"

"What? What is it? Some damn rat? I told you this was a bad idea. Damn creepy-ass place."

Dawn pulled out her cellphone and turned on its light, pointing it at the wall. Her eyes widened. She dropped her phone and screamed at the top of her lungs.

"Dawn! What the hell is wrong with you?" He walked toward her.

She pointed to the wall and he aimed his own cell phone at it. "It's a body, Steven. Jesus H. Christ, what are we gonna do?"

"Mother of God." He aimed his phone farther down into the walls of the abandoned shaft. "Wait. Oh no. Dawn, I think there's..." He moved closer and gasped before turning away and heaving out his guts.

Dawn looked at what he'd seen. She covered her mouth and tears streamed down her cheeks.Trembling, she turned to Steven. "We gotta get out of here." She ran toward the light at the end of the shaft, desperate to reach the entrance as though someone might emerge from the hole and take her and Steven too.

Reaching the end, Dawn made it into the light of day with eyes stinging from tears and the bright sun. Steven soon followed. Both seemed jolted back into sobriety.

"We have to tell the police." Dawn paced a four-foot area in front of the shaft. "Did you see them? It looked like they got eaten by rats or something. We have to tell someone now."

"Just forget about it," Steven said, pulling her away and back toward the trailer. "Forget what we saw, okay? You want them to start asking questions as to why we was here? No way am I going back inside. Three strikes and I'm gone. You know that, right?"

"Steven, we can't leave them there. We'll just tell them we were here messing around. Not that we were getting high. We'll just wait until the drugs are out of our systems, okay? Then we'll go."

"No. It's too risky. I don't need that kind of heat on me, Dawn, and you know that." He marched toward the trailer. "We're leaving right now and never coming back here." Upon reaching the car, he opened the driver's side door and waited. "You coming or not?"

She eyed him. "This isn't right."

"Just get in." He slipped inside and turned the engine. When she remained standing in front of the car, he raised up his palms.

Through the car's windshield, she saw his lips move as if asking her, "Well?" She finally walked to the passenger side and stepped in. "Fine. We'll go. But I ain't never coming back here again."

"Fine by me." He shoved the car into reverse, spun his tires and sped away.

4

As a profiling apprentice, Kate expected a certain amount of grunt work to be handed her way, and she was not wrong. But the arrival of Eva Duncan, the woman and team member with whom she hadn't yet become familiar, offered an unexpected reprieve from the monotony.

"Reid, you have a minute?" Duncan stood in her doorway in a dark pencil skirt and white blouse with her hair pulled away from her face. The woman was a sight to behold. All at once, she portrayed strength, beauty, and most of all, was unlikely to take guff from anyone. It also didn't hurt that she spoke with a mild Chicago accent that came off as fairly intimidating.

Kate liked her already. "Sure. Please come in."

"Thanks. I know you handled assorted duties at the WFO. Any chance you're familiar with ViCAP?"

"Funny you should ask." Kate eyed the pile of papers on her desk. "I just happen to have several case files that I'm entering into the system now. And yes, I'm very familiar with the database."

"Good, because I wanted to run something by you." Duncan

laid a file on Kate's desk. "I'm working on a theory that would require some restructuring of the database and would include additional markers but reduce the number of questions on the questionnaire."

"I remember back at San Diego PD, no one wanted to enter a case because it took almost an hour to do so and rarely yielded results."

"Exactly my point. Because far too few law enforcement agencies use it. Combine that with the budget cuts to the program, nearly two-thirds of the training staff has been cut. It all adds up to a failed system. Nothing like ViCLAS the Canadians use."

"But the difference is, the Canadians mandate the system be utilized, and they're not shy in funding it," Kate added. "Therein lies the problem. It always comes down to money."

"That's not a problem I can solve. If our higher-ups pulled their heads out of their asses once in a while, they could, but that's a conversation for another day. Theoretically, though, if we can reduce the size of the questionnaire, it should garner at least some additional support," Duncan continued.

"Assuming it covers the same information, yes. But why are you working on this? I know it's part of BAU. Have you spoken to the program manager?"

"Not yet," Duncan replied. "I wanted to talk to you because I know a little about your background. I know how the system brought you closer to finding the man who abducted you."

"That was where I first learned of the program." What Kate failed to mention was the man who brought it to her attention. A man she still dearly missed. "I think this is a very good idea and you should take it to the program manager. Any help we can get in improving the effectiveness of the system will make not only our jobs easier, but will make it easier for us to help the local guys."

"There's one other thing, would you mind reviewing the questions?" Duncan opened the file and pulled out the papers. "Maybe there's something I haven't thought of."

"Absolutely. I'd love to help."

Duncan studied Kate for a moment. "Look, I know the challenges you face by being here. This job is hard enough without having people think you got it because someone was playing favorites. But don't ever let anyone tell you that you don't belong here."

Kate raised the corner of her lips in a half-smile. "Are you speaking from experience?"

Duncan pushed up from her seat. "You could say that. I'll leave this with you. No rush. I know you're still getting your feet wet." She began to leave but stopped short. "I'm glad you're here, Reid. Sometimes the testosterone levels get pretty high in here. We need to keep that in check."

Quinn appeared in the doorway as she began to leave. "Duncan, how are you?"

"Doing just fine. Catch up with you later?"

"Sure." He continued inside. "Glad I caught you. You want to take a trip?"

"Where to?" Kate asked.

"The New York Field Office asked us to come take a look at something they think will be right up our alley."

"Sounds interesting."

"Should be. We're leaving now." Quinn slapped the doorframe with his hand. "Don't worry. We'll be back by dinner."

CALLING IN SICK FOR THE MORNING SHIFT AT THE GROCERY store was all Dawn wanted to do. But she couldn't afford to lose this job even if it was only part-time. She hadn't slept much and what little sleep she did get was riddled with images of the bodies in the mineshaft. Steven was wrong to stop her from going to the police, but she had kept her mouth shut like she promised.

Her first customer of the day and Dawn had to put on a smile. "Morning."

"Morning. How are you, Dawn? Good to see you."

"You too, Mrs. J." She began scanning the food and could scarcely look the woman in the eye. "That'll be $34.76, ma'am." Dawn continued to peer at the store's entrance, expecting the police to come in after her.

"Dawn?" The woman held the money in her hand, waiting for Dawn to take it.

"Oh, sorry about that, Mrs. J. Thank you."

"You all right, honey?"

"Just a little tired is all. Here's your change. Have a good day."

"You too and get some rest." She grabbed the bags and walked to the exit.

That was when Dawn overheard the conversation in the checkout lane next to her. She peered over her shoulder just for a moment to catch a glimpse of the woman who was speaking. It was Mrs. Waverly.

"Chief Tate sent his boys out to look for her yesterday, but still nothing. I'm getting real scared, you know, but I'm trying to keep up hope."

"Course you are. I'm sure Joanne's just fine. She'll turn up," the woman in line replied.

Mrs. Waverly nodded. "I know she will. Thank you."

"Anytime. You try to stay positive now, you hear?"

Mrs. Waverly revealed a half-hearted smile before heading toward the exit, right past Dawn's lane. She watched as the woman's listless smile faded until she passed through the doors.

"What's going on?" Dawn turned to the co-worker who rang up Mrs. Waverly.

"Joanne Waverly's been missing a couple days. Her momma's worried as you'd expect. I sure do hope that girl turns up soon."

"Yeah." Dawn returned to see another customer approach, but the words echoed in her mind. She wondered if it was Joanne Waverly inside that shaft. It was too dark and she was too frightened to be able to recognize anyone. Not to mention that the bodies were already almost unrecognizable thanks to the creatures that lived inside or those that smelled the rotting flesh from a distance. Her stomach turned as she tried to keep her wits about her.

"You already rang that up, Dawn." The customer furrowed her brow.

"I did?" She looked back at the screen. "You're right. I'm so sorry." Dawn keyed in a credit and continued on. If she kept making mistakes, the boss would notice. Maybe it was best just to claim she was ill and go home. They wouldn't fire her for just that —surely. Of course, anything was possible. But they would certainly fire her if she kept making mistakes, which right now seemed all too likely.

Once she finished with her current customer, she knew what to do. Dawn untied her apron and headed back toward the manager's office. "Excuse me, Ron, I'm just not feeling well. I should've stayed home, but I thought I'd be able to stick it out. I'm sorry. I just can't."

"Well, you don't look good, Dawn. Peaked almost. You go on home and don't worry about things here. We'll keep you covered."

"Thank you. I surely appreciate it, Ron." She backed out of the doorway and started toward the employee exit. Once outside, her nerves got the best of her. She retched into the planter near the door.

Dawn pulled back up and looked around to make sure no one saw what she'd done. A tear started down her cheek and she made her way to her car. With trembling hands, she tried to unlock it. When it finally opened, Dawn sat down, gripped the steering wheel, and sobbed.

There was only one place she could go, and she would have to convince him to go to the cops. It hadn't even been a day and she was a wreck. Living with this wasn't an option, not when she saw Mrs. Waverly suffering like that. Dawn pulled out of the parking lot and headed north to see Steven. If he knew that Joanne Waverly was missing, like she did, maybe that would change his mind. It had to.

Dry-rot had eviscerated much of the front porch of Steven's home, and when Dawn arrived, she trod lightly on the few secure sections that remained. He lived alone after losing his mother to cancer. His father left when he was only eight. When she knocked on his door with no answer, her concern for him grew. "Steven, open up. It's me, Dawn." She noticed his car wasn't in the driveway, which was unusual given that it was still somewhat early in the day. He didn't have a job and rising before noon wasn't common. "You in there?"

She waited for a moment longer before surrendering to the idea that he wasn't home. "Damn it. Where the hell are you?" Her nerves kicked in and she felt queasy once again. "Don't make me come look for you." She wanted to go straight to the police but feared his backlash. Her arrival was an attempt to convince him to do what was right, but now Dawn was on her own.

Her car was parked at the end of the drive and she figured it was best to have a look around for him first. Give him the chance to at least come up with a story that reconciled with her own.

Within minutes, she was back on the road in search of him. Few people lived in Crown Pointe and there weren't a whole lot of places to go. Only one bar, which hadn't opened yet. Three restaurants, a couple of small grocery stores, and a new e-cigarette store called Vape. The nearest Walmart was twenty miles away. Besides the schools and a small hospital, that was just about it. Steven wouldn't have been at either of those places. Then it occurred to her. Maybe he'd gone back. Maybe he did feel bad and went back. Now that they were sober, she wondered if he'd reconsidered.

Dawn turned around and headed back to Devil's Den, back to the mine shaft. "You'd better be there, Steven." She pressed her foot on the gas pedal and sped down the single lane, her car stirring up debris on the side of the roadway. Dried twigs, plastic bags, a few dead leaves all swirled in her wake. Her nerves settled once again, feeling assured that he would be there and that he had reconsidered, but maybe decided to take one last look to be sure they hadn't dreamt it all up. This was all going to be over soon.

A pullout on the road was just ahead and she spotted something tucked far back inside. Almost hidden, except for what now appeared to be the sun's reflection off of a taillight. She slowed down and peered ahead, squinting her eyes to shield them from the glare. As she drew nearer, her face masked in uncertainty. It was a car tucked into the pullout and she knew exactly whose car it was.

Dawn slammed on the brakes, turning the wheel until she was on the shoulder. She launched herself out and ran to the car. It appeared as though someone had tried to conceal it and maybe the winds blew away some of its cover. But the back end was unmistakable. She continued her approach, fearing Steven was inside. "Oh God. Steven?"

She reached the driver's side door and peered in. It was empty. He wasn't there, and nothing seemed to suggest anything nefarious had occurred. Dawn shook her head and surveyed the wooded area. "Steven? You out there?" A few steps nearer to the trees and she called out for him again. "Steven?" There was no answer. "Damn you." She walked back to her car and started the engine. A final glance at his abandoned vehicle, and Dawn pulled onto the road, still headed for the trailers and the mineshaft.

Up to this point, she was afraid of Steven's reaction to her insisting they talk to the police. Now she feared she would be talking to them anyway—searching for answers about him.

With her eyes fixed on the road ahead, Dawn continued. Only another mile and she would be there. A part of her worried the mineshaft might have another occupant. But she had to table those thoughts or risk losing her nerve and turning around altogether.

In the distance, Devil's Den appeared. Beyond that lay the abandoned mineshaft. Dawn drove as close as she could to the opening. The grassy clearing was low and had plenty of barren spots that made driving on it fairly easy this time of year. In the summer, the grasses grew much longer and the heavy rain spurred growth in the dirt areas.

She shoved the gearshift into park and stepped out of the car, hesitating for a moment and taking a calming breath. Her stomach was in knots. She was frightened of what else she might find inside the shaft while her courage faded.

Careful steps brought her closer. A glance over her shoulder confirmed she was alone. Any occupants in the trailers either ignored her arrival or were too high to come out. It was likely the latter. No one really lived in them, just used them as temporary shelter, such as they were.

Standing just outside the shaft's entrance, the rustic scent of damp earth reached her senses. Though inside, she would encounter the rancid odor of decay. "Just go in." Her legs seemed to refuse the order, but she had to do this. She had to know if Steven was inside. Why she believed that was the case remained a mystery, but she was most certain it was. What other reason could there be for his abandoned car? The missing Joanne Waverly. Disappearances in this town weren't that suspect because the people would eventually turn up dead from overdoses. But Dawn already knew what was inside the shaft, and the time had come to confirm her suspicions.

She forced her legs to move and walked inside. The tunnel became darker, the smell— more pungent. With her phone in her hands, she turned on its flashlight and aimed it at the wall where she stood only yesterday, staring at the bodies of people she didn't know, but now suspected at least one was Joanne.

Farther inside, a fresh mound of dirt was visibly shoved against the wall, as though someone had tried to replace it after digging it out. She slowly raised the light from her phone along that portion of the wall and stopped when a hand appeared. "Oh no. Lord, please no." The light quaked in her palm, but she pressed on, moving it higher. The body was wedged in the wall, fit inside like a cookie cutout, only it was shaped like a human body.

The face. Tears streamed down Dawn's cheeks as she saw his face. Bloodied, bruised. His eye so swollen it was hard to tell where it stopped and his cheek started. She dropped the phone and tried to scream, but nothing would come out. Instead, Dawn hyperventilated. There was no mistaking that this was Steven— and he was dead. He wasn't much more than skin and bone anyway, now he appeared even more gaunt, as though he'd lost every bit of blood in his body.

The light from her phone shone in her eyes as it lay face up in the dirt, casting a shadow on Steven's body, which was only feet from the other two. "No. No, no, no. Dear Lord, what happened?

Why are you here? You can't leave me. You gotta come back."
Sobbing, she reached for him but couldn't bring herself to place
her hand atop his chest. "I have to get out of here." She cast her
eyes away and toward the entrance. "I have to go. I have to tell the
police."

With strength that had deserted her only minutes earlier, she
sprinted away from him, away from the horrific scene and made it
back outside into the light of the clearing. As she made it to her
car, and from the corner of her eye, a man appeared. He stood
outside one of the trailers. The way he stood, almost swaying,
suggested he was high or drunk or maybe both. Dawn had to leave.
But what if he recognized her? What if he went to the police and
knew she had been there yesterday too?

Dawn couldn't think about that now. Steven was dead.
Someone killed him. The same someone who killed at least two
others inside there. But she couldn't be sure if one of them was
Joanne Waverly. The other bodies were just too disfigured and
had begun to decompose.

She slipped into the driver's seat and keyed the ignition.
Peering over her shoulder, she noticed the man walk back inside. A
visible sigh of relief overcame her. Her car spun around and she
fled the area as fast as her car would take her. The only place she
could go now was the police station. No matter what might
become of her and their decision to keep hidden what they'd seen.
She would do this for Steven. And for Joanne Waverly.

5

The jangling of keys in the door lock startled John Floyd from his morning newspaper as he sat at the kitchen table. When the front door opened, he peered around the paper until Lynn came into view. "That didn't take long."

Lynn Floyd held a plastic grocery bag in her hands and set it down on the kitchen counter. "Only needed a few things." She retrieved a pack of razors and held them up. "Got you them razors you said you needed. Damn things keep getting more expensive every time I buy them."

"Thank you. I'll do my best to make them last." John returned to his paper.

"I overheard something interesting while I was checking out."

"Oh yeah? And what was that?"

"I heard Kim Waverly talking to a couple ladies about how Joanne's been missing a few days," Lynn replied.

"What did them old hens say about that?" he asked.

"Said she was most likely on a bender, only they put it in more polite terms."

"Well, that's a damn shame. Not that I'm surprised. Seems most of the young people around here been doing the same kind of thing. What they need are jobs. Hell, what we all need are jobs," John added.

"No argument from me, but still, Kim seemed real upset and I do ache for her. She's got the sheriff's office involved and the chief sent his boys out looking for Joanne yesterday, but by all accounts, nothing's turned up." Lynn approached her husband at the table. "Listen here, I got two coming by later. You met them. I'll get you what they want."

"They want the same as before?" John asked.

"I reckon they do."

"Okay then. Get it ready."

DAWN PUSHED INSIDE THE CROWN POINTE SHERIFF'S OFFICE wearing panic while sweat dripped from her hairline.

Deputy Eric Slocum jumped from his desk. "Miss, are you okay?" He knew the young woman, but not well enough to call her by her first name. "What's wrong?"

Her lips quivered as she wiped her damp brow. "Steven's dead."

"What? You talking about Steven Schiller?" Slocum asked.

"Yes, sir. He's dead. And so are two others. I saw them with my own eyes."

Slocum raised his hands. "Okay. Okay, just calm down." He glanced at Lazaro, who was already on his feet. "Come sit down. You want some water?"

Dawn shook her head wildly. "No. I don't want nothin'. There are three dead people and you gotta come see them."

Deputy Shane Lazaro moved toward her. "Where are they? Do you know the other two?"

"No. But they're all in the mineshaft at Devil's Den. Like buried, or something. Kinda sticking out of the wall." Tears fell down her cheeks as she appeared to recall the gruesome images.

"Criminy sakes." Slocum turned away in disgust. "Are you sure about that? I have to ask, have you taken anything today?"

"No! I ain't high or drunk. I'm telling you, you got three dead people in the mineshaft. And Steven's one of them. You have to come quick. I saw his car."

"Wait," Lazaro interrupted. "You saw his car? Where?"

"Not far from the trailers," she continued. "It was inside a pullout, tucked inside like someone was trying to hide it. I saw it and stopped to look."

"Was this before or after you found the bodies in the shaft?" Lazaro pressed on.

Dawn stopped cold, appearing to realize she was going to have to choose her words carefully. They were going to ask why she was out there. Everybody in town knew there was only one reason to be out that way. "Um, it was um, before. I was just out looking for him because we were supposed to see each other, and well, I figured, knowing what he could be like sometimes, that he might've been out that direction. See, I left work on account I was ill."

"You went home from work, but you and Steven had plans to see each other?" Slocum asked.

"Yes, sir. Just for a while. He'd left something at my place. And, well, first I went to his house and he wasn't home. Wasn't answering his phone. So that's when I decided to go out to the trailers."

Lazaro peered at her with mild suspicion. "What made you go into the shaft? It's a dangerous place, you know."

"I can't say exactly. Just a feeling I got. You know, I saw his car. I got scared. So when I made it out there, I reckoned, I best take a look. Just to be safe."

"And that's when you saw the bodies?" Slocum added.

"Yes, sir." She peered anxiously at the deputies. "You gotta come out there. Please. I ain't lying."

"Okay." Slocum appeared to consider a solution. "I tell you what, you can ride out there with us, show us Steven's car and take us to the mineshaft."

Dawn nodded.

"Just let me get word to the chief and we'll head out." Lazaro headed toward the chief's office. "Excuse me, sir?"

He looked up from his computer. "Yes? What is it?"

"Dawn Murphy's out here and she says she seen three bodies in the abandoned mineshaft at Devil's Den. One of them she claims is her boyfriend, Steven Schiller."

"Dear Lord. Are you sure about this?" he asked.

"She seems very sure, Chief. Figured you might wanna join us on this one."

Chief Tate stood and grabbed his jacket off his chair. "Hell, yes. Lord knows what we're going to find out there. For Christ's sake, what is happening in this town?"

"I can't say, Chief, but I sure as shit hope we don't find Joanne Waverly in there. Slocum and me was just out there yesterday. Got no whiff of anything unusual."

The chief brushed past him. "Then let's hope Dawn Murphy is seeing things."

∾

DEPUTY SHANE LAZARO WAS BEHIND THE WHEEL WHILE THE

chief sat on the passenger side. He pointed ahead. "There's the car just a ways up."

"I see it. Pull on up next to it." The chief peered over his shoulder at Dawn, who was in the back seat with Slocum. "That Steven's car?"

"Yes, sir," she replied.

As the patrol car rolled to a stop, the deputies and the chief stepped out.

"You mind staying here, Ms. Murphy?" Slocum asked.

"No, sir." She watched as the men approached the vehicle, hands on their holsters, ready to shoot if something should go south. But Dawn knew no one was there. Just Steven's abandoned beat up Chevy Malibu he got from his momma before she died.

With tears in her eyes, she watched them open the doors, the trunk, the hood. Looking for what, God only knew, but she was helpless to do anything now. She just wanted to get him out of that shaft.

"Hey, Chief, you wanna take a look at this?" Slocum was hunched over the driver's seat and aimed his light at the floorboard. "Looks like a pill."

Chief Tate peered inside. "That it does, and I'll give you two guesses as to what kind of pill."

"I only need one. It's Oxy and I'll bet it's an eighty mil." Slocum used a card he found in the center console, one of those postcard advertisements that always slipped out of magazines. He slid it under the tablet and raised it up. "Eighty mil and I can bet this ain't the only one."

"Might be the only one we find in here, but let's bag it and tag it."

Slocum nodded. "Okey dokey."

One of the things that had gotten easier in the battle against the opioid problem had been the passage of new laws regarding

OxyContin and the formation of the new tablets. These new tablets were almost impossible to crunch with teeth and crushing one turned it into some kind of jelly-like substance. And still, the time-release ingredients inside made it hard as hell to get a decent high. Another benefit was that if anything was added to it, if it was laced with something, Fentanyl in most cases, it was generally easier to trace to a dealer. This could provide useful information as to Steven Schiller's last hours on this earth.

"I don't see anything else noteworthy in here, Chief. Should we head out to the shaft?" Slocum asked.

"Might as well. Let's call the doc and he can meet us out there with a truck." Chief Tate walked back to the patrol car and opened the rear passenger door. "We found Oxy in Steven's car. You don't know nothing about that now, do you?"

"No, sir," Dawn replied.

"Didn't think so." He closed the door and slipped onto the front passenger seat. "We'll be heading out to the mineshaft now. Called for the ambulance to come meet us there too. We'll get Steven taken care of and the others. Assuming that's what we'll find."

When Lazaro returned to the driver's side, he peered back at Dawn. "You sure there's nothing else you want to tell us before we head out there?"

She shook her head as Slocum entered the vehicle.

"Okay then. Let's go."

Within a few minutes, they'd arrived at the clearing. Devil's Den was in sight.

"Should we see if anyone's here first, Chief?" Lazaro asked. "When we were here yesterday, the place was deserted. Like they were warned the law was coming and they scattered like cock-roaches."

"That's right," Slocum added. "Knocked on doors, peeked through windows. Nothing."

Dawn remembered the man from the trailer who'd seen her run out of Devil's Den like a bat out of hell. She wondered when the deputies had made their visit, but didn't dare ask.

"Let's just get inside the shaft and get a handle on what we're dealing with. Then we'll figure things out from there," the chief replied.

"I'll show you where they are. It's sort of deep inside it, near the collapsed part," Dawn said.

"Fair enough." Chief Tate opened his door and the four walked toward the entrance of the mineshaft. He glanced at Dawn. "I'll just need you to stick close to me, you hear? Place is dangerous enough as it is."

"Yes, sir." Dawn followed them inside. "It's back a ways. I'd say at least thirty feet. You'll know it when the smell hits you."

"I'm still not exactly clear as to why you were in here, Ms. Murphy," Lazaro added. "But I guess the best thing is for us to see what it is we got in here." His nose crinkled and he raised the back of his hand to his face. "Lord Almighty."

"That's the smell I was talking about." Dawn stopped and put her hand on her stomach.

"You gonna be all right, miss?" Lazaro asked.

"Yes. I'm sorry. It's still just—just so shocking."

"My Lord." The chief stood in front of Steven's body. He reached for a handkerchief in his pocket and covered his mouth with it.

"We got another male and female over here, Chief." Lazaro pointed to the others with his flashlight. "When's the doc coming?"

"Should be in the next few minutes." Chief Tate approached the other bodies. "Any idea who they are?"

Slocum stood nearest to the female and aimed his light at her chest. "The necklace. Name on it says Joanne. Has to be Joanne Waverly."

The chief shook his head. "Son of a bitch. Who's the male?"

Slocum studied the body. "Can't say. But I can assume it's Tommy Conroy."

They all turned to the entrance at the sound of another vehicle.

"Must be the ambo." Lazaro looked at Dawn. "Okay, miss, I think it's time you waited outside. Let us get these poor souls out of here." He led her toward the entrance and spotted the ambulance and the doctor who stepped out of it.

"What y'all got in there?"

"Doc, you'd have to see it to believe it," Lazaro replied. "Chief Tate's in there waiting for you." As he led Dawn away, he spotted a man standing outside one of the trailers. "Hey, you know that man?"

"No, sir."

"Okay. Just have a seat in the cruiser. I'm going to go have a quick word. Just sit tight, you hear?"

Dawn dropped her head in her hands and sobbed.

"Excuse me?" Lazaro shouted as he approached the man still standing outside his trailer. "I'm Deputy Lazaro. Can I ask you your name, sir?"

The man, who appeared in need of a good bath and clean clothes, eyed the deputy. "I don't know nothing about whatever it is you got going on over there."

Lazaro moved closer, standing only feet from the man. "That's not what I asked, sir. Can I get your name, please? I just want to talk to you. That's all."

"Jensen. Name's Sterling Jensen." He folded his arms across his chest, making his protruding stomach appear even larger. Not an obese man by any means, but a man who didn't take much care with his eating habits. Fast food was cheap here. Sometimes cheaper than homemade. And overconsumption of such processed foods would lead one to appear much as Sterling Jensen did.

"Mr. Jensen, as you can see, we've come up on quite an unfortunate situation over there. You say you don't know anything about it. Fair enough. But I don't suppose you seen any unusual comings and goings around here in the past few days?"

"You do know what generally goes on around here, don't you, Deputy? You seem like a smart man," Jensen replied.

"I am familiar with the area's reputation. What I'm asking is, apart from what is normal for here, have you noticed anything out of the ordinary? Cars you ain't seen before. People you ain't seen before. That sort of thing. Cause I'll tell you what, I was out here with my partner yesterday and didn't notice you. You weren't hiding from us or anything, were you?"

"I'm not a permanent resident of this location. I'm only here when the mood strikes me. So, as I wasn't here yesterday, the only car I seen is the one driven by that blonde woman you came out here with. She was here only a short while ago. Nothing else before. Not that I took note of, anyhow, apart from y'all."

"Did you happen to notice what she was doing?" Lazaro continued. "As you say you weren't here yesterday. Was she alone?"

"Deputy, I don't pay any attention to the folks around here. I saw her come out the mine, left it alone, and went back inside."

Lazaro nodded. "Right."

"Figured nothing good ever going to come from inside that place ever again and whatever it was she was doing, I wanted no part of." He peered around Lazaro. "What'd you find in there? I imagine that ambulance isn't here just 'cause."

"No, sir, it's not. But I'm afraid I can't say much more than that right now. You be sure and let me know if you recall anything else. I surely would appreciate it."

"Will do." Jensen walked back inside.

Lazaro headed toward the car and spotted the chief approaching. "He doesn't know nothing. Just what Ms. Murphy already told us."

The chief glanced back at the mine and then to Lazaro. "Well, I think we ought to make contact with our federal friends."

"Louisville?"

"Feds got an office in Pikeville. Closer and might get a better response," Chief Tate replied.

"Why you think we need to call on them? Drugs?"

"I do believe that has something to do with it. They won't get involved in local murder investigations unless, of course, it's got something to do with drug trafficking. Right now, I'm leaning in that general vicinity."

Lazaro looked on with some confusion. "You think they were killed for drugs?"

"Can't think of no other reason just yet. Drug deals gone bad, most likely."

"Maybe even crossing state lines, figuring on how hard it's been lately getting anything here in Kentucky," Lazaro added.

"Exactly. Better to be proactive in a situation like this, in my humble opinion. I'll let them decide if they think it's worth their time. Right now, we should make a visit to Kim Waverly."

"What about Tommy Conroy's folks?" Lazaro asked.

"Best wait until we get confirmation from Doc on an identity. Shouldn't take but half a day or so. We'll start with Kim. She'll need to formally identify Joanne, but the necklace is somewhat of a giveaway." Chief shook his head in disbelief as he made his way back to the ambulance.

The doctor who ran the local hospital and morgue stood at the back of the truck and opened its doors. He spotted the chief's approach. "It'll take me and my team a while to get those bodies out with as little disturbance to them as possible."

"Appreciate that, Doc. Me and the boys are gonna pay a visit to Mrs. Waverly. How long you think before you get a positive ID on the male?"

"Not long. I'll give you a shout as soon as I know for sure." He turned his sights toward the truck. "Can't believe something like this could happen here."

"Don't I know it. Shoving them in there like that. Doing what they did to the bodies. Best guess is it's some outside group trying to move in and take over the trade. But that's something we'll have to get to work on ASAP."

"I'd better get a move on," the doctor replied. "I'll let you know as soon as I know anything, Henry."

"Much obliged, Doc."

THE CHIEF WAITED IN THE LOBBY OF THE HOSPITAL WITH Slocum and Lazaro. He checked the time on his phone. "Said he'd be here by 10am."

"Well, I bet that's him coming up to the door now," Lazaro replied. "Sure looks like a Fed."

A man who appeared to be in his late twenties, wearing a navy-colored suit, walked inside. He spotted them immediately. "Morning. I hope you haven't been waiting long." He offered his hand. "Special Agent Roger Ness, Pikeville Field Office."

Lazaro smiled. "Ness? As in Elliot Ness?"

"I assure you there is no relation."

"Sure, yeah. I'm Deputy Lazaro. This here is Chief Tate and Deputy Slocum."

The chief offered his hand. "Pleasure. We certainly appreciate you coming down here to take a look."

"Happy to help. I do apologize for the delay. It took a couple days to get the approval. Which, I'm hoping means you might have some additional forensics come through?"

"I'm afraid not. We got a positive ID on all three victims, but we're still waiting on tox screens and DNA testing." The chief started into the hall. "Doc's waiting on us. Best go on back and get started."

The agent followed him. "So you believe this is related to drug trafficking?"

"Right now, that's the only damn thing makes even the slightest bit of sense as to what happened to those poor people." He turned back to the agent. "You'll see in a minute what I'm talking about."

They entered the room where all three victims lay on gurneys. Doc approached the agent. "You must be with the FBI. I'm Dr. Powell, but everyone calls me Doc." He offered his hand.

"Special Agent Roger Ness. Pleased to meet you."

Doc smiled a little before glancing to the chief, whose face suggested he not mention the man's last name. "Right. Okay, so some good news. I just received the tox screens on two of our three victims here. Don't know why the delay on Steven Schiller's results, but anyhow, this will give us a start."

The agent moved closer to the only female victim. "Who's this?"

"That there is Miss Joanne Waverly. Nineteen," the chief began. "Her momma came to me a few days ago. Someone happened across the bodies the other day, and well, here we are."

The agent looked at the doctor. "Cause of death?"

"I was initially inclined to say blunt force trauma to the brain, however, after receiving these results." He turned to the chief.

"Henry, I'd say she very well could've been dying from the drugs in her system. And then someone decided to hurry along the process."

"What'd you find in her system that leads you to believe that, Doc?" Chief asked.

"OxyContin, as you'd expect, but it appears it was mixed with a toxic combination of chemicals."

"Like precursor chemicals?" Agent Ness asked.

"I'm afraid I'm not sure what those are, but according to the screen, she had elements of propanol, chloroform, and acetone, among others in her blood. And together, it was a highly lethal brew."

"What exactly are precursor chemicals?" Slocum asked.

"They're mostly used by the cartels to make counterfeit Oxy, in addition to things like Fentanyl," Ness replied.

"So this is sounding like it's outside dealers looking to get in?" Lazaro asked. "Like the chief suspected?"

"Except you can't sell drugs to dead people. Makes no sense creating a product intended to kill your buyers." The chief looked to Agent Ness. "And then crush their skulls and bury them inside the walls of an abandoned mineshaft. Agent Ness, after what Doc here has said, I'm starting to think this might be more to do with intentional murder than a drug deal gone bad. I might've been wrong to call you out."

"Could be both. It's hard to say, but I'll tell you what." Ness rubbed his chin as he continued to observe Joanne's body. "I'd like to get some input from our unit that handles unusual cases such as this. And given that there are already three unfortunate souls here, I think they might be interested in taking a look."

Chief Tate looked to his deputies and returned his attention to the agent. "Whatever it is we need to do to make sure no one else turns up like this, I'm on board with."

6

Daylight had drawn to an end and shadows crawled along the walls of Kate's office. It was then she recalled the standing dinner plans she would miss out on with Nick if she didn't leave soon. They both went to extreme measures to ensure their weekly dinner date didn't get pushed off the calendar. It seemed like a Herculean effort this week, but she would keep her end of the bargain. When Kate made her way into the hall and Quinn appeared with a look she'd seen before, it became apparent tonight might be put on hold after all.

"Are you leaving?" Quinn asked.

"I was about to, but I'm assuming you have other plans for me?"

"I just got a call from a field agent operating out of Pikeville, Kentucky. The main Louisville office referred him to us."

"Must be important," Kate replied.

"That's what I'd like to find out. A small town called Crown Pointe in the eastern part of the state now has three dead bodies. All discovered in an abandoned mine shaft, bludgeoned. They suspect drug trafficking deaths, but aren't sure as it stands right now."

"Drug trafficking? Given the condition of the victims, it sounds like the work of a cartel. That's not really our thing, is it?" she asked.

"No. But the reason for the request was the manner of the deaths, and the way in which the bodies were—stored—for lack of a better term." He handed her a file. "We head out first thing in the morning. Take a look so you can get familiar. I'll be studying it myself tonight as well." He turned on his heel. "Flight leaves at 8am."

Kate slipped the file in her bag and continued into the hall. Her low-heeled black shoes clicked softly on the tile floor. The tall windows that lined the corridor allowed the setting sun's rays to shine through. Arriving at Nick's corner office, she peeked inside. "Hey. I know we had plans tonight. In fact, I was just getting ready to leave when Quinn handed me a file. We're leaving in the morning for a town called Crown Pointe in eastern Kentucky."

"What's going on down there?" He pushed back from his desk and held her gaze.

"Three dead bodies. That's about all I know right now. I need to review the case file, which is why I need to reschedule our dinner."

"You know what, why don't we get some pizza delivered and we can go through the file together? If that's okay with you—and Quinn."

"It's okay with me. You're not too busy?" She walked inside.

"Sure I am, but I'd like to see what you've got. I'm a little surprised he didn't brief me on it."

"He was probably waiting to see if there was anything to it. Sounds to me like it's the work of a drug cartel anyway. Might just be a wasted trip." She placed the file on his desk.

Nick reached for the folder. "Let me take a look."

THE FBI's LOUISVILLE FIELD OFFICE WAS THE FIRST STOP ON the way to Crown Pointe. In a circumstance where a smaller satellite office was referred to Quantico, the jurisdictional lines and keeping open communication efforts were the best way to avoid situations like the mishandling of evidence. The agent in charge was cordial and left it up to Quinn to determine if the BAU needed to be involved. He also made it clear his office wanted nothing to do with the investigation, given that he already believed it was a DEA issue and not FBI.

But a cursory look into the case had already been agreed upon. And the next step was the drive to Crown Pointe. Agent Ness from the Pikeville office would meet Quinn and Kate at the local police station at which they'd just arrived.

Quinn pulled into a parking spot in front of the station. "Looks quaint."

"I've lived in 'quaint' before. Trust me, it's never what you think it is." Kate stepped out of the rental car and waited for Quinn near the entrance.

He met up with her and opened the door. "After you."

The chief stood just inside the entrance as if he was waiting on them. "You must be Agent Quinn, I'm Chief Henry Tate. I've heard a lot of good things about you and the work you've done at the BAU."

"Thank you. I hope Agent Ness hasn't raised your expectations too high. But I'll do my best." Quinn turned to Kate. "This is Special Agent Kate Reid. She's apprenticing for me right now after having spent the past few years doing similar work with the FBI's Washington Field Office in D.C."

"Agent Reid. Pleasure. This is Deputy Shane Lazaro and Deputy Eric Slocum, and of course, you know Agent Ness."

"Actually, we haven't yet met in person. Thanks for bringing us in on this, Agent Ness." She turned to the deputies. "Pleased to meet you both."

The chief clapped his hands and began, "Okay. Now that the pleasantries are over, let's get down to brass tacks." He approached Slocum's desk. "You'll have to forgive our paltry accommodations. I don't have a nice big conference room, so we'll have to convene here where Slocum can pull up the case files and I can brief y'all on this regrettable situation."

While the chief filled them in on much of what they already knew, Kate studied the crime scene photos again. She noted the meticulous placement of the bodies. The way their clothes had been fixed. Buttoned up, or straightened up, even though they were blood soaked. Care was taken with them. "Forgive my inter-ruption, but I'm noticing here on these pictures that the victims appear to have been cared for, in a way."

"I'm sorry? Cared for?" Slocum asked.

"Yes. As if whoever put them here felt bad for their deaths. Regretted them, even," Kate explained.

Quinn leaned over her shoulder to take a look. "You could be onto something." He returned his attention to the chief. "I under-stand there is some concern on your part that this could be a drug deal gone bad. And according to the file, only two of the victims were well acquainted with one another. The third murder occurred at a later date."

"That's right. The girlfriend of that third victim said she'd been with him the day before. But I do maintain that this is drug-related, given the toxicology reports, which are also in the file."

"Yes. We did review those," Kate replied. "Agent Quinn can correct me if I'm wrong, but the placement of these bodies." She paused for a moment. "I'm not DEA, but how many cartels would take the time to do this? Place them the way they did inside that mineshaft."

"Agent Reid, I have nothing but respect for the work you do," the chief began. "I simply can't imagine the horrendous things you must see in your line of work. However, here in Crown Pointe, we've been dealing with an epidemic for quite some time. Drugs have taken a whole lot of our fine people. If it's a drug deal, then so be it, but I've seen what happens here when deals go bad. And this is nothing like I've seen before. Which is why I asked Agent Ness for help. And he turned to you fine folks."

"These pictures only give us part of the story," Quinn said. "We need to see the victims. I think it will help us develop a more comprehensive understanding of these murders."

Chief Tate nodded. "I think that's a fine idea, Agent Quinn."

AGENT NESS LED THE CHIEF AND HIS DEPUTIES TOWARD THE small medical facility while Kate and Noah Quinn followed in their own vehicle.

"Sounds to me like the chief isn't sure which direction to take this investigation," Kate said. "I don't think Ness is confident either."

"I suppose that's why we're here. This isn't something the chief is used to dealing with. OD's, addicts, petty crimes; those are things they're used to. Bludgeoning and tox screens that show a deadly chemical compound, not so much," Quinn replied. "This must be the place. They're pulling in here." He cut the engine and looked at Kate. "You've been doing this for long enough, so I won't insult you by offering instruction on how to deal with the local authorities. So long as it doesn't end up in a shouting match like your last investigation."

"That's not fair. You knew we were dealing with a bad cop."

"You're right. I'm sorry I brought it up." Quinn pulled the keys from the ignition. "I will, however, suggest that we let the evidence speak for itself. If what we see doesn't jibe with their assessments, we will make ourselves heard. First and foremost, we're here to speak for the victims."

"Couldn't agree more." Kate stepped out of the car and caught up with the others.

Deputy Slocum nodded as she approached. "I reckon you're pretty used to this kind of stuff, Agent Reid."

"I'm not sure how used to it anyone could really be, but I've seen my share. And it doesn't get any easier."

"Well, we sure appreciate you both being here. I never seen nothing like this before. And I don't care to see it again." Slocum opened the door and they walked inside.

"Second time in a week, Henry," Doc began. "Let's try not to make a habit out of this." He offered a handshake. "And it appears you brought company."

"Yes, sir. This here is Agent Quinn and his colleague, Agent Reid. They're with the Behavioral Analysis Unit of the FBI."

"Ah yes. I'm familiar with the work y'all do over there. Can't say as I'd want to be doing that myself, but I reckon I got no choice at the moment."

"No, sir. I don't blame you," Quinn replied. "If you don't mind, could we go back and get started? We're a little under the gun."

"Sure. Of course. Come on back and take a look." Doc started back but peered over his shoulder at Quinn. "I'm still waiting on some forensics, unfortunately. Don't suppose there's anything you can do to expedite that for us?"

"We can certainly try." Quinn glanced at Ness. "Agent Ness? You think you could put in a call on your end?"

"I'll give it my level best."

They arrived at the room, the only one large enough to house the three victims while the case moved forward.

"As you can imagine, I've got the families of these poor souls waiting for us to release them," Chief said. "So the sooner we can get these results, the better for everyone involved."

The doctor opened the cold lockers and pulled out the trays. Each body was covered in a sheet.

Kate approached Joanne Waverly's body. "According to the file, these victims were struck from behind." She pulled down the sheet and examined the marks on her body, taking note of her legs. "This girl wasn't on her knees at the time of the blow to her head. I see no scratches or bruising on them, so I have to assume she was standing."

"You're thinking it would've made more sense for the perpetrator to force her to her knees, then strike the back of the skull. Better leverage for the desired effect," Quinn replied.

She looked to the doctor. "May we turn her on her side?"

"Of course. Let me give you a hand."

"Thank you." Kate continued to examine the trauma to the skull. "Your post-mortem exam suggests the victims were on the verge of death, likely from the drugs, before the final blows that would end their suffering."

"Well, yes. Although I'm not sure which would've been worse."

"The blow to the head would've been quick," the chief said. "Quicker than watching her mouth foam and her body convulse."

"Meaning the unsub might've shown compassion," Quinn replied. "Although that doesn't change the fact that whoever it was wanted the people dead in the first place."

"The strength that it would've taken to strike hard enough would also point to the unsub being a male." Kate walked around the body and toward the other victim. "This one here." She pointed to the skull of Steven Schiller. "This man is what, about five feet ten, 160 pounds?"

"Just about," Doc replied.

"A woman would've struggled to reach his head and still have the leverage needed to assert enough force." Agent Ness stepped in for a closer view.

"So let me get this straight. Y'all think we're dealing with a man, at least medium build, who has compassion for his victims?" The chief looked to his deputies. "Sounds like an oxymoron if I ever heard one."

"That it does," Quinn replied. "But would someone from outside, a cartel member or drifter, have known about the abandoned mineshaft? The trailer park and its reputation?"

The chief seemed to consider the probability. "Unlikely."

"I suppose that means it's someone here in town. I can't believe anyone in Crown Pointe would be capable of something so horrific." Lazaro appeared distraught at the idea. "This town's got its problems, but brutal murder isn't one of them."

"It is now," Kate replied.

7

The lights inside the plane were dimmed on the return red-eye flight to D.C. and most of the passengers were sleeping. But Kate wouldn't be going to sleep anytime soon. With her tray table down and her laptop open, she continued to work.

Quinn sat next to her and scrolled through his phone before taking notice. "You don't stop, do you?"

She peered at him. "Sorry?"

"Work. You don't stop working, do you?"

"Sure I do. Usually from the hours of midnight to about 6am."

Quinn checked the time on his phone. "It's after midnight now."

"Ah, but you see, I'm technically still on the clock. So..."

Quinn smiled. "I was impressed with your work today. And the way you handled yourself."

Kate furrowed her brow. "Did you expect anything less from me?"

"Well, let's just say the last time we worked on a case together, you were frustrated, verging on hostile."

She nodded. "I can see I clearly made a bad impression on you during that investigation. Which leads me to wonder why it was you still brought me on. And in all fairness, you weren't my supervisor at the time. Not to mention the fact that we were dealing with a corrupt cop in the process."

"Fair point. And as to why I still wanted you here, all I can say is I saw beyond your temperament. And I do feel that the circumstances were challenging with that detective. I can appreciate that. I should've prefaced my earlier statement by clarifying that you were surefooted. More confident in your conclusions than I'd seen before. Which leads me to believe that you don't need me as much as I thought you did."

"What can I say? I'm a quick learner."

"That you are, Reid." He tipped back the rest of his soda. "Time will tell if our—your—conclusions are correct."

"I hope I'm not proven correct when another body surfaces and that this was the end of it," Kate replied.

"It's in Ness' hands now. We've given them something to chew on. It'll be up to Chief Tate to decide how to move forward and if they need to get the DEA involved."

Lynn Floyd pulled away from the window. "They're here. Are you ready?"

"I am. Let 'em in." John Floyd poured the tablets into the prescription bottle and sealed the cap. "Remember, we agreed on a price."

"I know that." She opened the door as they approached her front steps. "Afternoon, boys. Come on in."

A young man, appearing to be in his early twenties, removed his baseball cap. "Thank you, ma'am. This here is Wyatt. I'm Kevin."

"I know who you boys are." Lynn closed the door as they stepped inside. "Go on in and see Mr. Floyd. He'll get you all fixed up."

The first young man still clutched his ball cap as he made his way inside the kitchen. "I was real sorry to hear about your daughter. She was a good person."

"Thank you. We miss her dearly. How did you know her?" John asked.

"Through some friends. Can't say as I knew her well, but we hung around with much of the same crowd."

"I see. Well, like we agreed upon. I assume you have the money?" John replied.

"I do, sir." Wyatt reached into his pocket. "Five hundred dollars, like you said." He placed the money on the table.

John pushed the bottle toward him. "There you go. You give us a ring if and when you're needing some more."

"Will do." Wyatt looked at Kevin. "Come on. Let's get out of these nice people's hair now. I'm sure they got better things to do than look at us." He led the way toward the door again. "Thank you, sir; ma'am."

Lynn nodded and let the boys out. She waited until they pulled away before closing the door again. "Should get us by for a while."

"Yep. I'm sure we can count on their speedy return." John handed his wife the money. "Keep this in a safe place."

"Always do." She began walking toward the living room again. "Oh, there's two more I came across yesterday. I reckon they'll be coming by before too long. Seeing as we still got the lowest price."

"What'd you do? Just go up and tell them you're a drug dealer?"

"Didn't have to. I made sure they saw me pull the bottle from my handbag. Made it real obvious for them. It was pretty easy after that."

KATE POURED A CUP OF COFFEE AND CAUGHT SIGHT OF NICK shuffling into the kitchen. "Looks like you could use a nice cup of hot java." She retrieved a mug for him.

"Why didn't you wake me when you got home last night?" he asked.

"Because I didn't get home until almost three in the morning. No sense in both of us suffering from lack of sleep."

He leaned in to kiss her. "I'm glad you're home. How'd it go?"

"We gave them our two cents. Not sure if they wanted to hear it."

Nick sipped on his coffee. "Weren't they the ones who asked for a consult?"

"Agent Ness with the Pikeville office did. Don't get me wrong, I think they appreciated our advice. I'm just not sure they'll heed it. The chief seemed reluctant."

"I'm sure it's not easy. Small town. Everyone knows each other," he added.

"Must be hard to imagine someone you know could've done such a thing. I think that's why they kept steering the case toward an outside cartel instead of looking internally."

"And you and Quinn don't think that's the right way to go?"

"I'm not convinced considering the evidence they presented. Though I wouldn't rule it out just yet," Kate said.

"You think you'll have to go back?"

"Hard to say. I think they'll need some time to absorb our suggestions. The problem is..."

Nick interrupted. "They still have a killer on the loose."

"Yes, they do." She placed her mug in the sink. "I'd better head out."

"Wait, did you eat?"

"I'll grab something on the way." She kissed him. "See you at the office."

In the halls of the BAU, agents and other staff busily carried on with their work. Meanwhile, Kate felt a little worse for wear but tossed back the last gulp of her Starbucks and continued toward Quinn's office. "Morning."

"Morning," he replied. "Glad you managed to make it in on time. What with only a couple hours of sleep. How are you holding up?"

"Fine. Couldn't be better." She was, of course, exhausted, but given that Quinn was a few years her junior, she didn't want to give in to any misconceptions about age, or being a woman.

"Great. Me too." He pushed up from his desk. "Hey, can I show you something?"

Kate watched as he started toward his door. "Where are we going?"

He glanced back at her as he stepped into the hall. "Downstairs."

Without the chance to even check her emails, Kate was already heading out again. This time, the reason was shrouded in mystery. "Downstairs" usually referenced the lab, but there were also classrooms and archival facilities.

"Does this have anything to do with the Crown Pointe murders?" She stepped quickly to catch up.

"You'll see." Quinn opened a door and switched on the lights. "I found something I thought would be useful."

"When? Since our flight arrived five hours ago?"

"I don't have anyone to occupy my time, so I spend a lot of it here."

His words were laced with a little spice, which confused her, considering his compliment on the airplane only last night. But rather than cause a dust up with her still-new boss, she let it slide—this time. "So, what is it, then?"

"Follow me." He made his way inside the small training room and opened a laptop, which projected an FBI screensaver on the wall ahead. He keyed in a command until an image appeared.

Kate studied the wall monitor. The image was of a shallow grave that contained four bodies. All lying face up. Arms resting at their sides and still fully clothed, except that it was clear there was a fair amount of decay. "What is this?"

"A case I pulled up from a few years ago. Ten to be exact. This was in rural Michigan in a vacant lot behind a house. These bodies were uncovered after neighbors complained of erratic behavior from the owner."

"Erratic how?" she asked.

"Loud noises, dog barking till all hours. The owner coming and going at night. Lights on in the backyard. That sort of thing. But it wasn't until the smell reached some of these neighbors that they finally called the police," Quinn replied.

"You said this might be useful. In what way?"

"Glad you asked. I pulled this case after I got a hit on a search for drug cartels here in the US. The ones that usually expand from Mexico. And what I found was that our Crown Pointe case isn't as atypical as it might appear." He grabbed a remote and clicked to change the image on the monitor. "In fact, I noticed some similarities, which is why I wanted you to see this too."

"The victims all appear to have been shot execution-style. That's not what we found in Crown Pointe," Kate replied.

"No, it isn't. However, take a look at the care in which the bodies were buried."

"So you believe this was also the result of a cartel? That the owner of the house was maybe part of it? Do we even know who did this?"

"We do." He clicked again and the image changed to three men in handcuffs being led to a jail or a courthouse. "These men were part of the Sinaloa Cartel. Members who resided in Michigan."

Kate peered at him. "Resided?"

"That's right. Apparently, the way they used to do business, outsourcing their shipments and deliveries to partners, they'd decided to handle themselves, bringing it in-house after discovering they could save not only money but reduce the risk of informants from said partners. The cartel members, in many cases, moved into the areas they controlled. They sent their kids to the schools; hell, they even mowed their own lawns. Just like every other red-blooded American."

"And dealt drugs," Kate added.

"As well as take care of those who tried to cross them." Quinn switched back to the grave site.

"Okay. Say this is the same thing. That doesn't explain the difference in techniques. The Crown Pointe victims weren't executed. They were bludgeoned and they weren't buried."

"I'd disagree with you there," Quinn began. "They were absolutely buried. That mineshaft is as much a grave site as anyplace else."

"But you said yourself, unless it was a local, how would they know about the abandoned mine?" she pressed on.

"Like I said, these people are moving into sleepy communities. And that's exactly what Crown Pointe is. A sleepy community with a very high ratio of addicts. What could be more perfect?"

"The only way this makes sense would be if the victims were also involved in dealing. Or else why kill them? You don't kill your customers," Kate added.

"I'm still working on that logic. Which is I why I think we need to go back and ask Chief Tate who moved into town in the past, what, few months maybe?" Quinn replied.

Kate considered his theory. "Maybe. But I'd say we could go back a year. People don't move into a place like that without causing a stir."

"We should speak to Ness then too. If we can all agree this could well be the work of a cartel, as this theory dictates, he will most likely want to refer this to the DEA."

"Yes and no. I'm not one hundred percent sold on the idea. I think it's another avenue to get to the truth. See, that's the thing about theories. If you aren't always trying to disprove them, then you aren't doing your job." Kate's earlier irritation at his perceived slight had vanished because he was absolutely right. And this was a legitimate lead. She knew how easy it was to get caught up in your own head. She'd done it before. And while in that instance, she was right, it was the time when she would be proven wrong that frightened her the most. Because that meant her blinders kept her from finding a killer.

"You want me to make the call or do you want to handle this one?" Quinn asked.

"I'd like to run on it."

He grinned. "That's what I was hoping you'd say."

❧

WITH HER HEAD FULL OF NEW IDEAS, AND A CONFIDENT stride, Kate was on her way back to her office when she almost collided with Nick. "Whoa! Hey there. Sorry about that. I was on the way to my office. Did you just get here?"

"No. I was in a meeting earlier," Nick replied. "What's going on? You look completely absorbed by something."

"Just a lead on the Crown Pointe consult. I need to put in a call to the local field office agent."

"That's good news. I was actually on my way to see Duncan. Have you seen her?" Nick asked.

"No, I haven't. I've been with Quinn since I arrived." Kate paused for a moment. "You know what? I think I'd like to run something by Duncan. When you're done with her, would you mind letting her know I'm looking for her too?"

"Sure thing. Hey, you let me know if something interesting pops up on that deal."

"You got it." Kate made it to her office and started compiling more information relating to Quinn's theory. Within a short while, she was ready to make contact with Agent Ness and reached for her phone. But before she dialed the number, Eva Duncan appeared.

"Heard you were looking for me. What's going on?"

Kate peered at her. "Oh, hey. I wanted to talk to you about what you're working on with ViCAP."

"Sure." Duncan walked inside and sat down. "About the questionnaire? Thanks for the input, by the way."

"Have you made any progress with the program manager regarding that?" Kate asked.

"Some. He seems receptive to it. In fact, I was going to bring it up in our meeting later today. I'm sure Quinn will want to put in his two cents. Maybe Scarborough too. Why do you ask?"

"Quinn and I got back from a consult on a case in Crown Pointe, Kentucky yesterday."

"I heard about that. Did something come of it?"

"I'm not sure yet. But before I move forward on Quinn's suggestion, I think I'd like to run a search on ViCAP to see if I can find any other similar cases. Quinn found some interesting similarities with a cartel investigation from ten years ago, but I'd like to enter different parameters and see what pops up."

Duncan studied her for a moment. "You two aren't on the same page?"

"Almost. Not entirely. I'm not quite ready to give up on my idea. Not that he's asking me to. He's just looking at alternative leads."

"He usually does," Duncan added.

"I figured. I got that from our first interactions. But, I don't know, I just get a different vibe and I'd like to start with ViCAP," Kate replied.

"You want some help with it?"

Kate laid out the files on her desk. "I thought you'd never ask."

ON HIS WAY TO SEE LEVI WALSH, NICK WAS STOPPED IN THE hall by the man himself. "I was just coming to see you," Nick said.

"Good timing, then. I'm heading to Quinn's office to drop off the archived files he requested."

"Oh yeah? Anything to do with the Crown Pointe consult?"

"Don't know." He raised the box he held in his hand to view the writing on the side. "This says—oh."

"What?"

Walsh looked at Nick. "I asked someone downstairs to pull the files, but I only gave him a number. Guess I didn't realize what it was."

Nick peered at the box. "What the hell does he want with this?"

"I'm sorry. I don't know. You'd have to ask him."

Nick walked alongside Walsh as they headed toward Quinn's office. There was no mistaking Walsh's marked change in demeanor. He appeared uncomfortable, verging on awkward, neither mentioning anything further.

As they arrived at Quinn's doorway, Walsh was the first to speak. "Got those files you asked for."

"Thanks. I appreciate you pulling some strings for me on this one." He glanced at Nick. "Scarborough? What can I do for you?"

Walsh placed the box on Quinn's desk and turned on his heel to leave. A move he'd made quicker in light of the situation.

Nick folded his arms and peered at Quinn. "Well, how about you explain to me why you requested the Hendrickson case file from the WFO?"

8

Quinn shed his gaze to the floor as he sat at his desk. "I was planning on running this by you and I'm sorry I didn't get a chance to explain before now."

Nick meandered inside and took a seat. "I'm listening."

"Look, you of all people know how valuable Reid's insight into the Hendrickson case is. I simply wanted to gain a better understanding of her motives, her problem-solving abilities. I think it's important I know how she operates."

"And you think the only way to get that information is by reviewing the case file?" Nick appeared doubtful. "Do you have any idea how long it took for her to put that behind her? That man hunted her. That man killed her childhood friend. And yes, I do know first-hand, her insight. And there was a time when I utilized that knowledge."

"You mean exploited it?" Quinn appeared to regret the comment.

"Frankly, I don't know what you could learn in those files that you wouldn't learn simply by working with her," Nick continued. "Wasn't that the whole point of bringing her on as your apprentice? And, I thought Reid made it clear she wasn't ready to discuss that case with you in any great detail."

"She told you I asked about it?"

"Of course she did. I'm her boss, for one thing. And I was there. I faced Hendrickson and I helped take him down." Nick stood again. "Now, if you'll excuse me, I was in the process of tracking down Walsh. I'd better go back and find him." He began to leave but stopped short and turned to face Quinn. "Something you should know about Reid. If she believes you're taking advantage of her, she'll become your worst enemy. You only need to look at the Copeland investigation to see that as fact. If you want to get inside her head, you'll only be there because she allows it."

Eva Duncan was stationed in the forensics lab when Kate arrived and caught up to her. "Good. I found you."

"I didn't know you were looking." Duncan swiveled away from her computer screen. "I haven't finished running your parameters yet on the Crown Pointe case."

"I know you're busy, but that's not why I'm here anyway. It does have to do with Crown Pointe, though. I made contact with the Chief over there and asked if he could send me data on the town's murder investigations," Kate began. "Oh, I also wanted to know the details of the murders. Domestic violence, drug-related, crime-related."

"He got back with you?" Duncan asked.

"He did." Kate held a flash drive between her fingers. "I copied the files to this. Mind if I show you?"

"Go right ahead."

Kate inserted the drive and loaded the files. "I put together a quick and dirty spreadsheet because I wanted to run something by you." She highlighted areas on the spreadsheet. "Take a look at this. Over the past five years, there have been almost thirty accidental drug overdoses, mostly Oxy, but some heroin."

"That's a lot," Duncan replied.

"It is for such a small town. We already know they have a problem with addiction, much like the rest of the country. Only it seems to have hit this community particularly hard."

"It's hit a lot of rural communities hard," Duncan added. "Big pharma made it so easy to get scripts, we're now dealing with a significant portion of the nation who's addicted to pain meds. Most have graduated to heroin because it's cheaper." She paused. "Sorry. Didn't mean to get off-track."

"Which is another reason why I wanted to get this data," Kate added. "These here that he sent over are accidental ODs. But in this file here are the cases classified as murder investigations."

"Is this case looking like it should be farmed out to the DEA?"

"I don't think so, despite the case histories Quinn found. Initially, the chief reached out to his local FBI field office because he believed the deaths were related to drug trafficking, which of course makes it a federal crime. However, based on what I'm seeing here. I think this investigation could be right up our alley. In the past five years, these deaths I've highlight were all ruled accidental. Every investigation that was opened was almost immediately closed once the labs came back. Then you have the murder investigations." Kate opened the other tab.

Duncan peered at the spreadsheet. "There's nothing on here."

"Exactly. There have been zero murder investigations in Crown Pointe. Only overdoses," Kate replied.

"What are you looking to get from this?" Duncan pressed on.

"Quinn suspects this could be a cartel moving in. Sinaloa, Los

Zetas, or whatever because it's happened before. There is precedence and I recognize that. However, I don't think that is the case here because there is not one drug overdose death on here caused by a drug-related crime. No deals gone bad, robbery, or the like. So what? These cartel thugs move in and immediately kill three people? Doesn't make sense to me."

"No." Duncan studied the screen. "What does make sense is that someone might've killed at least a few of those people for another reason. Someone who knew they'd be checked off as just another OD."

"Now we just need to find out what that reason was. Do you think we can take a look at the search? I'd like to know if we get any hits on similar crimes elsewhere. Markers are pretty clear in this instance. Head trauma, staged bodies, etc."

"Right." Duncan returned to her screen and began typing. "We should do that right now."

THE DISCOVERY OF THREE DEAD BODIES, HORRIBLY BATTERED, their remains tucked into an intentionally carved opening inside an abandoned mineshaft had everyone in Crown Pointe terrified. And Chief Tate still had no answers.

"I understand your fears. I'm fearful too." Chief Tate stood behind the podium at the high school's cafeteria that doubled as the drama department's stage. But this was no performance. He was afraid.

"What are you and your boys going to do about this, Chief?" One of the residents stood and wagged his finger angrily at him.

"Mr. Shepherd, I can assure you we are working day and night to get justice for those poor souls. We even got some advice from the FBI."

"Does that mean they're going to help you find the person who did these things?" another woman in the crowd shouted.

"Right now, they're consulting with us, helping us to gain a better understanding of the situation. As you all know, this sort of thing just doesn't happen here in Crown Pointe," the chief added.

"We sure as hell got enough problems down here without adding to it. We need answers, Chief. And I hear there are other folks missing too." He looked to a man and woman who were seated next to him. "When are you going to get us some damn answers?" Shepherd asked.

"As I said, we'll keep y'all informed of any new developments, but right now, please, just let us do our jobs. Thank you." He stepped away from the podium amid more questions. As Chief Tate made his way toward the side exit, Slocum approached.

"Hey, Chief. Can we hang back for just a minute?"

"Why is that?" he asked.

"Mr. and Mrs. Walcott would like to speak with you—in private."

The chief eyed Slocum, his nerves standing on end, already expecting the worst. "All right. Let this crowd leave. I'll stick around and talk to them."

It took another ten minutes before everyone filed out of the cafeteria. But one couple remained.

The chief approached them along with Slocum and Lazaro. "Evening, Charlie, Maggie. Deputy Slocum here says you wanted to talk. I can only assume your son Andy hasn't yet turned up. And I'm afraid we haven't had luck on our end either. We haven't forgotten about him. I can assure you of that."

"Go on, Charlie." Maggie nudged his arm.

"Well, Maggie here thinks our Andy is gonna turn up—well, like them others. And she..."

Maggie interrupted. "Chief Tate, you know us. You know our

boy. This ain't like him. You gotta find him before... Can't you just ask them FBI people to come here and help? No offense, but we only got the three of you here and we know that ain't gonna be nearly enough."

The chief peered at the couple. "Maggie, we are doing everything in our power to find Andy."

"Our son ain't no washed up addict like the others you found. You know that," she added.

"Andy's a good boy. I do know that. But I just don't have anything else for you right now. I wished to God I did." Chief Tate held his hat in his hand and he eyed Maggie. Both of them teared up. "It's best me and the boys head back to the station now. We know y'all ain't gonna sleep until Andy comes home, and neither are we." The chief pushed through the exit doors and his deputies followed.

In the high school parking lot illuminated by only a few working light posts as the sun had set, Lazaro began, "Chief, you think we should take a drive out to the mineshaft and have a look-see if Andy Walcott is there? We haven't checked out there since we took them others out."

Chief Tate stopped in his tracks and eyed his deputies. "If that boy's dead, and he's in that shaft like the others were, then we're dealing with a killer who's all kinds of stupid. Damn near the whole town was in there just now. They all know where those bodies were found. They'll be standing watch outside the mine, I know they will. No. If Andy Walcott is dead, I'd bet a dollar to a donut he ain't inside the mineshaft. But before we write this boy off, let's put all our efforts into finding him—alive."

Lazaro and Slocum nodded and spoke in unison. "Yes, sir."

～

WITH HER KEYS IN HAND, KATE OPENED THE APARTMENT door to see Nick on the other side. "Didn't expect to see you home already."

"I didn't see your text until I left and I thought, well, hell, why not surprise you." He kissed her lips. "Are you surprised?"

"I am. Pleasantly so." She shed her coat, and bag, and continued inside. "Eva and I had a particularly good day. I think she's warming up to me."

"Oh yeah? I knew they'd come around. What were you two working on?" Nick asked.

"Crown Pointe. We don't have what I was looking for just yet, but we're getting close. She's helping me look for hits on ViCAP regarding similar crimes."

He walked into the kitchen. "You want a glass of wine? Have you eaten yet? I could order something."

"Yes and no. Let's get something delivered. That'd be great. So anyway, you know Quinn was suggesting that the deaths were cartel-related."

"Sure. Makes sense."

"It does. And while I don't completely disagree with him, I am taking another path. One that I think seems a little more viable."

"And have you brought this up with him?" Nick retrieved the glass from the cabinet.

"In a roundabout way."

"He is your supervisor. I think it's important you maintain the chain of command. I shouldn't have to tell you that."

"And you don't." She reached for the glass full of Chardonnay. "I'm doing what I always do, Nick. And that is to find the truth. Find the real reason why those two men and that woman were murdered. Look, I think taking a two-pronged approach is the right course of action."

"I'm not saying you're wrong. I'm saying you should keep Quinn informed of what you're doing."

She sipped on the wine before continuing. "I didn't expect push back from you."

"Kate, I just need you to play by the rules here. I realize we had a lot of leeway at the WFO. It's not like that here. We're part of a much larger team. A team that I'm in charge of. And you're an apprentice. If Quinn decides you aren't the right fit, it's his prerogative to terminate the deal."

"I don't get where this is coming from. I'm not doing anything wrong. I did mention my theory to him. Are you telling me I can't do anything without getting his authorization? Duncan didn't seem to feel that way."

"That's because she has a permanent role on the team. She's been there long enough and has enough autonomy so that it's not an issue for her. And, if you play by the rules, you'll get that autonomy too," Nick replied.

"Did he say something to you about me and my work? Because honestly, it really seems as though he's more than willing to consider my points of view," Kate pressed on.

"I'm sure he is. At the end of the day, Quinn is a good agent, an exceptional profiler. But I think he wants to understand you better. How you operate."

"I don't have a problem with that. I thought that was the whole point of apprenticing for him?" She regarded Nick closely. "What are you not telling me?"

"Nothing. All I'm saying is that you need to keep him abreast of your ideas and leads and whatever else you're working on. You do that, and there won't be any problems. You'll learn the job and who knows? Maybe one day, you'll be better than him."

She scoffed. "You sure you weren't drinking any of that wine before I got here?"

He eyed her.

"I'm only joking. So, what's for dinner?"

As they returned to the station house, Chief Tate regarded his deputies. "We got a real damn problem here, boys. I suspect those three victims aren't going to be our last."

"No, sir," Lazaro replied. "How you want to handle this?"

"So far, we know these victims all had a manufactured form of Oxy in their system. And likely the Walcott boy will too, when we find him."

"You're assuming he's already dead?" Slocum asked.

"I hate to. I really do. But we need to be honest about this situation. It's time we backtrack to find out if they all got the drugs from the same place."

"Do you think it's a cartel? Like them agents said?" Slocum pressed on.

"I don't know. I spoke to the one lady, the profiler lady."

"Agent Reid?" Lazaro asked.

"That's right. She asked me to send her some info on recent cases. And I did. I also know she talked to Ness about the idea this could well be a case of drug trafficking or something along those lines. We're getting our fingers into too many pies here, boys. We're going to need some assistance. Lord knows we have enough on our plates and to deal with three murders, maybe four? Well, I don't see as how our small-town resources are going to get us very far."

"We can't just sit here and wait for them to show up," Slocum replied.

"Let's get back out there and start in on finding Andy Walcott again. Then I'll talk to Agent Ness about tracing the drugs, and maybe, if we're lucky, we'll find the dealer and go from there."

"You got it, boss." Lazaro turned to Slocum. "We should head out. It's already getting dark. I want to hit as many places as we can tonight."

The men headed out to the parking lot and stepped inside the patrol car.

With Lazaro at the wheel, Slocum began, "I think I might know where we should look."

Lazaro turned the ignition. "And where's that?"

"You heard the kids talk about a place called the cabin?"

"Can't say as I have. Where is it?"

"Not far from the trailers. About a mile out past them, I reckon," Slocum replied.

"You think we'll find the boy there?"

"Maybe. It's as good a place as any to start. By all accounts, the kids go there to get high. So, by my reckoning, the trailers were the same sort of place. And Chief says there's no way the killer would go back there after the whole town knows what happened."

Lazaro pulled out onto the road. "So you think the killer would've taken him there?"

"Taken him, or he was already there," Slocum replied.

"Okay, then. That's where we'll go first. You know what I still can't understand?"

Slocum glanced at him. "What's that?"

"Why on God's green earth someone would have beaten in the heads of them people. Makes no damn sense to me. Especially if the drugs would've killed them anyway. Leads me to believe Agent Ness might be right and them other agents."

"That it's the work of a cartel? That doesn't sit right with me because why would you kill your customers?"

"Hell, I don't know. I guess I'm just grasping at straws here. Same as everyone else."

Slocum nodded. "Let's just get to the cabin and have a look around."

"What if we find people there? Using the facilities, as it were? We planning on arresting them?" Lazaro asked.

"At this point, might be safer for them if we did." Slocum stared straight ahead. "Doubt anyone would want to be out there knowing there's a killer running round."

The next few minutes found the deputies silent as they quietly pondered what they might find in the dark of night.

"Make a right up ahead." Slocum pointed at the road.

Lazaro turned the car and began heading down a dirt road, like so many of the roads on the outskirts of town. "Is that it up there?"

"Yes, sir, it is." Slocum glanced at him. "Maybe you should kill the lights."

"I don't see any cars out there. Place could be empty."

"Dear Lord, I hope so."

Lazaro pulled to a stop a few feet from the cabin's entrance. "Doesn't look like anyone's taken care of the place in some time." He killed the engine. "Guess we should go have a look-see."

The deputies stepped out of the cruiser and walked toward the front porch.

"You reckon they got power out here?" Slocum asked.

"Not likely. And I don't see any lights on inside. Course they could have them LED lanterns," Lazaro whispered. "You want to head around back?"

Slocum nodded before pivoting toward the side of the house.

Lazaro knocked on the door. "Crown Pointe police. If you're inside, please identify yourself." He waited. No answer. "This is Deputy Lazaro with the Crown Pointe Police. Open up." Again, there was no answer. Lazaro placed his hand on the door knob and turned. It wasn't locked. He pushed the door that opened to a dark, single-room cabin that had seen its share of neglect.

As he walked inside, shining a flashlight, he spotted an old wood-burning stove, and on further inspection, noted it was cold. A few used needles lying around. Some pill bottles and a bong sat on a coffee table. The couch was well-worn. A small kitchenette was adjacent with a card table and a couple of folding chairs.

A knock sounded and Lazaro swung around, hand on his holster. "Jesus, Mary, and Joseph. You about got your head shot off."

Slocum had knocked on a window in the kitchen. "Sorry." His muffled voice sounded through the single pane glass. "You might ought to come on out here and see this."

Lazaro exited through the front of the cabin and walked around to meet Slocum. "What is it? What'd you find?"

Slocum shined his flashlight on a mound of dirt. "I don't know about you, but this mound looks pretty fresh."

"We got a shovel around here anywhere?" Lazaro cast his gaze about and spotted a small shed. "Let me see what I can find in there." He walked toward the shed and opened the door. It was the smell that hit him first. "Dear Lord!" His hand covered his mouth to control his gag reflex.

"What is it?" Slocum jogged to catch up to him.

Lazaro moved his light around until it landed on the source of the smell. "Oh, my."

"That's Andy Walcott, isn't it?" Slocum asked, already knowing the answer. "What the hell did they do to him? His damn brains are bashed in all to hell."

"Yeah, I see that." Lazaro reached for his radio. "Chief Tate, we found him."

The chief's voice sounded on the radio receiver. "Andy Walcott? Is he all right?"

"No, sir, he's not. He's most definitely not."

9

Floodlights mounted on stands were aimed at the shed where Andy Walcott's body was found. The secluded area was otherwise pitch black as the hour approached midnight.

"We appreciate you coming out, Agent Ness," the chief said. "I'll be honest with you, I don't have one damn clue as to what the hell is going on in this town. I've seen my share of wicked business, but nothing like this."

"And you're still waiting on the analysis of the drugs on the most recent victim?" Ness replied.

"We are. I see now I'm going to have to light a fire under the doc. See what he can do to move it along. I think this all goes back to the drugs, in some form or another."

"Hey, Chief." Slocum approached the men. "The ambulance is here and ready to move the body."

"Let's get him the hell out of there, then. Unless you have a need for him to stay put?" he asked the agent.

"No. I'm good. I've got the photos."

"All right, then. Slocum, go ahead and have them bring back the gurney."

Within minutes, the EMTs appeared, wheeling the gurney over the heavily weed-filled backyard of the dilapidated cabin. They approached the shed and entered.

"Be careful now. Show that boy some respect," Chief said.

"Yes, sir. I could use an extra set of hands," the paramedic replied.

"Slocum, go on and help them two out."

Slocum joined them and helped hoist the body of the young man onto the gurney. He swallowed down to contain his gag reflex both from the smell and the sight of brain matter exposed like the innards of some disemboweled animal. "Christ Almighty."

The chief and Agent Ness watched the boy as they took him away. It was then that they stood just outside the shed's entrance, aiming their flashlights into it.

"He wasn't killed here," Ness said.

"No. Whoever it was brought him here after the deed was done. What do you reckon that means?"

"I can speculate, but I think I'd like to call again on our friends at Quantico. They're the experts in this sort of thing. I think they'll need to join in on this situation. Can you ensure this remains untouched?"

"Absolutely. The sooner you can get them here, the better. Agent Ness, I fully believe I have a murderer on my hands and I don't care if it's some drug cartel or a drifter. I just need to catch the son of a bitch before I gotta tell another parent their child is dead."

$\sim$

Kate slept soundly until Nick's cell phone buzzed on his nightstand. He roused and eventually answered the call.

"Scarborough." He yawned and rubbed his eyes clear. "When?"

The one-sided conversation drew her attention when Nick sat up with interest. She turned toward him, waiting for the outcome.

"Of course. I'll authorize it. We can leave first thing in the morning. I'll let her know. Thank you." As Nick ended the call, he turned to Kate.

"What's happening?" she asked.

"We're going to Crown Pointe. Quinn's booking the 7am flight." He checked the time. "Meaning we've got about two hours of sleep left."

"They found someone else, didn't they?"

"They did."

Kate pursed her lips and nodded. "Are we all going? The entire team?"

"Fisher will need to coordinate with Agent Ness out of the Pikeville field office. And Walsh should be there too. It's his job to work with the local authorities. Quinn, of course. And then you and me."

"I'd like to request Duncan come along too."

"I need someone here who can run on research. That's what she does best, and for now, here is where we need her."

"Fine. But you'll be coming? Are you sure that's wise? I mean, that's not your main role—going into the field. Not anymore."

His side table lamp shone against her face and he noticed her expression. "Sounds like you don't want me there."

"I'm not saying that at all. I'm just saying that maybe you should let your team run the field. That's their job. And mine."

"Look, I know you want to prove to them that you're not under my wing. That you can handle yourself. And I get that. I do."

"You know I'm right, Nick." She placed her hand on his well-toned shoulder. "You wanted out of that part of the job. You should stay here. If they need you, they'll tell you."

He pushed his hand through this thick hair that had sprouted streaks of grey on the sides. "Yeah. I guess this is what I wanted, wasn't it?" He lay back down and turned away from her. "You'd better get some sleep. Five am will roll around quick."

Kate examined him as he kept his back to her. This was what he'd wanted. But in practice, it appeared he might be regretting his decision. She felt for him and was even a little sorry he wasn't going to be there with her and the others. Their work together was extraordinary. But she knew she could be extraordinary on her own.

Deputy Lazaro peered through the window near his desk as the sun rose in the sky. "Hey, Chief. Looks like we got us a whole horde of Feds here." He pulled back and turned to Slocum. "They're driving black SUVs, just like on TV."

"You shittin' me?" Slocum pushed up from his desk and walked toward the window. "I'll be damned. Just like TV." He chuckled but stopped at the arrival of Chief Tate.

The chief glared at them. "You boys done now? Because we got some serious work ahead of us. Unless you think this is humorous in some way?"

Both of them muttered their way out of trouble.

"That's what I thought." He stood in the center of the bullpen and waited for them to enter.

Agent Ness was the first to push through the door. He stood in place, door in hand as he addressed the chief. "Morning, Chief Tate. I got some people here wanting to lend a hand on this investigation." He nodded as Walsh entered. "This is Agent Levi Walsh. The lead investigative analyst."

"Pleased to meet you, Chief Tate." Walsh offered his hand.

"Agent Cameron Fisher. He's the official field coordinator. Meaning he's the guy I arranged this with. And of course, you already know Agent Quinn and Agent Reid."

Chief Tate greeted each of them. "Thank you all for coming and especially on such short notice. It wasn't without need, rest assured of that."

"I'm very sorry to be here again, Chief." Quinn shook his hand. "But let's hope we can resolve this quickly and without any more tragedy."

"From your mouth to God's ear." He returned the greeting. "Okay. Now, you all been briefed on the latest?"

Fisher removed the toothpick from his mouth. "We have, yes. I'd like to start by getting us set up here and let Agents Quinn and Reid do what they do best."

"I can only assume that must mean you two would like to take a look at our latest victim?" the chief replied.

"That's a good first step," Quinn began. "After that, we should see where the body was found, how it was staged. Things of that nature."

"Staged?" Slocum asked.

"Yes. Just as the others were staged in an upright position, essentially carved into the side of a mineshaft. I'm assuming this latest would've been staged in a similar manner."

"We believe the killer is making a statement," Kate added.

"You mean, you no longer believe this was the work of a cartel pushing their way into our town?" Chief asked.

"I still believe that could be the case, but as Reid has alluded, a statement is being made. Whether that is from a cartel or a serial killer, we need to decipher his message if we hope to understand what we're dealing with," Quinn replied.

"Then it's settled." Chief Tate turned to Slocum. "Why don't you help Agents Fisher and Ness get set up here. Get them a nice place to work. I'll head out with Quinn and Reid. And what about you, Agent Walsh?"

"You should join us," Quinn said. "As well as Lazaro, if that's okay with you, Chief?"

"Fine by me. The more sets of eyes we get on this beast, the better off we'll be." Chief Tate led the way outside and opened the door of his older model SUV. "I see y'all travel in style with all those federal dollars you got. I must admit, I'm a little envious."

"I'll tell you what, Chief. Why don't we drive? We'll spend some of those federal dollars on a tank of gas, so you don't have to."

"I like the way you think, Agent Quinn."

The five of them stepped into the black rented SUV with Quinn behind the wheel. "To the hospital?"

"Yes, sir." The chief pointed the way ahead before turning back to the others. "Y'all doing all right back there?"

"We're just fine, Chief," Walsh replied. "We appreciate you taking the time to get us acquainted. I know Reid and Quinn were here a few days ago, so they're more familiar, but now that we have a full-fledged investigation, it's best the team understands the entire situation as it has unfolded so far."

"Do I detect a slight southern accent, Agent Walsh?"

"You have a good ear, Chief. I've been in D.C. for the past ten years, but I was born and raised in Alabama."

"Ah, a 'Bama boy. I bet your momma's proud of you."

"I believe she is, sir."

This was the first time Kate had a chance to really spend some time with her team on her own, and it felt good. She knew Walsh had been at BAU for the past two years as an investigative analyst.

It was great she was getting to know more about him. And in turn, how she fit in this puzzle.

"What about you, Agent Reid?" Chief asked. "You don't sound like you're from the south."

"I'm not. I'm a California girl. Born and raised outside Eureka. I started with the San Diego Police Department before moving to Washington."

"I am in the presence of some very bright, young talent. I can see that. We might learn a thing or two from these folks, Lazaro."

"Yes, sir."

"Thank you, Chief," Kate replied.

"Okay now, you're gonna want to take the next right. If you'll recall, that's where the hospital is."

Quinn turned right, and ahead, the building came into view. "Looks like that's it just ahead."

"You are correct. Go on and pull in. Doc knows we're coming."

Quinn parked the SUV and the agents stepped out.

Kate walked to the sidewalk and waited for Quinn to lock up when Walsh approached her.

"I didn't know you were from Northern California."

She smiled. "I didn't know you were from Alabama."

"Guess we learned something new about each other, Reid." Walsh patted her on the back.

She studied him as he continued inside and wondered how it was he didn't know where she was from. Her past was an open book and she assumed everyone on her team knew exactly who she was. Especially considering Nick was their boss and had been knee-deep in the Hendrickson case, along with her.

As Quinn walked closer, she stopped him. "Hey, can I ask you something?"

He stopped in his tracks. "Shoot."

"The rest of the team... do they know about me?"

Quinn glanced at them as they continued toward the entrance. "I assume you mean Hendrickson."

She nodded, as if there was anything else to know about her.

"They know. Not in so much detail. But I've shared with them some of the information. I felt it was crucial before bringing you on."

"I was just wondering how it was Walsh didn't know where I was from."

"He was either being nice, making small talk, or maybe he didn't know. I don't recall shedding that much light on your background. Just that you'd been abducted from a small town in northern California," he continued again. "Take it as he's looking to get to know you. And that's a good thing."

They made their way inside and joined the rest of the team.

The doctor appeared to await their arrival and as they approached, he began, "Well, Chief, I can't say as I'm happy to see y'all again. And it looks like you brought even more friends."

The chief made the introductions and added, "These fine folks are going to be a big help and I'm sure glad to have it. You mind if we go on back? I'd like to get them started."

"Follow me." The doctor led the way back to the same room as before, except now there was another body. "As you can see, we're still waiting for authorization to release the other victims." He turned to the chief. "Any idea when that might happen?"

"You'll have to ask these folks."

"I'm afraid we'll need to keep them here until we can get all the results back," Quinn said. "I think it's imperative we don't overlook what might seem like even the smallest detail."

"That's what I was afraid you might say. I got these families wanting answers, as I'm sure the chief can attest."

"If at all possible, we'll just need to hold them off a while longer." Quinn walked toward the latest victim. "This is Andy Walcott?"

"It is." Chief moved in closer. "My boys found him late last night. Had to break the news to his folks shortly thereafter."

"I'm sure that must've been very difficult," Quinn replied.

"Difficult don't even come close to what it was, Agent Quinn." Chief eyed the others. "When we're finished here, we'll head out to the scene so y'all can see for yourselves."

Kate moved closer to the body. "The trauma appears to be more violent than what we saw on the previous victims."

"Maybe he put up a fight," Quinn added. "He's also larger, stronger than the other males. In fact, he doesn't look at all like a strung-out addict. He appears to have an athletic build."

"I don't think he was," Chief said. "His momma vehemently denies he was a user, though his daddy tends to believe he dipped his toe in occasionally. I know Doc here is still waiting for the tox screen to come back. And I suppose that will give us a clearer picture. But what you're saying rings true. I reckon he was using only on a recreational basis."

Walsh moved in next to the chief. "The time's come to put in place provisions to help safeguard the public. Let them know they would be putting themselves in danger if they engage in the purchase of the illegal prescriptions or any narcotics."

"Agent Walsh, I don't know how much you're aware of the drug problem down here, particularly opioids. But damn near half the residents here use, and I'd say of that, at least a quarter are addicts." Chief looked to the doctor. "Wouldn't you say that's a fair assessment?"

The doctor nodded. "Maybe even a little conservative."

"Right." The chief returned his attention to Walsh. "So to say to these people they need to stop buying drugs is akin to telling an alcoholic to stop buying booze. And that's legal. You understand what I'm saying?"

"I do, Chief. And I can't imagine the struggles you and your department have faced. But from what I know right now, danger surrounds them if they go in search of these drugs. Whatever we need to do to get through to them, I guess I'll look for your input on that. But they need to know what's happening—and why."

"I understand where my colleague is coming from," Quinn began. "But before we sound the alarm—not that these people don't already know about the murders—I think we should ascertain the extent of the victims' histories. Find similarities, and develop a profile on the killer himself. I still don't feel comfortable ruling out a gang or cartel trying to make a statement."

Kate wanted to say something, that she wasn't one hundred percent convinced of his theory. But she didn't feel comfortable doubting him in front of everyone here. She had zero clout and she would have to come up with more in order to prove her theory before bringing attention to it. But there was something she could bring to light. "One thing I do find interesting is that these bodies have been discovered in known drug areas, so to speak. These are places people go to get high or to make their deals."

"Which brings us back to the statement the killer or killers are making," Quinn added.

"Okay, if we're not ready to go public..." Walsh began.

"Oh, I've gone public. There's no two ways about it. We had a town meeting a few nights ago. These people are already scared. And frankly, I don't blame them because, right now, it doesn't appear like we know our asses from our elbows." The chief paused to collect himself. "You'll have to forgive me. It's been a long week and I'm starting to feel a little more than frustrated at the situation. I need something I can work with here, fellas. And I thought that was why all you people come down here."

"It is why we're here, Chief. And unfortunately, without a complete picture, without all the labs and forensics, it makes our jobs that much harder." Quinn looked to his team. "I think the best we can do right now is to go out to the crime scene and take a look. What I'm seeing here now is highly concerning. The killer is becoming more violent. I'll tell you one thing, the victims are being killed somewhere else and then brought to these well-known drug hangouts. What we need to understand is where are they coming from? This is a small town. And I can't believe no one has seen anything out of the ordinary. I think maybe someone has, but they're afraid to talk."

"Rightly so, I'd say," the doctor replied.

"Regardless, we don't have enough to go on right now. We need more. And with the help of you and your men, Chief, we need to get the word out that the feds are here. That just might jolt someone into talking."

"I think I can work with that, Agent Quinn. If you wouldn't mind working out the details with me, Agent Walsh? Between us and your Agent Fisher, maybe we can reach out to the community more effectively while these two over here work to find out who the hell is killing the people of this town."

10

The marching orders had been handed down. The chief and Deputy Lazaro, along with two members of the elite FBI Behavioral Unit, Walsh and Fisher, were to scour the town in search of anyone who could come forward with relevant information. The others would examine the crime scene in search of something that might have been overlooked.

The first person on the list was the man with whom Lazaro had already spoken, Sterling Jensen, an unreliable man who would certainly look out for his own best interests, and who wasn't bothered by the fact that people were dying all around him.

"I didn't get much out of him last we spoke," Lazaro said. "I can't even say for sure if he's still out there. Seems like he goes anywhere he can put his head down. Guy pretty much keeps to himself, by all accounts."

"He'll cooperate. Won't have a choice," Chief replied. "We can justify a search of the trailer. He doesn't own it. I checked already. Place was abandoned years ago like the rest of them. He was the only person to see Dawn Murphy and I reckon he saw other stuff he's keeping to himself too."

"Best option we have is to see if he's out there. Otherwise, we're just spitting in the wind," Lazaro added before turning to Walsh. "Unless you folks have a better idea?"

"No, sir. If he's there, chances are better than fair this Jensen guy would see his way to cooperating. Most people do when they see the FBI at their door."

"Better give it a shot." The chief headed out of the station and waited for Fisher to unlock the SUV. He stepped into the passenger seat and peered through the windshield while the others made their way inside.

Fisher pulled onto the road and headed out before glancing at the chief. "Why do you call that place the Devil's Den?"

Chief peered back at Lazaro before answering. "About thirty-odd years ago that mineshaft collapsed. It was run by a small operation that cut corners. Nothing like the big mines on the other side of town. Anyway, it ended up killing some of the miners. They're the ones who lived in them trailers. They never did find the bodies. They're still buried behind the wall of dirt that came down about forty feet inside the shaft. Company went belly up; didn't bother digging them out. And no one came to help. No one. People say the place is cursed. So that's how it got its name."

"Jesus," Walsh replied. "That's the saddest thing I've ever heard."

Chief nodded. "Yes, sir. It is."

"That's it, up ahead, gentlemen," Lazaro said.

Fisher eyed the grounds. "Place looks deserted."

"I imagine word got 'round. What with the town meeting and the police barricade in front of the shaft," Chief began. "Anyone foolhardy enough to stick around here must be in some kind of desperate shape."

Fisher pulled alongside the trailer where the man in question had previously been seen. "We might be in luck. There is a car here."

"Like I said, desperate. I'd appreciate if y'all let me initiate the discussions," Chief added.

"We'll follow your lead, Chief." Walsh emerged from the vehicle into the dusky light of a setting sun. He pulled on his jacket for warmth. "I didn't think it was supposed to get so chilly down here."

"Oh, make no mistake, we get our share of winter weather. Maybe no snow like where you fellas are from. But it can get downright nippy." The chief started toward the door of the tin-clad trailer and knocked on the screen. "This is Crown Pointe police. We'd like to have a word."

He turned to the others, and with a downturned mouth, shook his head. "This is Chief Tate with the Crown Pointe Police. Sterling, we'd just like to ask a few more questions of you is all."

When there was still no answer, Walsh began, "Any chance he's already vacated?"

"It's sure looking like that. Why he would've left his car is beyond me, though." The chief reached for the door handle. "Well, I'll be damned, it's unlocked. Reckon we should take a look round." Upon opening the door, the stench seeped out. "Good Lord." The chief covered his mouth and continued inside.

The rest of the men followed him into the small trailer.

"Smells like a dead body," Walsh said. "Is there a bedroom in here or is this it?"

The scope of the living space consisted of a two-burner stove, a bar-sized refrigerator, and a microwave that took up most of the counter in the kitchenette. There was a sofa and coffee table a few feet away. With windows covered in tin foil, it was nearly pitch black inside, except for the opened door, which let in some gray light.

Lazaro walked to one of the windows and ripped down the foil. "Oh hell." He peered at the two-seater sofa where a body lay sprawled across. "This isn't the man we're looking for."

The chief shuffled closer and studied the body. His shoulders dropped and a heavy sigh escaped him. "This is Wyatt Cavanaugh. Boy ain't more than twenty-five." The chief ripped off his hat and turned away. "Damn it!"

"I don't see any trauma to the head," Walsh began. "Not like the others." He examined the young man closer. "Could this have just been an overdose?"

"Appears so. Seems like one hell of a coincidence, if that's the case. Why here? In the very same place ol' Sterling Jensen was seen the other day." The chief turned to the agents. "Well, what do y'all think now? What words of wisdom can you impart on us that might explain what the hell happened here and why it don't match the others?"

Fisher stepped toward the victim. "Until we run a tox screen, we can't offer any answers for you, Chief. I'm sorry. I wish we could."

As evening fell, so did their chances of finding the answers they sought. Kate and Noah Quinn now stood outside the shed where the recent victim, Andy Walcott, was discovered. Only he was different from the others and died a much more horrific and violent death.

"He's the youngest of the victims to date, which is troublesome enough. And there's no doubt in my mind that whoever brought this young man here was male," Quinn said.

"You won't get an argument from me on that one. Andy Walcott was a strong kid. Looked like he played a lot of sports. So the person who brought him here was above average in height and weight. We're talking a sizable man." Kate continued to observe the surrounding area. "I know we're losing light, and I can't be sure, but I didn't notice any signs that the unsub forcibly entered the home. The shed either."

"No, but this doesn't appear to be the most secure place. Especially if it's generally used as a drug den."

"Your cartel theory," Kate continued, "it seems there would have been more than one person involved, wouldn't you agree?"

"Not necessarily. Not if you recall my thoughts that it could be someone who has recently moved into the community. A precedent has been set for that."

"Chief Tate is still waiting on county records, but he couldn't recall anyone new in the past several months. And he seems to be on top of things around here," Kate replied.

Quinn's phone buzzed in his pocket. "It's Walsh." He answered the line. "Quinn here."

Kate continued to examine the inside of the shed using the light on her phone. What was she missing? The killer couldn't possibly have been so methodical as to leave nothing behind. There was always something. Even something seemingly innocuous. She recalled a few of her past cases in which that had happened. She just needed to look harder.

A careful step inside the shed while Quinn continued his conversation and Kate studied the 4-foot by 6-foot metal box that someone had once used to care for their back lawn. But that must've been a long time ago. This was her chance to show them what she could do. There were plenty of times she laughed off her so-called sixth sense. Her ability to discover the minutiae and make a case. Nick always told her it was what made her remarkable. And while her modesty often got in the way of accepting such accolades, there were times when she felt absolutely driven by that sense. But could she summon that drive now, or would it fail her at this most crucial of times when more lives could be on the line and a killer or killers on the loose?

"What did you leave behind?" she whispered.

"Reid?"

Kate spun around, startled by the sound of her name.

"Geez, did I scare you?" Quinn asked.

"Sorry. I was deep in thought."

"We need to go. They found a body, but they don't think it's related. No physical signs. Probably an OD. We're needed back at the station for a briefing."

"Sure." Kate turned to leave and held up her phone to shut off its flashlight. And that was when she spotted it. A faint glimmer in the fading light. "Wait." She aimed the phone at the frame of the shed's door. "You need to see this."

"What is it?" He stepped inside and turned his sights upward. "Is that a splintered piece of wood?"

"Looks like it to me. Except you see that? Does that look like blood to you?"

"Hell yes it does. Could still be fresh. Looks almost wet in that light. You have a bag or something?" Quinn looked around.

"Hang on. I don't have a bag, but I have gloves." With the latex glove in her hand, she reached for the piece of wood, ensuring the glove was the only thing that made contact with it. As she pulled it down, they both examined it.

"That's definitely blood. In that little crevasse of the splinter," Quinn said.

"What are the odds we'll find prints or at least partials?"

"Won't know until we test it." He turned to her. "How the hell did you see that? Everyone's scoured this place."

Kate shrugged. "Dumb luck, I guess."

The headlights of the rented SUV cut through the black skies as Quinn and Kate returned to the station house. He pulled into the lot and turned off the engine.

Peering into the building, its window blinds still open, Kate spotted everyone inside. "Looks like we're the last ones to the party." She opened the door and stepped out, pulling on her jacket.

"Looks like it. I'm anxious to get this evidence into a lab. We'll ask Ness to take it with him tonight to process." Quinn held open the station door for Kate and both walked inside.

"Glad y'all made it back. I thought you might've gotten lost," Lazaro said. "It gets pretty tough to navigate the area after dark, especially on the outskirts."

"Did you find something?" Ness peered at the evidence Kate still held.

"A splinter, or rather broken chunk of wood, found on the door frame of the shed. Looks like it has blood on it. We were careful not to handle it. Any chance you can get this to your lab asap?" she asked.

"How the hell?" Ness' face masked in surprise. "We searched that shed several times."

"Don't ask me how she found it," Quinn started. "I didn't see it. Reid spotted it wedged in some crevasse in the frame. I can only imagine it snagged on something when the killer left or..."

"Or, the beating didn't happen somewhere else, like we thought," Walsh added.

"That was my first thought too, except Quinn and I didn't find any evidence it happened in the shed. No tissue or even blood, as

I'm sure you all figured out. Best we can gather is like you said, Quinn, whatever it was that was used to strike the victim was caught on something and splintered. But the sooner we get this analyzed, the better we'll be. If we can get DNA or fibers from it, hell, even identify the object itself, we'll be that much closer."

"That's one hell of a find, Agent Reid," the chief said. "Like pulling a rabbit out of a hat."

"Thank you, Chief. I just got lucky."

"My guess is luck didn't play into it." He eyed her as though he knew what she was capable of. "As you likely already heard, we found another unfortunate soul. Only this one doesn't appear to be related. The body was collected and sent to the morgue. I need to make a trip to see the boy's folks. Something I can't fathom having to do yet again."

"And we're sure it's unrelated?" Quinn asked.

"The doc will run a tox screen," Fisher began. "But it doesn't appear that the boy was a victim of the unsub. Like the chief said to us earlier, they get their share of ODs here."

"Seems awful damn coincidental to me," Slocum emerged from the back of the station. "I got y'all set up in the break room. Couple tables and your LAN connections. Should do for now. Better than squeezing everyone out here. Chief, you want me to accompany you to the Cavanaugh's?"

"No. Best if I go it alone. What's the plan for tomorrow? I assume you folks will need a place to put your head down for the night?"

"We will, Chief," Fisher chomped down on his toothpick before turning to Agent Ness. "You'll take the evidence Reid found and rush it through?"

"I will. I'll run it out now and expedite its processing. I'll head back down here at first light."

Fisher nodded. "Okay. We'll all meet up back here in the a.m."

"Then it's settled." The chief turned to Lazaro. "You mind getting these folks situated with some accommodations?"

"No problem, Chief."

WHAT COULD SCARCELY PASS AS A MOTEL APPEARED TO BE the only lodging in town. Either that or Deputy Lazaro was having a laugh at the FBI's expense. The team stood in front of the two-story building, its vacancy sign shining a bright green just below the name of the motel, the Moonlight Inn. Of course, Kate had seen worse and the day had been long, so none of it really mattered to her in light of their current situation.

She opened the door to her room and switched on the light. As she stood in the doorway, Quinn peered inside.

"Looks okay. You'll be all right in here on your own?"

"I'm a big girl. I'll be fine. Goodnight." She turned to Walsh and Fisher. "Night, guys."

Once inside, Kate secured the lock and retrieved her phone. A quick call to Nick to update him and she would turn in. Tomorrow was going to a long day too. But before she could press the call button, a knock on her door stopped her. Kate turned and peeked through the fish-eye lens.

"Reid, it's Quinn."

She opened the door. "Everything okay?"

"Oh, yeah. The guys and I were just talking and noticed that bar and grill across the street. Thought we'd see if their kitchen's still open. Maybe grab a beer too. Care to join us?"

"Why not? Sleep is overrated anyway." She followed him out, slipping her phone into her pocket.

They walked across the street, noting the parking lot had no cars in it.

"Is this place even open?" Kate asked.

Walsh opened the door. "It does appear to be." He waved her and the others inside before making his way to the bar and greeting the bartender. "Evening. Any chance you're still serving food?"

"Let me check. I'm sure they can whip up something. We sure are glad y'all are here." He started back toward the kitchen.

Walsh returned to the bar top table where the agents now sat. "He's going to check to see if they can make something for us." He pulled out his stool and sat down. "He says the people around here are glad we're on the job."

"Don't they trust what the chief is doing?" Fisher asked.

"Didn't say, but maybe they think he's in over his head."

"He's a good man, but he might be. Which brings to mind, Reid, Ness got the sample into his lab. Got the call just before we left," Fisher said.

"That was a hell of a find," Walsh added. "You must've gotten out into the field a fair bit at the WFO."

"I—we did, yes. I prefer to be hands-on."

"Well then, I'm not entirely sure you've come to the right place. Don't get me wrong, we get a decent amount of field action, but to be honest with you, there's a shit ton of paperwork, analyses, court appearances." Fisher looked at Quinn. "Must be why you were lucky enough to get help. Meanwhile, the rest of us are like chopped liver."

Walsh turned his attention to the approaching bartender. "What's the good word, barman?"

"They can do y'all up some sandwiches, chips. But that's about it. I can still get y'all some beer."

"That'll do us just fine. Thank you," Walsh replied.

11

The heat inside the motel room must've been set to eighty. In the early hours of the morning, Kate kicked off the thin bedspread and jutted her legs from beneath the sheets. "Good Lord." With sweat dripping down her hairline, she marched to the window where the heating unit blew out stifling air and shut it off. She then tried to open the window, but it was stuck. Looked to be painted shut. This motel was top notch for sure. "Well, now that I'm awake." Kate returned to the bed and her mind already started to spin with the investigation and how the day might pan out.

For a moment, she considered making that call to Nick since she'd failed to do so before having a beer and sandwiches with the team. Nevertheless, it was 4am. They were at least in the same time zone, but it seemed too early to call, and what did she really have to say anyway? Nothing new. No big breaks in the case. Not yet anyway. And she was tired. Her return from the fine establishment across the street last night had been much too late. The beers

—too many—for her. It had been fun, though. Unexpectedly so. She was beginning to gel with these guys. It felt good.

In the end, guilt prevailed and Kate reached for her phone. "Hey. It's me. I didn't wake you, did I?"

"No. I'm up. You doing all right? I was concerned I hadn't heard from you."

"I know. I'm sorry I didn't call you last night. It was—well, it was a little crazy, as I'm sure you can imagine."

"I can. How's it going down there? Any new developments?" Nick asked.

"Fisher didn't fill you in?" She soon recalled the time he left as well. "I suppose it was too late for any of us to call. We ended up grabbing some sandwiches and a beer at this dive bar across the street. It was a very long day. But I will tell you, we are making progress. I discovered a potentially significant piece of evidence at one of the crime scenes. Agent Ness with the Pikeville office submitted it to his lab last night after we all broke up for the evening. It could open this up for us."

"Why am I not surprised it was you?" He chuckled. "Listen, I know how it can get when you're working a case. I haven't forgotten. But just do me a favor and try to keep me in the loop. Or at the very least, have Fisher do it."

"I can't exactly tell the senior agent on the team to call you. How would that look?" Kate asked.

"No. I suppose not. I'll contact him myself and make sure he understands. I know he does, but I'll just make my point a little clearer."

"Okay. I'd better get going. I'm sure the others will be awake soon." She stood up.

"Hey, Kate?"

"Yeah?"

"I'm proud of you," Nick said.

"What for? I'm just doing my job."

"I know you are. I also know what you're up against down there. And I don't just mean the investigation. I want you to know that I have no intention of stepping in unless I'm asked to. This is your deal."

"Thank you. I'll keep in touch. Love you."

"Love you too."

No sooner did she end the call than a text arrived while she still held the phone in her hands. It was Walsh.

"Be ready in twenty."

"That's my cue. Four a.m. These guys don't mess around."

LYNN FLOYD STOOD AT HER KITCHEN SINK AND FILLED THE coffee pot with water. "You heard them FBI people are here now? Some kind of specialists, I reckon."

"I heard." John Floyd folded his morning newspaper and set it on the kitchen table. "I don't know what to think about that. Seems to me Chief Tate's starting to grasp at straws."

"Maybe. But I don't think they'll be leaving anytime soon. Might get pretty tough for us to move product with them nosing around."

"I doubt they give two hoots about us, Lynnie."

"Not yet." She poured the fresh brew into her cup and then John's before handing it to him. She joined him at the table. "How much we got left now?"

"Enough for another few days. Let's hope they leave by then."

"I got a feeling they'll be monitoring the buses, all things considered," she added.

"At least the ones going to Florida. Maybe Ohio too. Right

now, we need to just take this one day at a time. Let them do their digging around. Wait until we feel it's safe to continue."

"What if we can't wait?" Lynn sipped on her coffee.

"Don't you worry about it just yet. It'll all sort itself out in the wash."

Lynn stood again. "I best be getting ready, then."

"Why? You got work today?"

"Just for today, yes. They called and said they needed someone at the school. Just some janitorial work. I have to do it or they'll pull our bennies."

"I know. You just be mindful of who you're around and what you say."

She started to leave. "I always am, John."

JOHN DREW IN SKIMPY DISABILITY BENEFITS ALONG WITH HIS Social Security and Lynn had to pick up the slack. The added income from their recent venture, however, had proven helpful, relieving much of the stress they'd shouldered since their daughter's death last year. They were still paying for her funeral.

But neither of them was the same. They'd become numb to their surroundings, cared little for anyone else, and had pulled away from the community and church with which they'd once shared a close bond. It all changed the day they got the call. But that was neither here nor there anymore.

Lynn arrived at the school and checked in with the manager in charge of the janitorial staff.

"Thanks for coming in today, Lynn. It's good to see you out and about. We haven't seen much of you or John for a while."

"You know how it is, Chuck." Lynn reached for her bucket

and mop after slipping on her overalls. "Things just don't mean as much to us as they used to."

"I understand. Well, thanks again for being here. You'll be a big help." He handed her the keys. "You just let me know if you need anything."

"Will do." She pocketed the keys and rolled her bucket out into the corridor toward the gym.

School was due to start in about thirty minutes, which meant she had little time to get it ready for the breakfast crowd. Most kids here were in the National School Lunch Program, meaning they got free breakfast and lunch. So the place was usually packed for the free pancakes, French toast sticks, and chocolate milk.

Lynn worked her way from the front of the gym-slash-cafeteria, toward the kitchen where others prepared the meals. And the women behind the counter appeared upset about something. Lynn wasn't much of a socializer anymore, so she just listened as she moved the mop back and forth.

"I heard they found themselves another one the other night. Down at the old Mill Creek house," one of the ladies began.

"Do they know who it was?"

"I reckon they do; they just ain't telling nobody yet. They want to tamp down our fears," the other replied as she scooped scrambled eggs into the catering-size tin server.

"From what I heard, somebody bashed him in pretty good, but that's just a rumor."

Lynn listened to their conversation with growing interest. It wasn't until she stopped mopping that one of the ladies turned to her.

"Morning, Ms. Lynn. How are you doing?"

"Oh fine, thank you. And you?"

"Well, about as good as could be expected, all things considered."

"I suppose so. Terrible what's been happening around here. You and your family managing?" Lynn asked.

"Just about. Time will tell. I swear, they find anyone else dead in this town, I might just hole up in my house. This ain't right. It ain't right and it seems our chief can't stop it. Like he said the other night at the meeting."

"It'll be okay. We'll all get through this. This town's survived a hell of a lot. We'll survive this."

"I hope you're right, Lynn."

The bell rang.

Lynn checked the time. "Them kids'll be coming in soon. Best get back to work." She offered a perfunctory smile before seeing to her work again. Everyone around here was afraid. Rightly so, she supposed. It was a hard thing to face—losing all these kids, mostly to drugs and worse. She could speak to that first hand. Not too many around here knew what she and John had gone through.

Oh, there were others who'd lost their children to the opioid epidemic. Most of them, however, left town shortly after. No point in staying in a place that offered up so many reminders. But Lynn and John Floyd stayed. And their plans weren't changing anytime soon.

CHIEF TATE SPOTTED THE FEDS' BLACK SUVs ROLL INTO THE parking lot. "Looks like they're fixin' to get an early start." He turned to his deputies, who were sitting opposite him at his desk. "Best you fellas follow up with Ness and that lab and see where they're at. That'll be their first question. I guaran-damn-tee you."

Lazaro and Slocum traded a brief glance before Slocum started, "I'll get on the horn with the doc. Lazaro, you want to give Agent Ness a ring? See if he's got anything new?"

The boys left the chief alone. He watched as the agents exited their cars and headed toward the entrance. It was as if he was trying to mentally prepare himself for whatever the day held. Seemed every day since all this started had gotten more upsetting than the last. "What more could possibly happen?" He stood up, inhaled a breath, and walked into the main bullpen awaiting their arrival.

The door opened and the chief plastered a warm smile on his face. "Morning. How'd y'all sleep last night?"

"Just fine." Walsh held open the door for the rest of the team.

"Wanting to get an early start?" Chief nodded. "I like that." He clapped his hands and turned toward the deputies. "I've asked the boys here to put in some calls in hopes of getting answers ready for you, which I'm sure you'd appreciate."

"Absolutely. Thank you." Fisher walked toward the coffee machine. "Mind if I help myself?"

"Not at all."

"Thank you, Agent Ness. We'll see you real soon." Slocum hung up the phone and looked at the others. "That was Agent Ness. He says he's got some preliminary findings on the tox screen from Andy Walcott that Doc ordered and that pill we found in Steven Schiller's car. He's heading down now to discuss. By the sounds of it, he reached out to the DEA. Says that's the best way to find out if they know who's dealing this shit these kids are taking."

"Any luck on the wood sample from yesterday?" Kate asked.

"According to Ness, not yet. Lab's still analyzing the blood and fibers. They're hoping later today, if not first thing tomorrow," Slocum replied.

Kate appeared disappointed by the delay, but not surprised. These things were rarely completed in less than forty-eight hours. Expedited or not. It was just the way the system worked. "It's all we can hope for."

~

AGENT NESS ARRIVED BY MID-MORNING AND HE WAS NOT alone. "I apologize for my late arrival. However, I brought reinforcements." He looked to the man who accompanied him. "This is Agent Brent Tucker, DEA." As they entered the bullpen where the others waited, Ness made the introductions. "This is Supervisory Special Agent Fisher, Agents Walsh, Quinn, and Agent Reid. All with the BAU in Quantico. I reached out for their assistance in light of the circumstances surrounding the multiple homicides in Crown Pointe. And this is Chief Tate, along with his deputies, Lazaro and Slocum."

"Pleasure to meet you all, though it's unfortunate that it has to be under these circumstances. However, Agent Ness has filled me in on the investigation as it now stands. And I think I can offer my two cents."

"Thank you for joining us, Agent Tucker," Chief said. "Forgive me, but we haven't seen this sort of activity around here before, let alone having two different federal agencies getting involved. I don't mind saying that I think my boys and I are beginning to feel outnumbered."

"That's certainly not my intention by being here today." Tucker looked at the others. "Like my other federal colleagues, I believe we want to expedite a resolution to this investigation before any more lives are taken. And we'll defer to your judgment on any decision-making. This is still your town, Chief."

"Thank you." He cast his gaze around the room. "First of all, I suppose we should discuss your part in this, Agent Tucker. You've seen the forensics on the chemical makeup of these opioids?"

"I have. And I had an opportunity to run it through our system to see if we've come across this before. I understand there is some consensus these deaths are being caused by a cartel attempting to move in?"

"That is the prevailing theory, though not definitive," Quinn added.

Tucker moved toward Slocum's desk. "Pardon. You mind if I set my things down here?"

"Be my guest."

Tucker opened his carrier bag and retrieved a file. "About a year ago, we began seeing a synthetic version of an opioid called 'shady 80s.' Genuine OxyContin tablets are available in 80 milligrams and are marked with an '80' on the tablets themselves. These synthetic pills, which are bluish-green, contain a compound known as W-18, a highly potent chemical over 100 times stronger than fentanyl. We believe the precursors are coming in from China, however there is a Canadian company that manufactures W-18. But here's the real kicker. The compound isn't even listed as a controlled substance in the US. Hell, it's not even on the DEA's list of 'drugs of concern.'"

"And what's in these pills, like the one from Steven Schiller's car, is one of these 'shady 80s'?" Kate asked.

"It appears so. What we don't know is if these pills are tied to a cartel. So far, we haven't seen enough of them on the streets and we honestly don't know where they're coming from," Tucker replied.

"What about the tox screen from our latest victim, the Walcott boy? The earlier victims appeared to have a bunch of these so-called precursor chemicals that Doc listed off," Quinn began. "Is it possible this W-18 chemical compound might not be in their systems?"

"From what I've seen in those tox screens, I'd say the similarities are enough to raise eyebrows. Of course, we don't have the screen back from the OD victim Ness mentioned last night. We'll have to wait to see if that victim is related." He handed Quinn the report. "This is what Ness gave me this morning."

"I've got copies for all of you," Ness replied.

"According to y'all, no one thinks the Cavanaugh boy is related. Just another overdose. But now you think he might have taken the same drug?" Slocum asked.

"I don't want to rule him out until we get a definitive answer," Quinn replied. "At any time, the killer could change his M.O. and I don't want to make the mistake of assuming he hasn't."

Chief reviewed the report before he began, "Well, we sure appreciate you coming in to tell us this, Agent Tucker, but I can't see how it's going to help us find the killer. Please let me know if I'm missing something here because I honestly don't know where we go from this point."

Kate wanted to tell the chief that this was all part of the process. Each piece of the puzzle would fit together, but that it took time.

"You're not missing anything, Chief," Quinn began. "But this still offers us some extremely valuable information. And I think Agent Tucker can take this back to his team and search for any other instances where this drug has appeared in the region."

"Yes. That's exactly what I'd like to do. Because if I can find a concentration of this pill's compound in a certain area, that might bring you closer to determining if a cartel is involved. My first inclination is to submit it is not. And the only reason I say that is the cartels, most of the established ones, anyway, understand the power of this new synthetic. They aren't looking to kill off their buyers. And that's essentially what this drug has done in many instances. Not all, but many. So, whoever is formulating this dangerous new compound, or has purchased it, is doing it for other reasons. Or at the very least, doesn't yet understand, or can't yet control its process. And that perhaps this is merely a testing phase for the product."

Agent Fisher pushed off the edge of Lazaro's desktop. "We appreciate any help the DEA can offer on this situation. While it may not provide us with immediate answers, it does give us insight into who we're dealing with. This is intentional. The drug is given with intention to kill or slow down the victims long enough to physically do the job. This tells me, with almost certainty, and Quinn can correct me if I'm wrong, but this feels like revenge killings."

Quinn appeared to consider that prospect before beginning. "I can see that as a possibility. Revenge is a powerful motive. But why so many? And revenge for what? Money?"

No longer able to hold her tongue, Kate began, "Whoever is doing this, I believe, isn't after money. You're right, Quinn, revenge is a powerful motive. But to bludgeon to death someone because they owed you a few bucks, or maybe more, doesn't seem as likely to me as being given a lethal dose of narcotics, then being beaten to death, in an effort to take revenge for something deeply personal."

"Where are you going with this, Reid?" Quinn continued. "I'm with you on your train of thought. But personal on what level? If not money, love? Betrayal? Hate?"

"Well, pardon me for saying, but that could cover just about every crime ever committed," Chief replied.

"Yes, it could, Chief," Kate continued. "We've decided the killer must be a man, given the strength and force of the blows. However, the care given to the bodies post mortem, the staging, suggests the possibility of an accomplice. So, to get back to your assertion, Quinn, I'd say the personal level could be anger. The killer is likely expressing deeply embedded anger."

"But that the assumed accomplice could be the one picking up the pieces. Making the message clear to whoever finds the victims," Quinn added. "Also, the appearance of some form of remorse is evident in the staging." He looked at Kate again. "Go on."

"That's right. Which leads me to believe we are dealing with someone local. Whether this person or people are tied to a cartel remains to be seen. And Agent Tucker will have to help us on that front. But the evidence, the profile all point to someone who calls Crown Pointe home. Someone who's been directly impacted by the addiction problem here."

"An addict himself?" the chief asked.

"It's possible. Someone who hates himself for what he's become and is lashing out at the others afflicted with the same disease." She paused for a moment and again cast her glance to Quinn. "Or, someone who's lost a loved one to the epidemic. Anger at the people who take the drugs. Anger at those who supply the drugs."

"And an attempt to wipe out everyone associated with the person they lost," Quinn said.

Kate raised her brows. "Right."

12

The news of yet more federal agents arriving to help solve the horrific murders had already spread throughout the tight-knit community. And the Crown Pointe Police station received an onslaught of calls and visits from those demanding answers.

Deputy Slocum set down the receiver at his desk and headed into the chief's office. "Excuse me, Chief. I just got another call. Me and Lazaro been fielding them all day. Folks are real nervous right about now. Have you thought about asking the agents to speak to the community? Might help subdue their fears. We're spending more time talking than we are on the case. Something's gotta give."

Chief Tate stood from his desk, and with a deep breath he thrust his hands in his pants pockets. "Maybe you're right. Maybe if they hear it from the feds themselves, they'll be able to understand what it is we're up against."

"They're scared, Chief," Slocum continued.

"I'm well aware of that. I know people are losing sleep over this. Hell, I'm losing sleep. But short of evacuating the entire town, there isn't much more I can do other than what we're doing."

"I understand that. How about I contact Agent Fisher? I believe he said the team was headed to Pikeville to meet with Agent Ness. I'll ask if he and his people can address the community tonight. Best to get it done sooner rather than later."

"You mean before another body turns up?"

The deputy turned down his gaze. "Yes, sir."

"Get on it, then."

"Thank you, Chief." Slocum returned to his desk and dropped into his chair.

"Well? What'd he say?" Lazaro asked.

"He said to ask and see if they'll do it. I'll make the call to Agent Fisher now. See if we can't get something on the books for tonight or tomorrow."

Lazaro nodded. "Good idea. And who knows? Best case, we'll have some answers by that point."

Slocum dialed the number and glanced at his partner. "I ain't gonna hold my breath."

"Fisher here."

The deputy pulled up in his chair. "Yes, sir, Agent Fisher, this is Deputy Slocum. I was speaking with the chief and we thought it best if you and your team could speak to the community as soon as possible. You know, 'cause y'all are here and folks are scared."

Fisher was on the passenger seat of the SUV while Walsh drove to Pikeville. "I'm afraid we don't have anything new to offer in terms of progress. What's the chief hoping for?"

"Well, you see, we're getting an awful lot of calls from nervous citizens. People are afraid to leave their homes. They're afraid to send their kids to school. We were hoping y'all could help calm their fears. Give them an update."

Fisher pressed the mute button on his phone. "They want us to address the community asap."

Walsh furrowed his brow. "Why? What good would that do?"

"They say the people are scared and it's getting worse. I think they're drowning in calls by the sounds of it."

"Well, shit. I don't know what we can tell them that the chief can't."

Kate sat in the back seat along with Quinn as they continued toward Pikeville to speak with Agent Ness. "We could ask Scarborough. He has a knack for calming the masses during an investigation. And, it would show unity among the team and give the people reassurance—having leadership come and address them." She waited out their silence before adding, "Look, I know it's been an adjustment, but Scarborough, despite what you might think, is an exceptional communicator. And, truthfully, I think the time's come for him to jump into the weeds with us. We're spinning our wheels until we get something back on that shred of evidence we pulled from the Walcott scene. Scarborough and Duncan are sitting at Quantico twiddling their thumbs."

"They're hardly twiddling their thumbs. It isn't like we don't have other cases we're immersed in right now," Quinn added.

"Fair enough, but I think it's time we move forward as a team." The changes Kate had experienced since joining Quantico were obvious with each passing day. She was becoming a leader herself, even if she hadn't known it. And this was a leadership call.

Fisher returned his attention to the call where he heard Slocum ask if he was still there. "I'm here. Sorry about that. I'll get it scheduled with our senior unit agent. We're on our way to meet with Ness right now. If we find out anything, I'll call you back." He ended the call and peered over his shoulder at Kate. "Chief Tate already thinks he's outnumbered. Adding two more agents to the mix..."

"I think Reid is right," Walsh began. "We should have the rest of our team here working with us. It would be unwise to turn away extra hands on this investigation. The deputies aren't much help and frankly, neither is the chief. Don't get me wrong, they have good intentions, but their resources and experience don't measure up to a case like this. We have four dead bodies. Possibly a fifth, if it's connected. A deadly narcotic being pushed on these streets by someone motivated by revenge. If we don't shut this down soon, you better believe Unit Chief Cole will start stepping on toes. I don't think any of us want that."

NICK SLIPPED HIS PHONE INTO HIS POCKET AND WALKED OUT of his office on a mission to track down Eva Duncan. He now stood in her doorway. "Hey, I just got a call from Fisher. You feel like making a little trip?"

She peered up from her desk. "Let me guess, we're going to Crown Pointe?"

"If you can fit it in, yes."

Duncan nodded. "Well, it's about time."

"I'll get us on the next flight." Nick began to leave.

"We could requisition a charter flight. It'll get us there quicker."

He stopped on a dime and returned to her doorway. "I hadn't thought of that. You know, sometimes I forget the resources we have at our disposal here."

"Yeah. It's a lot different than at the WFO." Duncan smiled. "I've done it before. Let me handle it. I'll let you know when to be ready."

"Thank you, Duncan. I appreciate it."

"No problem."

There was only one person who could authorize the use of a chartered flight and that person was Nick's boss, Unit Chief Cole. Duncan approached his office. "Sir? Can I have a quick word?"

"Duncan." He pulled off his reading glasses. "Of course. Come on in. What can I do for you?"

"We've been asked to join the rest of the team in Crown Pointe and I'd like to request a charter flight. The sooner we can get there, the better."

"I agree. Scarborough has kept me briefed on the situation over there and I think it's a wise move to get all hands on deck. Do you have the authorization form?"

"I do, sir." She handed him the form.

Cole scribbled his signature and returned it to her. "Let me know if you need anything else."

"Yes, sir."

❧

THE FLIGHT WAS READY TO BOARD AS NICK AND EVA DUNCAN walked along the tarmac.

"Thank you for arranging this so quickly." Nick trailed behind her.

"You haven't had much of a chance to get out into the field since coming here," she added. "Honestly, it's the one thing I regret about transferring here to Quantico."

Nick smiled. "You like getting out there too, huh?"

"I do miss it occasionally," she replied.

"Same here. I thought I wanted out of all that, but I guess I really do miss it."

They boarded the small charter plane and once they were

seated, the door closed and the announcement from the captain began.

It had been almost a year since Nick was in the field. It felt strange, but also familiar as though this was where he belonged. He turned to Duncan, who sat across the aisle on the small ten-seater aircraft. "Can I ask you something?"

She peered back at him. "Sure."

"What was the team's relationship with Cole?"

Duncan appeared to consider the question. "Well, he was our team leader for a long time. Several years. He was the one who recruited me, actually. So I do have maybe a closer relationship with him than the others did or still do."

"But as far as his style, would you say it was better suited to the team?"

She eyed him. "You mean does the rest of the team accept you as Senior Unit Agent?"

"I guess that's what I'm asking—yes. Sometimes I don't feel as though they do."

"I think things have improved. It's taken a while for us to click, to get to know you, but I think we're well on our way. Look, I know what a difficult decision it was to bring Reid aboard." She raised a preemptive hand. "And before you say it was Quinn's call, we all know that it was. But we also know that it was impossible for him not to consider you in his equation. I like Reid, I really do. And to be honest, I think the others are coming around."

"Where does that leave me?" Nick pressed on.

"We all know what you've done for the Bureau in the past. Your commendations, the cases you worked on. You've had an exemplary career, with few exceptions. That said, I think having you there on this investigation will go a long way to proving yourself in their eyes. Not that you should have to, but that's just the way it is. I'm sure Reid feels the same way."

He nodded. "I'm sure she does."

"So let's just see how things go. I think you'll be surprised at what we're all capable of doing when we're together," Duncan added.

"I won't be surprised. I know what you're all capable of. That's why I wanted to work with you in the first place."

AGENT NESS AWAITED THE TEAM'S ARRIVAL AS HE SAT IN HIS Pikeville office. He continued to refresh his computer screen, anticipating news. Perhaps news that could provide them with a breakthrough on the investigation. But still there was nothing. "Damn it."

The phone on his desk buzzed in and the speaker came to life. "Ness, you've got visitors—from Quantico."

"I'm expecting them. I'll be down in a minute." He refreshed his screen again. "Shit. What the hell am I supposed to tell them?"

Upon his arrival at the lobby, Ness tried hard to disguise the disappointment on his face. With a faux smile, he offered his hand. "SSA Fisher, thanks for coming down."

"Sure. We're getting pressure from the local authorities to make a statement to the public. I would love to tell them some-thing—anything that would help put their minds at ease."

Ness peered at the hopeful gazes of the rest of the team. "I was expecting results on the wood shard, which was why I called. The lab said they'd get them to me this afternoon. I guess I jumped the gun." Ness' phone vibrated in his pocket and on retrieving it, he noticed an incoming text message. A smile slowly appeared before he returned his attention to the team. "Will wonders never cease? Come on, let's head up to my office and take a look."

"You got it?" Fisher asked.

"I sure as hell hope so." Ness appeared almost giddy as he hurried toward the elevator, holding the door while the others entered. "It was only a matter of time before the chief would start leaning on you all for answers. I feel for him. I really do. They aren't used to this sort of thing."

"No," Kate began. "But, sadly, the rest of us are."

The doors parted and Ness led the way to his office. "Right through here. Take a seat wherever you can find one." He moved toward his desk and opened the file on his computer. "Let's see what our guys in the lab came up with."

He scanned the monitor and his eyes darted back and forth with scrutiny and speed. "They ran the screen again for that W-18 compound in the first three victims. It's not the forensics on the sample, though, as I'd hoped." Ness entered commands on his keyboard until he arrived at the desired information. "It's a match." He looked to the others. "It's the same drug in all of them."

"Then we are dealing with a single supplier. But nothing back on the wood splinter?" Quinn asked.

Ness shook his head in disappointment.

"Damn," Kate began. "I was hoping for results on what I have to believe was the murder weapon."

"Yes," Ness mirrored her expression. "Until we can get that, this is all you have to run on. But this is something you can give the chief. And offer progress that might soothe the fears of the community." He again peered at the others. "I'm sorry you came all the way here for just this. I'd hoped..."

"We know," Fisher said. "We appreciate your follow-through. This will give us something. We'd better head back to Crown Pointe and prepare to brief the rest of the team on arrival."

"You want me there?" Ness asked.

Fisher twirled the toothpick in his mouth, considering the

idea. "No. We're better served if you're here, following up on the labs and pushing those guys. It'll still be quicker than starting over and sending it out to our labs. Time isn't on our side right now."

Ness showed them out. "Good luck. I'll be in touch as soon as I know anything."

THE TEAM'S RETURN TO THE CROWN POINTE STATION WAS met with the early arrival of Scarborough and Duncan.

As Walsh made his way inside, he spotted them. "Didn't expect you all to get here so quickly. Did you take the chopper?"

"No. A charter," Duncan replied.

"Cole must be getting nervous to have authorized that expenditure." Fisher walked into the small bullpen.

"We all are," Scarborough replied. "I hear you all were meeting with Ness at the Pikeville field office. Any news?"

As the rest of the team entered and found seats, Slocum and Lazaro emerged from the chief's office, followed by the man himself.

"Good. We're all here," Chief Tate began. "I've had the pleasure of talking with Agent Scarborough briefly and I'd just like to start by saying that I appreciate your willingness to address the community. And Agent Duncan's input will also prove valuable, I'm sure. So, let's get down to business. What happened with Ness?"

Walsh made his way to Slocum's desk. "You mind if I print up an email?"

"Go right ahead."

Walsh proceeded to log in to his email account and print the report he'd received from Agent Ness. "This morning, we went to Ness' office in hopes he received forensics on the possible weapon used to bludgeon the victims." He walked toward the printer near the coffee maker and pulled the pages as they appeared. "Instead, it was the results of a retest on the first three victims. The narcotics compound was the same in all of the victims. They were given the same drug." He handed out copies of the new report.

Nick studied the results. "So we need to find the distributor."

"Yes. The dealer either sold these drugs to the unsub or is the unsub. That part, we haven't been able to figure out yet," Quinn replied.

"Well, hell." Chief Tate hooked his thumbs through the belt loops on his pants. "I was hoping for a little more than this."

"We're still waiting for results," Kate said. "But at least we have something that connects our victims to the same unsub, apart from the manner in which they were murdered. That's still an important element and will help lead us to him with the DEA's analysis as well."

"Chief Tate, you'll have to forgive us while Duncan and I catch up to the others," Nick began. "But I do know my team has been working tirelessly to find the killer. And as I have often been tasked with, I can help by addressing the concerns of everyone involved, not just the people of this town."

"I think what my boss is trying to say is that these things never happen quickly," Fisher added. "This is an important lead and we'll continue to pursue it while we wait for answers from Forensics."

"Chief Tate, do you have something lined up for me today?" Nick asked.

"As a matter of fact, yes we do. Tonight. At the high school auditorium. Seven o'clock, isn't that right?" Chief glanced to his deputy.

"Yes, sir. That's the plan," Slocum replied.

"Okay, then." Nick pushed off the corner of an empty desk.

"I'd like to spend the next few hours getting up to speed. Then I can prepare a statement with all the information we have to date."

Chief Tate approached him and extended his hand. "Thank you, Agent Scarborough. I guess me and the boys here will just have to sit tight and let you folks do your jobs."

13

The high school's cafeteria filled quickly with the frightened people of Crown Pointe. Chief Tate approached Nick, who stood to the right of the podium. As he walked along the aisle, he noticed the people of his community once again waiting and praying that the federal agents would offer deliverance from the terror that gripped them. "Agent Scarborough, you just about ready to get started?"

Nick checked the podium. A water bottle sat on a shelf tucked inside. A thin microphone extended from the top of it and chairs were placed on either side of the stage in the event he needed to call on his team to answer questions. He felt as though he was about to make a political speech instead of an update on the status of an investigation. Nick was used to the press. He had been forced to handle them plenty of times. But it wasn't often he had to look real people in the eyes and tell them he and his team were doing everything they could to stop a killer.

The families would be out there. The ones who'd already

suffered losses from the brutal slayings. Nick quickly recalled the reason why he left the field. The pain and anguish of the families could be overwhelming at times. It seemed especially difficult since he was with Kate now, a woman he'd hoped to begin a family with—someday. Although, she'd made it clear that wasn't an option for her. He felt he could persuade her to adopt, but then, what for? In times like this, it seemed unfathomable to want to raise a child, but people did it all the time. Still, the thought of being one of those parents out there tonight...

"Agent Scarborough?" the chief repeated. "Is everything all right?"

Nick pulled himself back from his wandering thoughts. "Yes. Could you just give me two minutes to run through it one more time with my team?"

"Just holler when you're ready." Chief took his leave and spotted Fisher heading his way. "Agent Fisher."

"Chief." He chewed on his toothpick and continued toward Nick. "You ready to get this show on the road? Looks like we've got a packed house."

"I'm ready. Just wish we had more to give them."

"We all do." Fisher peered out into the growing audience. "You think he could be here—the killer?"

"The thought had crossed my mind." Nick turned to him. "You and the others keeping watch?"

"Got it under control. We know what to look for." He patted Nick on the back. "Good luck. And who knows, maybe we'll get lucky and find the son of a bitch right here, tonight."

"Here's to hoping for miracles." Nick made his way toward the chief once again. "I'm ready."

"Okay, then." Chief Tate approached the podium and tapped on the microphone with his index finger. "This thing on?" The feedback indicated it was. "Evenin' folks. If y'all wouldn't mind taking your seats so we can get started." He waited just a moment for the room to settle down. "Much obliged. First of all, I want to thank each and every one of the people here in Crown Pointe. Lord knows, this hasn't been easy. And it's been a whole lot tougher on some than others. The boys and I have been getting a lot of concerned calls—and rightly so. We reckoned the best way to address your concerns was to have the bright and talented FBI agents talk to you directly."

A man in the audience stood. "Ain't you running the show no more, Chief?"

"Rest assured, we are all working as a team. But the fine folks here have dealt with this sort of thing more times than I'd ever care to know. They got the technology and resources we just don't have at our fingertips. So, to answer your question, Bill, we're working as a team on this. Now I'm gonna turn this over to Senior Unit Agent Nick Scarborough. We're lucky to have him here as well as the rest of his team." The chief presented the others as they stood on the sidelines. "So without further ado, I'll let Agent Scarborough get started."

Nick approached the podium. "Thank you, Chief Tate." He turned to the audience. "And thank you all for coming tonight. I know you have a lot of questions, but if you'll let me just give you an update as to what we know right now, then I'll try my best to answer them. First of all, I'd like to thank the Crown Pointe police department, headed up by Chief Tate. The cooperation between his team and mine has been exceptional." He stared at the faces in the audience. Anger, grief, sadness, fear. They wanted answers, and he had precious few to give. "I've only just joined the investigation, but my team, who has been here for the past few days, has brought me up to speed. What we can tell you right now, without jeopardizing the investigation, is that we are dealing with a complex case. We have received some forensic information, which has pointed us in a new direction. However, we are waiting on much more that could offer the break we need."

"So you're telling us you ain't got nothing? Is that right?" A middle-aged woman stood in the center row, her face masked in anger. "My dearest friend lost her child and you don't have diddly squat, do you?"

"Ma'am, if you'll let me continue."

"With what? Blowing smoke up our asses?" she added.

The chief stepped forward. "Now, Sharon, that's not fair to say."

Nick raised his hand. "No, it's okay. Ma'am, we are working night and day to track down the person or persons responsible. I can assure you that we do have leads. Strong leads that we're working on as I stand here and speak to you tonight."

"Then tell us, Mr. FBI man, what kind of monster is doing this to our children, to the people of this town?" Sharon continued.

"There are certain things that I'm afraid I can't divulge without jeopardizing the case, but we are working to bring this community some peace of mind and closure to this terrible situation," Nick replied.

Another woman stood and turned to Sharon, "Let the man speak. Sit down now."

Nick waited for the woman to take her seat again. "The best advice I can offer you is to help each other. Keep an eye out for suspicious activity. And, more importantly, if you or someone you love suffers from opioid addiction, please, please do not consume or let them consume any pills they might have recently purchased. We believe there are dangerous synthetic drugs being distributed right now that could very well be part of this investigation."

In the audience, Lynn and John Floyd cast a glance to one another. Kate, who stood near the back of the cafeteria, noticed the exchange. She nudged Duncan, who was next to her. With a shift in her gaze, Kate looked at the couple and then back to Duncan.

A quick sleight of hand and Duncan took a picture of the couple, appearing to catch on to Kate's meaning.

After several more minutes of tense exchanges between Nick and the people of Crown Pointe, he concluded his statement by bringing the chief back to the stage. "I'll let your chief finish up. Thank you all for your time." Nick stepped away from the podium and headed toward Fisher, who stood to the right of the stage. "Well, that could've gone better."

"None of us could've handled it any better," Fisher began. "You did well with the information you had. Don't be too hard on yourself."

"Thanks. Anything catch your eye?" Nick peered into the audience as they began to disperse.

"Not really, no. But we should catch up with the others to see if they spotted anything."

As they headed toward the rest of the team, Chief Tate stopped them. "Thank you, Agent Scarborough. I know that wasn't easy, but it was necessary. You did a fine job up there."

"Appreciate that, Chief. I didn't have much to give them."

"No, but I truly believe you gave them some hope that this will all be over soon enough." He tipped his hat. "You boys be sure and get some rest tonight. Tomorrow's a whole new day."

"Yes, sir. We'll see you first thing. We've got some work to wrap up yet tonight. You don't mind if we work at the station?" Nick asked.

"You go on ahead. Just lock up when you're through." He turned away, but stopped short. "Oh, and you know, you get a hold of me any time—day or night—if y'all need anything. Now I mean that."

"We will, Chief." Nick led the way with Fisher in tow as they headed toward the rest of the team. "I see Reid and Duncan over there."

"Walsh is coming too," Fisher replied. "Maybe we got that miracle."

"Hey." Nick pressed his back against the wall as the team converged. "Anything look interesting out there tonight?"

"As a matter of fact," Duncan retrieved her cell phone and opened the photos, "Reid spotted these two earlier when you talked about buying the drugs."

"What'd they do that caught your suspicions?" Fisher asked.

"Just as Scarborough said the whole thing about not taking any recently purchased drugs, these two looked at each other. And, I don't know, it just gave me a bad feeling," Kate replied.

Nick had learned not to discount Kate's "bad feelings," because nine times out of ten, she was usually onto something. "Suppose we should ask Chief Tate if he knows who they are."

"You had a feeling?" Quinn asked.

"I did. They know something. I just don't know if it's relevant."

"Well, after the other day, spotting that splinter of wood, I wouldn't dare disregard a feeling coming from you. Let's look into these two," Quinn replied.

"We can still catch the chief. I see him over there," Nick replied. "Did you happen to see them leave already? That couple?"

"They left almost immediately," Duncan said. "Which raised a red flag, that's for sure."

"I'll grab him." Walsh's quick stride was almost military-like. He approached Chief Tate, who was speaking with a couple. "I'm so sorry to interrupt. Chief, would you mind having a quick word with us before you leave?"

Chief seemed to note Walsh's look of concern. "I'm so sorry, Maggie; Charlie. Would y'all excuse me?"

"Go ahead, Chief. I can see we aren't gonna get any information about whoever killed our boy, Andy. Nothing left for us here, I reckon," Charlie Walcott replied.

"Y'all try to get some sleep." He turned and followed Walsh. "I hope this is important. Those folks lost their son. They need some damn reassurance."

"It is." Walsh led the way until he reached the rest of the team. "Duncan, you want to show Chief the photo?"

She pulled up the image on her phone. "Reid noted an unusual exchange between these two people when Scarborough mentioned the drugs. Any chance you know who they are?"

Tate took hold of her phone and studied the image. "They look suspicious to you, Agent Reid?"

"It's just a feeling. You know them?" she asked.

"I do. That there is Lynn and John Floyd. They lost their daughter to drugs a year ago. You think they got something to do with this, do you?"

"They lost their daughter?" Kate asked.

"Yes, ma'am. Bright girl too. Had high hopes for her. But like most things here in Crown Pointe, hope vanishes quicker than a blue-ribbon chili on a cold winter's day." He handed the phone back to Duncan. "I gotta be honest with you, I think you're barking up the wrong tree. I've known them for years. Honest, good, hardworking people. John was until his back problems got the better of him. But Lynn Floyd works damn near every day."

"I'm not saying they're the killers, but I would like to speak with them," Kate continued.

"Sounds like a plan," Quinn replied.

"Well, if you folks think they got something to do with this, then I can't stop you. You mind if I come with you? Or at least, send one of my boys? I think they'd feel better having one of us there too. No offense, but you feds make people nervous sometimes."

"That would be fine," Kate replied. "I know it's getting late, but do you think we could do this tonight?"

"I should say so. None of us wants another death on our hands. So if you think it's a worthwhile conversation to have, then the sooner the better. We can go right now."

"It might be a good idea for just the pair of us to go along with the chief," Quinn said. "Too many of us will shut them up, I think."

"Quinn's right," Fisher said. "The rest of us will head back to the station and catch up with Ness and whatever else we can do to speed things along while you're out."

The chief reached for his keys. "Then let's hit the road."

THE CHIEF DROVE ALONG THE SINGLE-LANE, TREE-LINED ROAD until a small structure appeared in the distance. "That's it. Up ahead." The yellow beam from the older-model Chevy Tahoe's headlights cast an eerie glow on what appeared to be a Craftsman-style home tucked into the wooded region.

"This is where they live?" Kate surveyed the area. "It's very remote. I don't see a car in the drive. You mentioned Lynn Floyd still worked. How does she get around?"

"Well, that's a good question. One we might ought to bring up," Chief replied.

"Isn't this the road we took to get out to the mineshaft?" Quinn asked.

"The very one." The chief turned the wheel and drove along the half-paved, half-gravel driveway that led to the home. "These folks have been here since I can remember. This is where they raised their daughter."

"Did they have any other children?" Quinn asked.

"No. Just the one. And then they lost her." He stopped near the top of the driveway and cut the engine. "Let's get this over with."

"Chief, do you think we're spinning our wheels?"

He turned to Kate. "I can't say with any certainty that's the case, Agent Reid. But my gut says you are." He opened the door and stepped outside. With his boots sinking into the soft gravelly driveway, Chief Tate tugged down on his hat and awaited his companions. As they approached, he continued. "Y'all don't mind if I start the conversation? Just to put them at ease."

"Not at all," Quinn said. "We'll take your lead here, Chief."

"Much obliged." He stepped up onto the front porch deck and knocked on the door. A single light burned in the window. "Looks like they're here."

A moment later, Lynn Floyd opened the door only slightly. "Chief Tate? What's going on? Everything okay?"

"Everything's fine, Mrs. Floyd. Thank you for coming down tonight. I know it couldn't have been easy, all things considered."

"No, it wasn't."

"The—uh—FBI wanted to have a brief sit-down with you and John, if that's agreeable to you both. Won't take but a few minutes of your time and then we'll leave you be."

Lynn peered at him with noted suspicion. "What about? Have we done something wrong?"

"Not at all, Lynn. They just want to talk to you about Jenny, if that's all right."

The chief put her at ease with the mention of her daughter's name, something Kate hadn't thought to do. Guess he was the chief for a reason.

Lynn pulled open the door farther and peered at Kate and Quinn. "Y'all think Jenny's death got something to do with what's been going on here in town? Cause she died some thirteen months ago."

"I know it's getting late, Mrs. Floyd," Quinn started. "But we really would like to just talk to you and your husband."

Lynn looked again at Kate. "Well, that's fine, I reckon. Come on in. You'll have to excuse the state of my house. We don't have no maid or nothing. It's just me and John and he's disabled."

"It's fine, ma'am." Kate stepped forward but waited for the chief to enter first.

Chief Tate removed his hat and bent down slightly to pass under the door's threshold. His six feet four-inch frame generally towered over everyone around him. "John, it's good to see you. Thank you for coming out tonight." He offered his hand.

"Don't know why we did. Sure didn't get much out of it 'cept a bunch of bureaucratic nonsense."

"I'm sure that's how it seemed to you, Mr. Floyd. But we are working very hard on this investigation, which is why we're here tonight." Quinn turned to the chief. "Chief Tate mentioned you lost your daughter about a year ago to addiction."

"That's right."

Lynn closed the front door and walked toward her husband. "Now, John, we're not heathens. Show these kind people to the sofa so they can have a seat."

"Fine." He gestured to present the small living room. "Have a seat."

The agents and Chief Tate sat down.

"Can I get y'all something to drink? I was fixin' to make some tea before," Lynn asked.

"Thank you, that's very kind," Kate replied.

"I'll take you up on that offer," the chief said.

"I'll have some too, thank you, Mrs. Floyd," Quinn added.

She turned away. "No need for formalities. You can call me Lynn. I'll be right back. Go on with your questions."

Quinn looked at John. "So your daughter suffered from opioid addiction and passed away."

"Did you not hear me right, son? I said she did," John replied.

"Of course. I guess I'd just like to know, well, at the meeting tonight, Agent Reid noticed the two of you." He looked at Kate to continue.

"Yes. It seemed as though you were concerned about something our supervisor said. About the drugs being pushed here in Crown Pointe."

"Of course we're concerned. There's some kind of crazy killer on the loose and we got this man telling us if we see any drugs coming through, we should say something. Pardon, but that don't make no sense to me. So, I looked at Lynnie and she shook her head too. Like we ain't been looking out for drug dealers here or something. I mean, what's that got to do with the price of bread anyway?"

"I can understand that," Kate added. "But the reason being is that we think the killer could be selling or forcing his victims to take a very toxic synthetic drug and that's what we're trying to track down."

Lynn Floyd returned with a tray of glasses and iced tea in a pitcher, placing it down on the coffee table. "Here you are." She handed each of them a glass.

The chief took a long drink. "That hits the spot. Thank you, Lynn."

Kate sipped on her tea, or rather the sugar water that contained a small amount of tea. She cleared her throat before continuing. "At the meeting tonight, I noticed you both showed great concern. Is there anything you can tell us about your daughter?"

"You mean, do we know who gave her the drugs?" Lynn sat down next to her husband.

"That could be useful to us," Kate added.

"Even after all this time?"

Kate tossed a brief glance to Quinn. "I think so, Mrs. Floyd. Any leads we can get. Anyone we can talk to who might be acquainted with other dealers would be helpful."

John peered at his wife and returned his attention to Kate. "Look, we don't know who sold Jenny the drugs. If we did, I guaran-damn-tee you, he'd be dead, you understand me?"

"Yes, sir. I'm sorry if I've offended you."

"Darlin', you didn't offend us," Lynn said. "He's just sensitive to the issue, as I'm sure you can understand. Look, I wish we could help you. John and me are doing the best we can just to survive this. You have any little ones?"

"No, I don't," Kate replied.

"Just as well. This world isn't what it used to be."

"If that's all the agents needed, I suppose we should mosey on out and leave you two be." The chief began to rise. "I'm sorry if we wasted your time."

Kate knew she wouldn't get anywhere with the Floyds, especially with Tate here, and that wasn't the only reason why she wanted to talk to them anyway. "Yes. I'm very sorry, but we certainly do appreciate your time. Oh, I was wondering, did you drive to the school tonight?"

"We did," Lynn replied.

"I didn't see a car in your driveway. We thought maybe you weren't home."

"Oh. A neighbor borrowed it. Had to run to the store for something or other."

Kate smiled and followed the chief and Quinn to the door. "Well that was nice of you. Thank you again for your time and I hope you manage to get some rest."

John shook his head. "That's a tall order, miss, considering you ain't found the killer yet. I doubt anyone's getting any rest till you do."

14

There was something to be said for living in a small town, despite the current and terrifying circumstances in which the residents now found themselves. But now, at night, Crown Pointe appeared serene and beautiful. The sky was filled with stars, unobstructed by light pollution. The air was clean and smelled of earth and trees. But what lay beneath this outward beauty was a tragic secret of poverty, addiction, and a people who suffered at the hands of both.

The chief arrived back at the station. "Looks like your compadres are still hard at work." He killed the lights and cut the engine. "Best go see if they have any news and let them know our visit with the Floyds appears to have been for naught."

Kate eyed Quinn as the two emerged from the vehicle and started toward the entrance behind Chief Tate.

Kate lowered her voice. "It wasn't for naught."

"I know. We'll wait until we're alone with the team. I wouldn't mention anything with these guys still here," Quinn said.

"Understood."

Inside, Lazaro, Slocum, and the agents appeared to be hard at work, which led Kate to wonder if it had bore any fruit.

"You're back," Nick began. "How'd it go?"

"Well, like I was saying to your cohorts, what we got was a big fat goose egg from the Floyds," the chief began. "Whatever Agent Reid here thought she saw seems to have amounted to nothing more than concern on the part of Lynn and John Floyd."

"Oh. I see. That's too bad." Nick eyed Kate and seemed to pick up on the fact that the chief might not be fully informed. "We did make contact with Agent Ness. He's still waiting on the labs from the sample. So, at his request, I put in a call to the lab and begged for their prompt attention. We'll have to see if that carries any weight."

Agent Walsh emerged from the hall, holding a paper cup with steam rising from it. "Nothing on your end?"

"Not really, no," Quinn replied.

"Seems like we're back at Square One, then," Slocum replied. "Guess we just keep doing what we're doing."

"You boys should head on home. It's late and you both have put in enough hours. We'll reconvene here in the morning," the chief said.

"Okay, boss." Lazaro shut down his computer and grabbed his keys from his desk. "Anything turns up, you'll let us know?"

"You bet. Say goodnight to the missus for me, Shane. And Eric, say goodnight to Gunner."

"Will do. He'll be missing his dinner by now. Night, y'all," Slocum replied.

After the deputies left, Agent Fisher looked at the chief. "Is Gunner Deputy Slocum's kid?"

"Nope. His dog."

"Ah. You know, Chief, we can head out so you can call it a night. There's plenty we can do from our hotel rooms."

"All right, then. I'll lock up behind you."

THE ONLY PLACE STILL OPEN WAS THE BAR ACROSS THE street from the motel where the team stayed. Late nights and early mornings weren't usually the norm for them. However, once or twice a year, a case would come across their desks that brought them out of their Quantico shell and into the heart of an investigation.

Every member on the team had done their time in the field and so the adjustment period was short lived. In fact, some relished the chance to get back into the thick of things. Kate hadn't had that luxury yet. She hadn't been office-bound long enough to experience the desire to escape it. Nick had. And she sensed, despite all he'd said in the past, that he was invigorated by returning to it.

However, sitting here almost like old times with the team, eating wings and drinking beer, Kate wondered if Nick could handle it. Not the field work. The drink. He was still attending the AA meetings and this was, to her knowledge, the first time he would face temptation in a social setting—with his subordinates. No one knew about his battle with alcohol. They couldn't know. It would undermine his leadership abilities and Nick had only just begun to gain a foothold on that front.

Fisher tipped the bottle of beer to his lips before beginning, "So, what was your impression of the Floyds, Quinn?"

"I'll let Reid tell you. This was her call. It was the right one."

"All right," Kate replied. "When I first spotted them, and the way they reacted to one another at the meeting, something didn't feel right. It was as if they were worried."

"Wasn't everyone worried?" Walsh asked.

"Yes, but this was different." Kate glanced at Duncan for affirmation.

"I was there. It seemed odd to me too. She ran with it."

"They were worried not because of what Scarborough said early on, about the killer and the tainted drugs, it was when he mentioned the dealers. Warning the people off them. That struck me as odd. Duncan had her phone out, so I asked her to take a picture of them."

"What was your end game in going to talk to them at their house?" Nick asked.

"The purpose of the visit was to, first of all, gauge their reaction to our presence. Were they going to be nervous, like they had something to hide?" Kate said.

"And were they?" Fisher asked.

"No," Quinn interrupted. "Not from my point of view."

"Mine either," Kate continued. "So that's when I started taking notice of their home. It hadn't been touched in a long time."

"Yeah. It looked like Archie Bunker's house," Quinn replied.

Kate smiled at him. "Something like that. But what I did notice were a couple of things. There was a bus schedule on the coffee table—Greyhound, and a highlighted destination was Tallahassee."

"Strike one." Quinn took a swig of his beer.

"We all know what that could mean," she added.

"The Oxy Express," Duncan replied.

"That's right. And then I noticed that while the house was in desperate need of updating, there were items dotted around that clearly cost some money and appeared to have been recently purchased."

"Such as?" Fisher asked.

"A newer-looking television. I'd say at least a fifty-inch. For a couple with barely one income and some disability, that would have been a big expense. And a box, a locked case, that sat on the kitchen table. Both of us noticed it as we walked in. That was the reason, I bet, why Lynn Floyd excused herself to get the drinks."

"A gun. They own a gun and she wanted to hide it," Walsh replied. "But I don't know why, unless…"

"It was illegally purchased," Kate added.

"And the chief said nothing about any of this?" Nick continued.

"To be honest, I'm not sure he picked up on it. Then again, he might know something we don't. They could've saved for the television and maybe they got a gun after their daughter died." Kate looked at Quinn. "But to me, it seemed more than that. Would you agree?"

"I would. The husband's demeanor." Quinn shook his head. "He seemed almost unconcerned about the fact that a murderer was wandering the streets of his town."

"Like he had nothing to worry about," Kate added. "And I felt that her response to the question of her car seemed odd. It was late and I didn't see any neighbors close enough that would've asked to borrow it. Oh, and I have to say, and this is completely off-topic." She again turned to Quinn. "What the hell was that tea? It was almost pure sugar."

At this, they both laughed.

"Okay, okay. So how do we want to handle this?" Fisher appeared ready to get back to business. "Do we tail the Floyds? See if they take any trips on the Oxy Express?"

"Hang on," Nick said. "They could be dealers. Hell, I suspect a lot of people in this town are, but that doesn't mean they're the ones pushing the bad drugs and killing people. We need more than this. Kate, what else you got?"

Kate felt mild heat rise in her cheeks. Nick had just referred to her by her first name and embarrassment at his familiarity set in.

They were working. And on this team, that just wasn't how they spoke to each other. The last thing she wanted to do right now was to remind everyone that she and Nick had a personal relationship.

Kate did her best to gloss over it and continued. "I believe these people fit our profile. We considered the idea there could be two assailants or one killer and the other cleans up the mess. They lost their daughter to drugs. They have reason to be angry and to seek revenge."

"I have to say that I agree with Reid," Quinn added. "What we saw there tonight, their behavior, the few things that really didn't seem to fit, and the profile. I say it's worth checking into this couple a little more. At least until we get something back from Ness and his forensics team."

"Okay, then. We'll go with that." Nick tossed back his tonic water. "We'll get back at it again in the morning." He approached the bartender and handed him a credit card.

"Are we meeting up first thing?" Duncan asked.

"Bright and early, and let's hope no one else turns up dead in the meantime." Walsh stood from the table.

"Let's remain positive, yeah?" Fisher added. As Nick returned, he continued. "Thanks, boss. And, if we haven't said it already, it's good to have you here. You and Duncan."

Nick eyed him. "It's good to be here."

THE HAPPY COINCIDENCE THAT THE BAR WAS ONLY STEPS away from the motel was the only thing the BAU team had going for it at the moment. When they returned in the late night hour, each of them headed to their respective rooms.

Quantico was only slightly more generous than the WFO in its lodging allowance, so at least no one had to share. However, it escaped no one's attention when Nick followed Kate into her room.

She glanced at Quinn and noticed judgement in his eyes. "Night, Quinn."

"Night, Reid, Scarborough." He continued toward the adjacent room and walked inside.

Kate opened the door and stepped in while Nick followed. "This doesn't feel right," she said.

"What do you mean?" Nick closed the door behind him.

"I mean us, together in this room."

"Kate, they all know we live together. Sharing a room should come as no surprise."

"I know. It's just, I don't want to remind them of the fact that we're together. I mean, Nick, come on, you called me Kate. No one here calls each other by their first name."

"I'm sorry. I didn't even realize I'd done that. It won't happen again, okay? I'm sure no one else picked up on it."

"Quinn did. I saw it in his eyes."

Nick stepped closer to her and placed his hands on her arms. "I am sorry, Kate. I truly meant nothing by it. It was a slip of the tongue. At the WFO..."

"I know what we did there. I remember. But this isn't the WFO. It's not just you, me, Dwight, and Alicia anymore. But I do want to say that I'm proud of you for, you know."

"Skipping out on the booze?" He smiled. "You think anyone noticed?"

"Everyone else was drinking beer, so maybe. I don't know. But no one seemed to care," she replied.

"No, they didn't. And the fewer questions we raise on that whole issue, the better."

"Come on, we should get some sleep," Kate added. "Who

knows what we'll be dealing with tomorrow. Like you always used to say, get sleep when you can..."

"It might be days before you'll get it again," he finished.

"Yep."

Nick stepped toward her and unbuttoned her blouse. He traced the edge of her lacy bra with his fingers. "You're not too tired for..."

"Nice try, but no, not a chance. These thin walls and my boss on the other side? No way."

Nick sighed. "Fine. Your loss." He unbuttoned his own shirt and pulled it open like a Chippendale dancer. He rubbed his toned chest and flat stomach. "You sure I can't tempt you?"

Kate threw back her head in laughter. "Oh, it's definitely my loss." She placed her hands on his bare chest and kissed his lips. "Goodnight, Nick."

WHEN THE STEAM FROM THE SHOWER ABATED, KATE STEPPED out and wrapped a towel around her petite frame before spotting Nick on the edge of the bed with his phone at his ear.

"Thanks. I'll let everyone know. Appreciate your help." He ended the call and peered at her. "That was Ness."

"And?" Her heart raced with anticipation of the break they so desperately needed.

"He got DNA back on the wood shard you found, but there's no match. Whoever it belongs to isn't in the database. The only thing we know for sure is that it isn't Andy Walcott's DNA."

Kate dropped her head to her chest. "Damn it. We've been pinning all our hopes on those results."

"Look, you know the drill as well as anyone. This is still good news. We have DNA on someone. So when we bring in a suspect, we'll get a swab and see if there's a match."

"We don't have a suspect," she replied.

"The Floyds?"

"Possibly. Although I really don't want Chief Tate to get wind we're tailing them."

"He won't." Nick stood from the bed and approached her. "I'll get cleaned up and we'll head out."

LYNN FLOYD GRABBED HER OVERSIZED HANDBAG FROM THE kitchen chair. "We're going to have to lay low for a while."

"We can't afford to lay low," John replied.

"It's either that or we go to prison. Your call."

John folded his arms across his chest. "Sons of bitches don't got nothing on us. They got no cause to even discuss anything. Yet there they were, sitting on our sofa, drinking our tea."

"Just cool your heels. This is the way it's gotta be for now. We'll just have to figure a way through is all." She started toward the door. "I best get to work. Can't afford to lose that job. What are you going to do?"

"Hell, I don't know. Sit here twiddling my thumbs, I reckon."

"How 'bout you put your noodle to use and figure out how we can get some money to keep us going?" Lynn closed the door behind her. As she walked toward her car, her attention was captured by a passing vehicle. In any other circumstance, this wouldn't have been an unusual occurrence, but at this hour, it struck her as odd. And in fact, it didn't look like the car belonged to anyone from Crown Pointe. It was a brand new SUV. No one around here could afford a car like that, which made her even more concerned.

As she slipped inside her ten-year-old Toyota Corolla, Lynn drove down the lengthy driveway toward the road. She recalled the woman agent asking why her car hadn't been in her driveway last night. Fortunately, her quick thinking appeared to satisfy the lady.

With her eyes darting from the rear-view to the road ahead and back again, she made her way into town toward the elementary school. No one followed her. Maybe she was just being paranoid. Difficult to say since she'd already been paid a visit by the G-men and women, and now it felt like eyes were on her everywhere.

Lynn regretted this life they now had. A life without Jenny. A life without morals. Nevertheless, they'd been forced into it by circumstances beyond their control. Jenny had been a good girl. Got good grades in school, was kind to people. In fact, she wouldn't have hurt a fly. She'd worked at the movie theater, which had since shut down. The added income helped the family. But just a few years out of high school and that was where it all started to go wrong for Jenny. And Lynn did nothing about it. Neither did John. Both buried their heads in the sand. When her daughter's appearance began to change—the weight loss, the black circles under her eyes—they didn't ask her why. They refused to see what she was becoming.

The day they got the call from Chief Tate was the worst day of Lynn's life. But even then, she and John denied the truth of her death. The root cause of it. Like so many other parents who faced similar situations, they couldn't come to terms with the fact that their loving and beautiful daughter was a drug addict.

Flash forward a year and the Floyds were dealing the very same drugs that took their daughter away. The jobs were so scarce and the money so tight, it was the only way to survive. Their lives had been reduced to nothing more than survival.

Lynn was yanked into the moment by the sound of sirens

drawing near. She glanced into the rear-view mirror and a patrol car with flashing lights quickly advanced. She checked her speed. If anything, she was going too slowly. Her mind ran through anything else that could be cause for one of the boys to flag her down. A broken taillight? Expired tags? No. It was none of those things.

She pulled over onto the shoulder, now only a mile from the school near the grocer's and the mobile phone store. The patrol car stopped behind her and Deputy Slocum stepped out. Lynn's brow knitted. She rolled down her window and felt the blast of cold air come through.

"Morning, Mrs. Floyd. How are you?" Slocum leaned into her window.

"Fine. Fine. Was I speeding, Eric?"

"No, ma'am. I just wanted to talk to you for a second."

"About? I'm on my way to work. Can this wait? You and me both know I can't afford to lose this job."

"It'll only take a minute. I understand them FBI came 'round your place last night, along with the chief."

"That's right. They were asking questions about Jenny," Lynn replied.

"What kind of questions?"

"About her—life, I guess. Her school and friends and, of course —well you know—how she died."

Slocum nodded. "That must've been tough to talk about after it's only just gone a year now."

"Yes, sir, it was."

"And they didn't ask nothing else?"

"Well, like what?"

He raised from the window to peer over the car while his eyes squinted in the sun's rays. Returning his attention to her, Slocum continued, "I'm just trying to figure out what they're planning, I reckon. I sure don't want them questioning everyone who's lost someone here in Crown Pointe. A terrible thing to have to relive."

"I suppose so. That'd take them some time to get through."

"Yes, it would." Slocum tapped the door frame with his palm and stood upright again. "I won't keep you. Best be getting to work now. Thank you for your time, Mrs. Floyd. You have a good day, now."

"And you too, Deputy." Lynn rolled up the window and pulled away, leaving Slocum standing on the shoulder. Through the side view mirror, she noticed his stare as she drove away.

15

A gangly man, not more than twenty-two, pushed back his unwieldy blonde hair from his face and surveyed the street ahead. Just bare trees and dirt roads. No other cars. He walked to his car and stepped inside.

"This is all they got." He held a baggie containing several pills.

"What about what them FBI people said last night? About not buying no more drugs from around here."

"Look, I got no reason not to trust these guys. I bought from them before. You don't got to take them if you don't want to. But I'm gonna. Shit, those cops don't know nothing anyway."

The woman next to him was younger, perhaps still in her late teens. She licked her lips and clicked her tongue as though she was parched. "Can't we get some Big H instead?"

"Don't you think I tried that? Nobody's got none right now. This is it." The man swallowed down two pills.

"It's gonna take forever to get a high that way," the woman said.

"You got a better idea?" He shoved his hand toward her. "Just take the damn pills and stop your bitchin'. We got to get out of here before someone sees us."

She took the pills and swallowed them down.

"There. All better." He started the engine and pulled away. As he made his way through the side streets of town, a car pulled up behind him. He checked the rearview. "Hey, you know who that is behind us?"

The woman turned. "No."

"Don't turn around!"

"What? You asked if I knew who it was. Don't need to be a dick about it."

"Never mind." He verified the car was still following. "I'm taking you home. I don't know who the hell that is back there, but I best get you back. Maybe they'll turn off somewhere else." He pulled into the Sunny Hills trailer park and stopped at number 4.

She opened the passenger door, but stopped when he hadn't moved. "Wait. You ain't coming in? I thought we was gonna, you know, get high."

"I gotta go." He peered over his shoulder, noting the car no longer trailed behind. "I'll see you later."

"That car's gone now. What are you going to do? Might as well come in."

"Just get the fuck out. I gotta go."

"Fine. Asshole." She slammed the car door.

He drove out of Sunny Hills and returned to the main road, veering right. That was when his chest started to feel heavy and nausea whirled in his belly. "Shit. Shit. Shit." Sweat poured down his brow and he grew lightheaded. The car swerved erratically. "No. This can't be happening."

The all-too-familiar feeling had happened twice before. Each time, he'd pulled through. But this time felt different. Worse. Much worse. The gag reflex kicked in and made him convulse. His vision blurred as he continued to drive, attempting to reach the nearby hospital. But it was too late. He lost control of his limbs and yanked the wheel. The car turned sharply off the road, skidding to a stop. He threw open the driver's side door and retched before tumbling out of the car and purging what could only have been the bad drugs the FBI man warned them about. Splayed on the ground on the side of the road, his face rested in the pool of vomit as his body seized.

With whatever consciousness remained, he spotted a shadow approach. Whoever it was had been obscured by the sun but he begged for help.

"No one's gonna help you now, boy." A large bat in the hands of the shadowy figure came crashing down on the man's chest.

Two more crushing blows to the stomach. The man lurched with each one, powerless to move away in defense.

The final strike was imminent. With wide eyes, he watched the bat fall. A swift crash against his skull, and the man was gone.

Exasperated, Chief Tate listened as Nick relayed the lab results. "So, no DNA match. Where the hell does that leave us now?"

The rest of the team looked on as tensions inside the small station house grew.

"Ness has his DEA contact working to find the origins of the synthetic pills. We need to know who's shelling out this deadly drug," Nick replied.

"Well, hell, son, I can give you the names of half a dozen dealers in this town right now. But I'll tell you what, not a one of them has the wherewithal to pull off something like this. This sorta thing just don't happen here."

"Respectfully, Chief," Quinn began, "the sooner you come to terms with this situation, the easier this investigation will go. I understand you don't want to believe anyone here would be capable of such a thing. But we've given you plenty of cause to change your mind. Your citizens are being murdered. And someone is giving them these lethal drugs and then finishing them off in a horrific manner. How many more people are going to die before you get with the program?"

"Now you just wait a hot minute." The chief pointed his finger at Quinn. "I don't know who the hell you think you're talking to. I've been in law enforcement since you were wiping your nose on your momma's skirt, so don't..."

The door burst open and Deputy Slocum rushed inside. "We got another one."

"Say again?" Lazaro shot up from his desk.

"We got another body. Off Oakhill Drive."

"Son of a bitch." Nick yanked his coat off the back of a chair. "We need to get down there now. You call emergency services?"

"I think that goes without saying," Slocum replied.

The team followed Nick and the deputy out to the parking lot.

Chief stopped Quinn for a moment. "I'm sorry for what I said back there. It's just..."

"Me too, Chief. I think we're all on edge right now. Come on. We'd better go see what happened out there."

THE ONSLAUGHT OF CARS—SOME POLICE, SOME CIVILIAN— caught the attention of everyone in the area. The ambulance had arrived and had already put the body in the truck.

Agent Fisher was the first to approach the EMT and pulled the toothpick from his mouth. "Hey. You moved this body?"

"Yes, sir. Couldn't very well leave him out here till the animals got him."

"Jesus!" He turned to Nick. "He just contaminated the whole damn scene!"

"Calm down." Nick stopped just short of the obvious location of where the body had been. "Everybody, stop where you are. We need to document this scene as best we can."

"I'm sorry. I—I didn't know..." the paramedic replied.

"It's okay. How could you have known? It wasn't your responsibility," Nick replied.

"He's right. It was mine." Slocum approached. "I screwed this up, didn't I? Christ." He turned away.

"We'll work through it. Let's just collect as much as we can and go from there." Nick turned to Kate and Quinn. "I'm going to need you two to jump in on this."

"We'll get photos," Quinn said. "Walsh and Duncan are baggin' and taggin'. Walsh is collecting soils samples too.

"I need to see the body before they haul him out of here." Fisher stepped into the ambulance.

Nick headed toward the chief. "You think we can get some crowd control over here? These people have dealt with enough. No one needs to see this."

Chief nodded. "Lazaro, get everyone back."

"Ten-four, Chief." He walked toward the growing crowd. "Okay, everybody. We're gonna need y'all to step back so we can do our jobs, you hear?" His modest stature and inexperience aired in his tone.

"I'd say the last thing y'all are doing is your jobs," a woman in the crowd began. "I was there last night. You people are a damn joke. None of you are gonna find the person killing all these poor people."

Lazaro stepped closer. "Ma'am, I'm gonna have to ask you to step back, please. I'm sure you're just scared."

"We're all scared!" another shouted.

Nick turned back at the sound. "Shit. We need to get control of these people." He looked at Kate. "You want to help him out?"

"I'll try." She approached Lazaro and the unruly pack. "I'll tell you what would be a great help to us," she said to the crowd.

"And what's that, Ms. F-B-I?" the woman continued.

"We sure could use your help in identifying who this car belongs to. Any of you all recognize it? Or maybe one of you might've seen something?"

The woman revealed a modicum of guilt. "I—I don't know." She turned back to the other people around her. "Anyone know whose car that is?"

A few people stepped forward. One of them was Lynn Floyd. Kate immediately recognized her.

"Mrs. Floyd? What are you doing here?"

"I work over there at the school. Heard the commotion and the ambulance and walked over along with everyone else."

"Did you happen to see anything?" Kate asked.

"No."

Kate thought she noticed a spark of recognition in Lynn Floyd's eyes. "Nothing, huh? What about the car? We can't show you who's in the truck. Not until we can find next of kin. But maybe knowing who owns that car, maybe that'll help us out in identifying the victim."

"I don't know whose car that is." She stepped back in line.

"Thanks anyway." Kate returned her attention to the crowd. "If anyone happened to see anything—anything at all that you might be concerned about, please reach out to one of us. An anonymous call, anything." She eyed the people once again before turning away.

"Thank you, Agent Reid," Lazaro said.

"No problem. They just need to feel like they have some control. And right now, they don't. We'll be able to pull registration on the vehicle, but just asking for their help puts some power back into their hands." She headed toward the scene again and approached Quinn.

He was squatting next to the blood-stained soil and peered over his shoulder at her. "You should take a look at this."

Kate joined him, squatting down, her arms resting on her thighs. "What'd you find?"

"Judging by the size of our victim, this shoe print right here doesn't belong to him."

"It looks like a boot." Kate looked at him. "A work boot?"

"Possibly." Quinn retrieved his phone and snapped a picture. "We'll have this analyzed. By the way, you handled the crowd like a pro. You've done that before."

"Sort of. Different situation. But my thoughts on Lynn Floyd haven't changed. I'm sure she recognized this car. I saw it in her eyes."

"All the more reason to keep moving forward on our idea. With or without the chief's knowledge," Quinn replied.

Agent Fisher approached the two of them. "Anything good here?"

"Shoe prints," Quinn replied. "It's something."

"At first blush, the body appears to have been struck by something along the lines of a bat, markings are similar to the others," Fisher said. "Forensics will have to make the final call, but it sure as hell looks like that to me."

"And drugs?" Kate turned back to where the body had been. "There's vomit all over here."

"We'd better get a sample of it. Tox screen will tell us for sure, but hell if I want to wait that long. We'll get results from a sample of the stomach contents a lot quicker."

Dispatch sounded on the patrol car radio. The chief picked up the receiver. "Say again, dispatch."

"A 911 just call came in. OD at the Sunny Hills Trailer Park. Unit 4."

"Damn. Is an ambo on the way?"

"Affirmative."

"Ten-four. We'll head over now." Chief dropped the radio and returned to the team. "Agent Scarborough? We got an OD down the road. 911 was called."

Nick eyed Fisher for confirmation.

"Go. We'll catch up. Take Quinn and Reid. Could be another one of these," Fisher said.

"Quinn? Reid? We need to go now." Nick started toward their vehicle while the agents caught up with him.

"What's going on?" Kate asked.

"An OD at a trailer park. Could be related. 911 was called, but I don't know if EMTs are on scene yet. Let's get down there before they touch anything."

NICK PULLED INTO THE TRAILER PARK WHERE SEVERAL residents had already gathered. "Should've brought Lazaro with us. We might need to cordon off the area."

"You're assuming the victim is already dead," Quinn said.

"That seems to be the current trend at the moment." Nick stopped in front of the trailer and next to the ambulance that appeared to have just arrived.

The EMTs rushed out of the truck and pushed through the front door. The three quickly jumped out of the SUV and ran toward the entrance. Nick led the way inside. "FBI. Chief Tate sent us."

The paramedics worked on the young woman. One began chest compressions while the other started CPR.

"She's still alive." Kate wore relief.

"God willing, she'll stay that way," Quinn replied. "She might know the other victim." He walked toward the paramedics. "Anything we can do to help?"

"Blankets. Towels. In the truck." She continued the chest compressions.

Quinn rushed back outside and soon returned with the requested items. "Here."

"We still got a pulse!" she said. "Check her vitals!"

The other EMT strapped a cuff around the young woman's arm. "BP is 170 over 90."

"Shit. Okay."

"Pulse ox at 94." He looked to his partner. "I think she's going to pull out of it. Just need to get that BP down."

Kate noticed next to the female paramedic was a vial of Narcan; a nasal spray used to treat overdoses. And it seemed to have worked.

"BP is now 150 over 85." The man looked to his partner again. "She's improving."

Within about a minute, the young woman regained consciousness.

"Miss? I'm Stacy, a paramedic. Can you tell me your name?"

In a groggy voice, she began, "Lori."

"Lori, can you tell me what you took?"

"Oxy."

"How much?"

"Two 80s." She started to blink and looked around. "Is Kevin okay?"

"Who's Kevin? Is he here?" the paramedic continued.

"No. You need to find him. He took the same thing as me." She grew agitated.

"Lori. I'm going to need you to calm down, okay? We'll find Kevin. I'm sure he's fine. But right now, I'm concerned about you." She turned back to the agents. "Kevin?"

"You taking her to the hospital?" Nick asked.

"Yes. We'll load her up now."

"We'll follow you." He pulled Quinn and Kate aside. "What are the odds our vic is named Kevin?"

"Pretty damn good, I'd say," Kate began. "She can tell us where they got the drugs."

As THE EMTs RUSHED THE WOMAN THROUGH THE GLASS doors of the hospital, Nick, Kate, and Noah Quinn were close behind in their own vehicle.

"I don't see the others," Kate said as she stepped out of the car.

"They aren't far behind. Once the doctors check her out, we should get the 'all clear' to talk to her," Nick replied.

"Are we going to tell her about her boyfriend?" Quinn asked.

"Not until we know for sure that was him on the side of the road." Nick checked his phone. "Speaking of that, let's see if Chief Tate can run the plates for an owner." He made the call, but the chief walked in before it connected. "Good. You're here. Any chance we can run the plates on the vic's car?"

"Already ahead of you on that one, Agent Scarborough. Car belongs to Erin Sadler, fifty-eight-year-old mother of two."

"Was one of the kids named Kevin Sadler?" Quinn asked.

"Kevin Adams. Ms. Sadler remarried. You have reason to believe our victim is Kevin?" The chief asked.

"They just brought in the OD, a young woman who said Kevin had taken the same drugs only an hour earlier. That's too much of a coincidence to not be Kevin Adams."

"She'll pull through?" Chief asked.

"They're treating her now. The EMTs did amazing work bringing her back," Kate said. "They had Narcan with them."

"Standard protocol now. What with all the overdose calls we get nowadays."

"I imagine it has saved a lot of lives."

"Yes, ma'am. It has." The chief removed his hat as they made their way inside. "I thought the rest of your team would've been here by now."

"Is the scene secure?" Nick asked.

"My boys are still out there waiting on the tow truck. Once they get that car hauled off out of there, I asked them to meet me here."

A doctor emerged from the corridor. "Chief Tate."

"Hey there, Doc. What's the good word on the OD that just came in?"

"She's in stable condition. The paramedics saved her life. We're just making sure she's hydrated and that she didn't sustain any injuries, which it doesn't appear she did, luckily."

"Do you think we could talk to her? We believe a man, likely her boyfriend, was attacked and killed after taking the same drugs."

"Do you believe this is tied to your case?"

"It sure could be, Doc. Which is why we really need to speak to her, with your permission," Nick said.

"I had one of the nurses notify her family. Could be a few minutes to an hour before they arrive. I suggest you speak to her before they do. I'll take you back." The doctor stopped and turned toward them again. "Um. I'd prefer it if just one of you goes. Maybe you?" He looked at Kate.

Kate was usually called upon to handle female victims. It was just a comfort thing. "Of course." She followed him back.

"Just keep it as brief as you can. She still needs to rest." The doctor opened the door for her. "Hello, Miss Lori. There's someone here from the FBI who would like to speak with you for just a minute. Would that be all right with you?"

The feeble young woman turned her head to see Kate. "Sure. I guess. Something bad's happened to Kevin, hasn't it?"

"I'll leave you to it," the doctor said to Kate before leaving.

"Is Kevin your boyfriend?" She approached the woman's bed.

"Sorta. Wouldn't call it anything serious, though. Just had a few laughs, got high." Tears streamed down her face. "I told him I didn't want to take those pills. After what y'all said about the bad shit someone was selling. I said I was scared and he said it'd be fine cause he knew them. But it isn't fine, is it?"

"The car Kevin drove belonged to a woman named Erin Sadler. Do you know her?"

Lori turned away. "That's his momma's car. He was driving it when he dropped me off."

Kate touched Lori's hand. "I'm so sorry."

"That psycho killer found him, didn't he? Someone beat the shit out of him? Just like all the others?" She sobbed harder. "How? I don't understand. How could you let this happen?"

"We're still trying to find answers for you, Lori," Kate continued. "But right now, it would be really helpful if you could tell me where Kevin got the drugs."

Lori was hesitant, or afraid of retribution. Difficult to know for sure.

"It's okay. We won't let anyone hurt you. But we need to stop this person. We don't want anyone else harmed the way you were, or Kevin. Please. If you know who it is, you need to tell me. This needs to end, Lori. And you can help us."

Lori swallowed hard and looked Kate directly in the eyes. "He only got them from two people. He didn't say which one it was this time, but it was either Billy Horton or the Floyds."

"Lynn and John Floyd?" Kate asked.

She nodded.

"Thank you, Lori. I'll let you get some rest." Kate pushed through the door and marched back into the lobby. "The Floyds. It was the Floyds."

"That's what she said?" The chief's face masked in shock.

"She said it was either a guy named Billy Horton or Lynn and John Floyd." She looked at Quinn. "We need to bring them both in."

16

Convincing a kind-hearted chief of police that the people in his town, people he trusted, might be the root cause of a murderous rampage proved difficult and frustrating for the seasoned agents. Chief Tate's refusal to accept that the Floyds played any part in the deaths of now six people in his town would hinder their progress at the expense of the citizens of Crown Pointe.

"Chief, I understand what a shock this must be for you, but the longer we sit here, the lower our chances become of bringing in the Floyds, or this Billy Horton. Word will reach them and they'll be in the wind." Nick's stance was unwavering, knowing the time to act was now.

"Where are the Floyds going to go? They don't have money," the chief replied.

"I'm sure they must if what the girl said is true," Quinn added. "Agent Scarborough is right. You brought us in to help and now we have a legitimate lead and we have to follow through on it. Lives are still at stake. Do you really want to sit on this?"

Deputy Eric Slocum peered at his boss. "They're right, Chief. As much as I hate to admit it. Just seems downright mind-boggling. But we got no other choice." He placed his hand on the chief's shoulder and looked to Lazaro for backup.

"I agree. The sooner the better," Lazaro said.

"I'll be damned. So everyone's against me?"

"We're not against you, Chief," Kate said. "We're following the only lead we have. The time is now."

He eyed each and every person in that room. Every federal agent and his own men. They all had the same look. They were right and he was wrong. "Bring 'em in then. I guess hell has frozen over if the Floyds would do something like this after losing their own child to drugs."

With renewed conviction, Nick began, "We'll split up. Walsh and Duncan, find this Horton kid and contact Agent Ness. He'll want in on this. Reid and Quinn can go to the Floyds' home and Fisher, you and I can go to Lynn Floyd's workplace. Cover all our bases."

"Now just hold up a minute," Chief began. "Look, I know y'all got more authority than I have, but these are my people. I'll send my men to get them."

"It's your investigation, Chief. If that's what you want, we'll stay here, but you're risking one of them slipping through your fingers," Nick replied. "We have the manpower to tackle this quickly and efficiently."

"This is what I want," the chief replied. "Shane, you and Eric go see if Mr. Floyd is home. I'll go check the school for Mrs. Floyd."

"And Billy Horton?" Lazaro asked.

Chief seemed to realize that he was, in fact, short-handed. "Scarborough, I'll let you send your people to find him."

"Will do." Nick watched them leave. "At least he's bringing them in. I thought we might have a real problem brewing."

"We'll still need to search the Floyd property," Fisher said. "I'm scared shitless they're going to trample over evidence, just like at the scene earlier."

"When they get back, I'll suggest we search the home while they're busy questioning the Floyds. Right now, let's get on the horn to Ness. Walsh, I want you and Duncan to find Billy Horton."

THE MIDDLE-AGED WOMAN BEHIND THE FRONT DESK OF THE high school lobby appeared surprised to see the chief of police walk through the door. "Why, Chief Tate, what are you doing here? Everything all right?"

"Afternoon, Ms. Abigail. Can you tell me if Mrs. Floyd is here today?"

"Well, I believe so. She's been here every day this week. Why?"

"You think I could have a word with her?" The chief took pause. "Actually, you reckon you could tell me where she's at right now? I don't need to disrupt anything you're doing. I can find her if you just point the way."

"Sure." The woman looked at the clock on the wall. "She should be cleaning up from lunch. You'll find her in the cafeteria. You sure I can't get her for you? Wouldn't be any trouble at all."

"Thank you, no. I'll catch up to her." The chief left and made his way toward the cafeteria. He wanted to avoid run-ins with anyone else for fear of questions. Inconspicuous, he was not, and the only way someone might miss seeing the chief was if his eyes were closed. The sooner he could get in, the sooner he could get her out, and hopefully, with little notice and few tongues wagging in his aftermath.

The cafeteria was just ahead and he peered inside the window. It was empty. Lunch was over. The heels of his cowboy boots clicked on the old linoleum floor as he walked toward the kitchen area. He pushed through a swinging door and spotted the ladies cleaning up dishes and mopping the floor. That was when he saw Lynn Floyd, hunched over a mop and bucket, not realizing he'd entered. "Afternoon, ladies." He tipped his hat.

Lynn turned and her face masked in fear. She dropped the mop and eyed the door.

Chief Tate noticed the guilt she wore. "You aren't fixin' to do anything stupid, Ms. Lynn, are you? You mind coming with me to the station for a quick word?"

With a cracked voice, she began, "Well, what's this all about, then? I can't just leave work."

"I'm afraid I wasn't really asking for permission. We just need to clear up a few things. Won't take long."

Lynn glanced at the other ladies and picked up on their judging eyes. "I suppose if it's only a short while. No harm in that." She picked up the mop, leaned it against a wall, and tugged at her shirt. "I just need to collect my bag if it's all the same to you."

He extended his arm. "After you."

Deputies Slocum and Lazaro arrived at the Floyd home and approached the door.

"You think he's home?" Lazaro asked.

"No. I think he's having afternoon tea at the Rainbow Room. Of course he's home. The man ain't got no job."

"All right." Lazaro raised his hands in surrender. "What's gotten into you?"

"Nothing." Slocum knocked on the screen door. "Mr. Floyd? It's Eric Slocum. You mind opening the door, please?"

"I don't hear anything," Lazaro continued.

"Give him a minute. He don't get around all that well. Christ." Slocum waited for a few more seconds before knocking again. "John? You in there? We just need to ask you some questions."

A crash sounded through the door.

"What the hell was that?" Lazaro placed his hand on his gun.

Slocum wasted no time drawing his own weapon. "John? You okay in there? I'm gonna need you to open this door or we'll have to force our way inside. I know you don't want me busting this door down."

"You think he fell?"

Slocum eyed Lazaro with some contempt. "Just get ready. I think we're gonna have to bust our way inside." He pounded on the door again. "Mr. Floyd, this is the last time I'm gonna ask. Open the door now!"

"I don't think he's gonna let us in."

"Son of a bitch." Slocum took a few steps back. "Get back. I'm gonna kick it in." He pulled open the screen and kicked the door with all the force he could muster. His days as a star athlete in high school paid off. The door splintered from its frame and swung open.

The deputies walked inside with Slocum leading the way, gun drawn. "John? Now we just want to talk. Where are you?"

"In here, you damn fools. I ain't armed. I'm hurt is all."

"Shit." Slocum holstered his weapon and walked into the kitchen where John Floyd lay on the floor.

"Holy hell, are you okay, John?" Slocum knelt down and quickly checked him for injuries.

"I'm fine. I fell down. I heard you knocking and I was pouring a cup of coffee. Spilled the damn thing and slipped on it." He looked at the deputies. "What the hell is going on, anyway? Why you here?"

"Come help me pull him up," Slocum said.

"Oh, right." Lazaro joined him and the two hoisted the large man and placed him in a kitchen chair. "We're so sorry, Mr. Floyd. We heard a crash. Must've been that coffee pot. Are you sure you're all right?"

"I'm fine. Just bruised my ego more than anything." He adjusted himself into the chair. "Now, you mind telling me why you boys are here?"

"The chief would like to have a word. We need to take you to the station. Can you walk?" Lazaro replied.

"Course I can walk. I ain't an invalid. Why does he want to talk? I don't understand."

"He'll explain more when we get there," Slocum replied.

"Well, I'll need to leave a note for Lynnie. She'll worry if I'm not here when she gets home from work."

"John, she's probably already at the station by now." Slocum offered his hand. "I'll help you up."

THE DEPUTIES RETURNED TO FIND LYNN FLOYD SITTING AT A desk with the chief on the other side and the head FBI guy behind him. Their arrival was quickly noted when John Floyd became agitated.

"Lynnie? What are you doing here? Would someone mind explaining to me what the hell is going on right now? Chief?"

"It's okay, John. Everything's going to be fine. I just need you to sit down and we'll explain everything."

He pulled away from the deputies. "I will not sit down."

Fisher was near the entrance and watched the dust-up, ready to draw down if the situation got out of hand.

"Whoa, whoa, now," Chief said. "Let's just settle down. There's no need for this."

Fisher looked at Nick for direction.

"It's okay. He's not going to hurt anyone," Nick said. "Let's all just calm down and talk this through. Mrs. Floyd, you want to tell your husband everything is okay?"

She turned around to face him. "They think we're drug dealers, John. Just sit down before you get yourself shot."

"What in the world?" he replied. "Drug dealers? You think you people might ought to be on the lookout for the murderer running loose in this town?"

"That's exactly what we're trying to do, Mr. Floyd. But we'd like to ask you some questions," Nick said. "Quinn, you and Reid better head over to the house now."

"What? My house?" Lynn said. "You can't just waltz into my home. You gotta have some sort of warrant or something. Ain't that right, Chief?"

"Ma'am, we have a warrant." Kate retrieved the document.

"Fisher, I'd like you to stay with me. Ness should be here soon. Quinn, find out if Walsh and Duncan tracked down our other lead. If not, have them meet you at the Floyd residence to expedite the search," Nick added.

"You got it."

"No. You can't. We ain't done nothing wrong," John said.

"Then there's nothing for you to worry about, Mr. Floyd," Fisher replied.

"What should we do, Chief?" Slocum asked. "This don't feel right. Should I go with them to the Floyd's?"

Chief Tate eyed the only other man in the room who anyone

was taking orders from, Agent Scarborough. "You got a problem if I send one of mine?"

"No problem, Chief."

"Lazaro can stay here. Slocum, go with them. You know the way anyhow."

"Well, all right, then. Let's go." Slocum pushed through the doors while Kate and Quinn fell in behind him. "I'm driving."

Slocum pulled out of the station and headed toward the Floyd home. "Y'all really think the Floyds are murderers and drug dealers? You do know their daughter died of an overdose?"

"We are aware," Quinn replied. "You were there this morning, Deputy. You saw what we saw, and know what the girl said."

"I suppose so. Just can't seem to wrap my head around it."

"Appears Chief Tate's having the same problem." A text came in on Quinn's phone. He read it while continuing, "Unfortunately, this is what we deal with all the time. It's usually the ones you least suspect." Quinn looked over his shoulder at Kate. "Just got a text from Walsh. No luck finding Horton. They'll meet us at the Floyds' inside of ten minutes."

It appeared no one had anything left to say on the topic of whether the Floyds were killers or just dealers. It wasn't long before they arrived at the home.

"This is the place. Looks like your buddies just arrived too." Slocum peered into the side-view mirror, spotting the SUV.

They exited the patrol car and walked toward the front door.

Walsh and Duncan caught up to them on the front porch. He looked at Quinn. "It appears as though no one's ever heard of Billy Horton."

"Of course not." Quinn shook his head. "Let's see what we find in here. If we come out empty-handed, we might need to put out a BOLO on Horton." Quinn looked at Slocum and the busted door. "What happened here?"

"I had to knock it down. Mr. Floyd fell and there was this whole thing." Slocum walked through the doorway.

"Reid, you want to take the back room?" Quinn began. "Duncan, you can take the family room over there. And Deputy Slocum, if you want to check the bathroom and the other bedroom, that'd be a big help. Walsh and I can take the front of the house and kitchen."

Slocum nodded and started down the hall.

Kate walked toward Quinn and lowered her tone. "You sure he'll be thorough?"

"Why wouldn't he be? I know these guys are small town, but that doesn't make them incapable of handling a case."

"That's not what I meant. I just meant we're getting a lot of pushback from them. That's all," Kate replied.

"We have to trust the job they're doing. Just like they have to trust us."

"Okay." She continued through to the rear of the home, but not before eyeing Duncan as they passed in the hall and shrugging her shoulders. Kate made it inside what appeared to be the master bedroom where there was a queen-sized bed draped in a country-style quilt, side tables, a chair in the corner, and a dresser. All of which looked to have been purchased probably around the time their daughter was born.

"Hey."

Kate spun around. "Geez, you scared the crap out of me. You find something?"

Duncan walked inside. "No. Wasn't much there, so I thought I'd see what you got going on in here. Quinn's still checking out the kitchen and Walsh is out front. What about our guy, Slocum?"

"Don't know. I just came straight here. And so far, nothing out of the ordinary. Help me check the closet." Kate pulled on the knobs of the wooden bi-fold closet doors, the kind with the slats on the top. "Wow. Not much in the way of clothes in here."

"No. Not for two people." Duncan pushed aside the hangers in search of anything of interest. "So I hear you have some sort of sixth sense about this stuff?"

"I wouldn't say it's my claim to fame, but I guess I've gotten lucky a couple of times."

"You mean like the shed the other day? Finding that wood shard?" Duncan pressed on.

"I guess so. Too bad it was a worthless find."

"No, it wasn't. We got DNA from it. We just need to figure out who it belongs to." She peered inside, moving shoes, shifting boxes. "It must be difficult working for your boyfriend."

Kate shot her a look.

"No offense. I'm just making conversation. Look, Reid, I like you. We all do, despite what you might think. I just imagine you must feel like you have to prove yourself all the time so people don't think you got some sort of preferential treatment. I know that's how I'd feel if it was me."

"It does sort of feel that way, I guess."

"You guess?"

"Okay. It definitely feels that way," Kate added.

"Well, we know you're good at your job. Quinn talked to us quite a bit about you before making his decision."

"I didn't know that."

"He did. We're a team, after all. But I want you to know that you're a part of it now. You and Scarborough both. So whatever happens to you two also happens to us. I guess what I'm saying is..."

Kate jumped in. "You hope nothing happens to us that might shake things up for the rest of you? I get that. And it won't. I promise you. Scarborough and I have worked together for years.

We don't let our relationship get in the way of the job." Kate looked away for a split second, guilty about the white lie she just told because, in fact, there had been times, plenty of them, when their relationship had gotten in the way. Even before they had one.

"Good. That's good to hear." Duncan returned to the task at hand. "Now here's to praying that sixth sense of yours starts kicking in right about now."

Slocum stood in the door way. "Anyone check the attic yet?"

Kate turned to him. "Nope. Feel free to tackle that one."

"Will do." He started back into the hall, lowering the ladder for the scuttle attic.

"Doubt he'll find anything there," Duncan said. "John Floyd is disabled and Lynn Floyd looks like she'd struggle to get up there too."

"We'll let him do what he feels he needs to do. He seems like a decent guy and all, and I do understand where the chief's coming from, but it took too long to get them to come around. And if that girl hadn't given us the names, we'd still be trying to convince them the Floyds were a concern."

"Hey, I got something up here, y'all."

The voice came from the attic.

"Looks like we spoke too soon." Duncan made her way into the hall.

Kate followed closely behind and Quinn caught up to them.

Deputy Slocum made his way down the steps of the attic ladder. "Looks like y'all might've been right about the Floyds. Who'd have guessed?" As he stepped off the bottom rung, he held a prescription bottle in his hands. "What's this look like to y'all?"

"Oxy," Quinn replied. "This will need to be tested ASAP."

17

With the discovery of the drugs inside the Floyd home, all that remained was to test the compound to see if it matched the pill found in Steven Schiller's car as well as the chemical compounds discovered in the victims. Though they still hadn't yet learned the makeup of whatever drug was in the body of Kevin Adams, it was almost guaranteed to be a match. On their return, the team felt reinvigorated by the breakthrough. Even Deputy Slocum appeared to revel in the find.

The chief, however, appeared shaken and demoralized. "I don't understand how, after everything you two went through with the loss of Jenny, how you could do this?"

"It's not ours, Chief, you have to believe me," Lynn pleaded as she held John's hand. "We didn't kill nobody and we didn't sell no drugs neither."

"Well, how the hell do you explain the bottle? John been taking them? You? And why the hell was it in the attic? Like you were trying to hide something." Chief grew more agitated as she pursued her rebuttal.

"Chief Tate." Nick approached him. "Maybe you should take a step back for a minute. Emotions are running high right now and we don't want to say or do anything we might regret." It seemed what Nick feared the most was a comment that might threaten the investigation and so pulling the chief back into line was the only way. He turned to the Floyds. "We're going to have to remand you into custody until we can get the results of the analysis on the pills. However, you will remain in the custody of the Crown Pointe police, not us."

"Lynnie's right." John's eyes reddened. "Y'all are making a big mistake. We ain't no killers. Chief, you know us."

"Okay, okay." Fisher inserted himself into the mix. "Scarborough's right. There is one thing we'll need from both of you, Mr. and Mrs. Floyd, that will help clear all this up. We're going to need a DNA sample. A simple swab. You want to prove your innocence? That's how you'll do it."

"The hell you say." John wiped his eyes. "We need a damn lawyer by the sounds of it. I don't take kindly to being railroaded by you feds. And I'll be damned if I let you come near me for anything, you hear?"

"I was hoping we could do this the easy way, Mr. Floyd," Fisher replied.

"Yeah, well, you hoped wrong, son."

Kate turned to Duncan as they stood near the back of the room. "This is going to get ugly."

"What can we do?" Duncan asked. "We can't make them submit to a swab, not without bringing charges first."

"And without that, we can't prove if the DNA on the shard belongs to either one of them."

"What about prints? We could go back to the house and collect prints," Duncan said.

"There weren't any viable prints on the splinter. Only partials," Kate replied.

"There has to be some other evidence left behind." Duncan paused for a moment. "Hang on. The shard. We know the DNA doesn't match Andy Walcott's."

Kate folded her arms. "I'm with you."

"So, we're assuming it's the killer's. Which would mean, the killer injured himself or was injured in the process of doing the deed."

"Oh my God. You're right. We need to check them for cuts and scrapes. Something that would've drawn blood."

"Yeah, we do." Duncan walked to Mr. Floyd. "Can I see your arms?"

"What? Why?"

"I need to see if you have any recent abrasions."

Nick furrowed his brow, but let Duncan continue.

John Floyd held out his arms and rolled up his sleeves. "Nothing. Okay? You satisfied?"

"What's this here?" She spotted a fresh gash higher up on his right arm."

"I bet that's where you cut yourself earlier today, isn't that right, John?" Slocum said. "He slipped on some spilled coffee and dropped the glass pot. Must've shattered everywhere."

"That's right. You boys scared the piss out of me, banging on my door like you did. Slipped and fell. Must've caught some broken glass."

"I see." Duncan shot a suspicious look to Fisher. "Well, we should probably attend to that wound for you."

Kate pulled Nick aside. "I'd like to run back down to the hospital and talk to Lori Stewart."

"Why?"

"We're not going to get anything out of those two, and I

183

imagine at any moment, they'll ask for a lawyer. What if Lori can tell us who else buys from them? She seems pretty connected to that world. Maybe it'll lead to Billy Horton too."

"I'm not sure how he fits into this picture now," Nick said.

"Well, John Floyd hardly appears capable of the physical aspects of the murders. He's got the size, but not the mobility. Duncan had good instincts to check him for cuts. I don't know. They could be pushing the drugs, but I'd be hard pressed to say John Floyd bludgeoned those people to death."

"Okay. If you think it'll yield results, go for it. Take Duncan and Quinn with you, though. I don't want you on your own and they'll be useful. The rest of us can handle things here and I know Walsh wants to head out again in search of Horton."

KATE OPENED THE PASSENGER DOOR AFTER QUINN PARKED IN front of the hospital. "Thanks for indulging me. I'd like to check up on her and see how she's doing."

"Nothing else we can do right now," Duncan said. "We've got the latest victim awaiting autopsy, DNA on three others." She stepped out. "What have we got to lose?"

"Let's go have a talk, then." Quinn locked the car as they headed inside.

The woman behind the counter regarded the agents as they approached. "I hear you got Lynn and John Floyd in custody for all them murders around here." She seemed to notice their looks of concern. "It's a small town, so when the chief comes and takes someone away, word gets 'round. I'll tell you what, though, you people are making a big mistake. Ain't no way those good folks did nothing like that. They lost their only child to drugs, you know."

"We know. And they're only being held for questioning," Kate replied. "We'd like to see how Lori Stewart is doing. Can we stop in for a moment?"

The nurse appeared put out by the request. "Go on. She'll be staying here tonight and they're going to release her tomorrow. Best go ask her what it is you came here to ask her. My guess is she'll be back on the drugs by tomorrow night." She peered down at her desk and continued working. "That's what usually happens."

Kate led the way through the corridor and to the young woman's room. She pushed open the door. "Lori? It's Agent Reid. I'm here with some of my colleagues. Can we come in for a minute?" She opened the door farther and stepped inside. "Lori?"

They continued in and it was Kate who spotted her first. "Lori? Are you okay?"

With swollen eyes, she turned to the agents. "They told me for a fact Kevin's dead. That he got beat up real bad, like you said before."

"I'm really sorry." Kate reached for the girl's hand. "But you're going to be okay. You're a survivor."

"Who killed him? Who could've done such a horrible thing as that?"

"We're going to figure that out," Duncan assured her. "That's what we're here for."

"Well, I don't mean no disrespect, but y'all sure ain't very good at your jobs." Lori turned away again.

"Listen." Quinn approached her bed. "We're questioning the Floyds right now. We found some drugs in their house and I was hoping I could ask... Do you know who else might've been buying drugs from them? Just so, you know, we could warn them, or maybe protect them from harm if they still have the drugs lying around."

Lori snorted a caustic laugh. "First of all, ain't nobody leaving nothing lying around. Not in this town. If people was buying from them, them drugs are already gone."

"Do you know how long they've been dealing?" Kate asked.

Lori shook her head. "I can't say for sure. A while is all I know. I never bought from them directly. Seems odd, though."

"Why is that?" Quinn asked.

"Cause they lost their daughter and all last year to the same thing. Probably needed money or something just to pay to bury her properly. No one 'round here has that kind of money, 'cept those dealing. And the old folks is the only ones who can get the Oxy. Shit gets harder to come by every day. Most people are turning to heroin. It's cheaper, but the high ain't as good."

"Is that why Kevin risked buying the pills even after the warning at the meeting last night?"

"Probably." Lori's lips quivered again. "With all the shit going down here lately, guess he just wanted to feel good and forget about it. Like the rest of us."

"We should let you get some rest," Kate began. "If you need anything at all, here's my card. Call me anytime, okay? I'll answer."

Lori examined the card and nodded.

The team headed out again.

Duncan walked alongside Kate. "What's wrong? Your spidey-sense kicking in or something?"

"She says they've been dealing for a while. Why kill now? Assuming they're the ones pushing the deadly drugs." Kate eyed both Duncan and Quinn. "Why, after a year, decide to take revenge for your daughter's death?"

"You raise a good point. And then what, partner up with someone to do the physical killing?" Quinn replied.

Duncan stopped in the hall. "Wait. Are you two suggesting

the Floyds aren't the killers?" She eyed them while they remained silent. "Well, if they aren't, then who the hell is?"

THE CHIEF STOOD AT THE HEAD OF THE ROOM WHERE SEVERAL folding chairs and lunchroom tables from the high school had been set up. "It appears as though we might run out of room here soon. Never thought our kitchen would be used as a command center."

"This is just fine, Chief. Thank you." Nick stood next to the chief while his team and the deputies convened to discuss the questions raised by Agents Quinn, Duncan, and Reid over their visit with Lori Stewart. "Quinn, would you like to start?"

"Actually, I think Reid should explain our idea."

"Sure," Kate began. "As you know, Quinn, Duncan, and I visited Lori in the hospital earlier this evening. She mentioned that she believed the Floyds had been selling drugs for a while, and likely had started as a way to pay for their daughter's funeral and other expenses that came along afterward. Like John Floyd's inability to work and that sort of thing." She stopped and turned to Quinn. "So, I got to thinking, and I think they both came to the same conclusion as me. But I wondered why, if they're the ones selling the bad drugs, why now? Why start killing people now, a year after the death of their daughter? Did they snap? I don't know. Which is why we thought it best to come together and work through this. Because as I see it, I think the time's come to start looking into the background of our victims. We've been putting out fires with every victim we find and haven't been able to stop and figure out why them. Why were they chosen? I don't think they're random and I do believe they are connected—somehow."

"Connected to the Floyds?" the chief asked.

"Maybe. Or their daughter."

Slocum appeared confused and folded his arms in a defensive stance. "Wait, now the other day, y'all thought the killer was someone or more than one person who likely had lost a loved one to drugs. Or even a cartel moving in. And that was why they were killing. Now y'all think it was someone who knew the Floyds or their dead daughter? I don't mean to sound like an asshole, but it's like y'all ain't got a clue as to who is doing the killing."

"It's another avenue to explore," Walsh began. "It would make sense if there was a connection among the victims. It's doubtful now it's the work of a cartel, considering what we know about the Floyds. I know we've tossed around that theory before. But this— this is something we haven't looked into and it's worth our time in my humble opinion. However, I'll defer to the bosses." He glanced at Fisher and Scarborough.

The senior agents eyed one another and Fisher appeared to concede to the new man in charge. "I'll let you make that call, Scarborough. Our resources are currently being underutilized. And I don't see that changing unless we get a confession from the Floyds, or we get labs back. According to Ness, it doesn't appear that will happen for another day or two on what we found in their home."

Nick considered the proposal. "We've got nothing to lose by searching for a connection between the victims. Just like in any other investigation, that could be key to finding answers. I say we start now."

SSA CAMERON FISHER WAS METICULOUS, BORDERING ON pathological, in his approach to an investigation. But this case was different. No one had yet looked for the bond that tied all these victims together. There simply hadn't been time when all they'd done was find dead bodies and drug dealers. And in his typically New York cop way, he nudged Kate at the end of the meeting. "You got a good head on you, Reid. We've got our marching orders. I'll head out with Duncan and talk to Joanne Waverly's mom."

"Thank you, sir." He still outranked her and she was nothing if not respectful. "I appreciate that."

"Save the 'sirs' for Quinn and Scarborough. We'll be in touch." He caught up with Duncan and both disappeared beyond the doors of the station house.

Fisher unlocked the driver's side door and stepped into the SUV. Duncan hopped into the passenger seat. As they drove toward the center of town to a small apartment building, Fisher began, "Reid seems to be doing well in the field."

"She hasn't been away from it long enough to lose her touch, I guess. So now that we've had practical experience with her and the new boss, what are your thoughts?" Duncan asked.

"I'll be the first to admit, so far, so good. Reid's finding her stride. I like her personality. She's a team player."

"And Scarborough?"

"You know, I was hesitant. Especially when he championed Reid to be brought onto the team."

"Well, I don't know if 'championed' is the right word. It was she who wanted to apprentice under Quinn," Duncan replied.

"Anyway, I think he'll do right by us. Cole wouldn't have left us with someone who couldn't handle the way we do things." Fisher turned to her. "And you?"

"Scarborough's all right. And I like Reid. She's smart. Talented. I think she'll do well." She laughed a little. "Hell, maybe it's Quinn who should watch out."

"Maybe." He smiled. "I think this is it up ahead." He pulled into the parking lot that fronted the building. "Building 2, apartment 104. Suppose that's the bottom floor?"

"That'd be my guess."

They exited the vehicle and headed toward the unit, which was on the first floor not far from where they parked.

"I spoke with the mother. Seems like she'll cooperate," Duncan said.

"I hope so. Whatever we get out of this little expedition may not amount to much, but it could mean everything." He knocked on the door. "Mrs. Waverly, it's FBI Agents Fisher and Duncan."

"Ma'am, we spoke on the phone?" Duncan added.

Within a moment, the door opened and a woman appeared. She was young. Younger than they'd expected. She must've been only a teenager when her daughter was born. "Please, come in. You'll have to excuse the place. I work two jobs and don't have much time for cleaning."

"It's fine, Mrs. Waverly. Thank you for seeing us." Duncan walked inside. "We'd just like to ask you a few questions about your daughter, Joanne."

"Certainly. Have a seat. Can I get you anything to drink?"

"No thank you, ma'am," Fisher replied and sat next to Duncan. "As you know, we're here investigating the deaths of not only your daughter, but several other victims in the community."

"I was there at the meeting and I've kept in close contact with Chief Tate. I know what's going on. But unfortunately, it doesn't seem like you do."

Duncan peered down, looking almost embarrassed.

"No disrespect. It's just with all the money the FBI has, sure seems like y'all might've been able to find my daughter's killer by now. Hell, you won't even let me bury her."

"We absolutely understand how you feel, Mrs. Waverly, but if we could just ask you some questions," Fisher continued. "Can you tell us if your daughter knew Jenny Floyd?"

"Lynn and John's girl?"

"Yes, ma'am."

"Well, sure she did. They went to school together. I mean, I don't want to speak ill of the dead, but I reckon it was Jenny who got my Joanne hooked on the pills. Of course, she started using heroin shortly thereafter because the Oxy was getting tougher to find."

"So you were aware of your daughter's addiction?" Fisher asked.

"Course I was. What, you think I didn't try to do nothing to stop it?"

"That's not what I'm saying at all." Fisher rolled the toothpick over his tongue; a habit that worsened when tensions grew. "Ma'am, we're trying to find your daughter's killer. Can you give us a list of names of people she hung around and where you think she might've obtained the drugs? Even the heroin. Any information you can give us will be helpful."

"He misses working with you," Quinn said as he sat in the passenger seat while Kate drove to the family of Tommy Conroy. "You could see he was disappointed he wasn't coming with us."

"As a matter of fact, I didn't see that. He's got plenty on his plate keeping the chief at bay and coordinating with Ness. And he was confident that his team could get the job done."

Quinn conceded. "My mistake. You know, there's no need to get defensive every time someone mentions Scarborough's name." When she didn't reply, he added, "So, what do we know about this family?"

"Not much other than it appears they didn't see their son

often. He didn't live with them. So I'm not sure how much help they're going to be," Kate replied.

"Maybe we should find a friend or two who can help?"

"Might be worth a shot. We're here now anyway. Might as well see if they can give us anything." Kate opened her car door when Quinn placed his hand on her arm.

"Just so you know, after working with you on your last case and now this one, I wasn't wrong to bring you on board. So just remember that you did earn your spot, regardless of what anyone else thinks."

She stepped out. "I sure hope they all think I earned it." Kate led the way to the door of the modest home. It was the nicest one in the neighborhood, but unfortunately, that didn't say much. The area was run-down like much of the rest of Crown Pointe.

Kate knocked on the door. "Mr. and Mrs. Conroy? It's Agent Reid and Agent Quinn. We spoke to you earlier."

The door opened almost immediately. A man who appeared to be in his fifties, rotund, but handsome, spoke. "Thank you for coming. Please come on in. I've got some iced tea, if you'd like."

Kate remembered the last time she accepted tea from one of the people in this town. "Thank you, but I'm all right. We won't take up much of your time."

"Have it your way. As I said, come on in and take a seat. The missus will be down in a minute. I called her back from work. I took off early too. We're hoping you had some news about our son."

"I'm sorry, Mr. Conroy. We are here about your son, but I'm afraid we only have questions, no answers just yet," Quinn replied.

"I see." His face masked in disappointment. "Well then, I'll do my best to answer your questions, though we've already talked to the chief."

"I know, sir, and we appreciate your cooperation." Kate caught sight of Mrs. Conroy walking down the stairs and waited for her to join them. "Mrs. Conroy, thank you for taking the time."

"It's all right. Anything we can do to help."

Kate noticed her devastation over the loss of her son, the pain of the fresh wound still wide open. "I'm very sorry for your loss. I can't imagine what this must be like for you, which is why we're working non-stop to find the person responsible." She cleared her throat and eyed Quinn before beginning. "We were hoping you might be able to tell us a little about your son's friends. Who he hung out with, aside from Joanne Waverly. And whether he knew Jenny Floyd."

The parents turned to each other and the mother looked back to Kate. "Well, sure he did. Everyone knew Jenny Floyd. The girl was one of the most popular kids in school. Cheerleader. Smart kid too. She could've been..." The mother trailed off. "Anyway, yes, he knew her."

"Did they hang out together often?"

"Not that I'm aware of. He fancied her; all the boys did. But no, I don't think they palled around after school or nothing. And of course, Tommy quit school and that's when all the trouble started happening. But he was a good boy. Just got involved in that garbage like most of the people in this God forsaken town." She reached for her husband's hand.

"Do you know where he usually got his supply from? And maybe when you think his addiction started?" Quinn added.

"Well, I could think of a few names of who might've sold him the drugs. Unfortunately, a lot of people around here do, but I got his cell phone still. I can look inside there."

"You have his phone?" Kate looked at Quinn with some surprise. "I didn't think he had one. It wasn't on him when..."

"No, it wasn't. His daddy and me took over the payments for him a couple months ago, and well, we knew he was getting desperate for money and so not too long before he passed, we sorta took it from him."

"How long before did you take it?" Quinn asked.

"A couple days. A week, maybe. We knew he was gonna sell it and so just thought it best to hang on to it till he got past the worst of it." She teared up. "But he never did, as it happens."

"Mrs. Conroy," Kate pressed on. "Could we take the phone with us and go through it? It could be a huge help to see who he'd been talking to and when. That is, if you know how to get into it." Kate tried not to lose hope, knowing how difficult it was to get into a smartphone. In fact, it was near impossible.

"As it turns out, we do know his passcode. The boy was loving, but he wasn't the sharpest tool in the shed. His code was his birthday. I'll go get it for you."

Kate and Quinn looked at one another with resolve, knowing what this could mean.

Quinn smiled. "Well done, Agent Reid."

18

The Crown Pointe police station teemed with federal agents, local cops, and now a lawyer. Never had so many law enforcement officials gathered in the small community where the worst things that happened were drug overdoses. Chief Tate appeared lost, as though he no longer had a place in his own investigation.

Agent Ness had arrived and now the Floyds' attorney. He was a local accident and injury lawyer who moonlighted as a court-appointed attorney. Michael Dumont was a man who appeared long in the tooth and in well over his head.

He wiped his nose and tucked his handkerchief back into his shirt pocket. "As I see it, you've got nothing more than circumstantial evidence, here, Chief. The Floyds have a prescription for that bottle your deputy found."

"Then why was it found in the attic?" Nick asked. "If it was legal, why feel the need to hide it?"

"Because, Agent Scarborough, if you knew a damn thing about this town, you'd know that some addicts will do anything to get their hands on the drugs. Breaking into people's houses ain't off-limits to the likes of those people," John Floyd replied.

"Look, Mr. Floyd." Levi Walsh carried himself in a manner that could be intimidating. His solid features and piercing eyes could set anyone to shrink away. It seemed he was doing his best to intimidate John Floyd right now. "You can put all these accusations to rest by submitting to a DNA swab. What have you got to lose? If you didn't hurt anyone, then you didn't hurt anyone. But if those drugs come back as a match for the ones found in the victims' systems, then I'd say you'll have some problems."

Lynn looked at her husband. "He's right. We got nothing to hide. We never hurt nobody. Mr. Dumont? What is your opinion on this?"

Nick eyed the lawyer as if to suggest he do the right thing for his clients.

"If you got nothing to hide, then so be it. Agent Scarborough, you may commence with your DNA swabs as the Floyds have acquiesced."

In that moment, Kate and Noah Quinn returned to the station. She quickly approached the others. "Scarborough, Walsh, we need to talk—privately."

The agents stood, appearing concerned, and followed the two back to the briefing room.

"What happened?" Scarborough folded his arms and stood at attention. "Where's Fisher and Duncan?"

"On their way back," Quinn began. "From what we gathered, they were able to get some useful information, but I think Reid has exactly what we need to move this case in the right direction."

"And that is?" Walsh asked.

Kate held the cell phone into view. "This belonged to the young man in the mineshaft, Tommy Conroy. His parents took it from him. They've been paying his bills and took it before he could sell it."

"Great. How do we plan on breaking into it?" Walsh continued. But stopped as Duncan and Fisher entered the room.

"Chief says you're all convening in here. What's going on?" Fisher asked.

Kate peered at her colleagues' arrival and held up the cell phone in full view. She soon continued, "We don't need to break into it. The parents had the security code." Kate entered the code and unlocked the phone. A picture of the young man with Joanne Waverly appeared as the phone's background photo.

"Text history," Duncan began. "That's where we should start." She pulled up a chair next to Kate and sat down.

"We'll need to make a list of the names and numbers or just numbers and start looking into his contacts. What about social media?" Nick said. "Can you open a Facebook or Twitter account?"

"Facebook has fallen out of fashion with most Millennials," Duncan continued. "Instagram, Snapchat. That's likely where we'll find something of value."

"You're the expert," Fisher said. "Whatever we need to do to find out who this kid was talking to."

"Walsh, we should head back out there," Nick said. "The lawyer has just convinced the Floyds to give us a swab. Anyone have a kit ready?"

"I've got one." Fisher opened his carrier bag. "Like every good Boy Scout. Always prepared." He followed Nick and Walsh back into the bullpen.

Kate continued to view the contents of the text messages and retrieved her own cell phone. "Let me get some shots of these numbers. We can start pulling them up."

"If we can find a history of contact with the Floyds, we'd have enough to hold them," Quinn said. "It appears Jenny Floyd was a popular girl. Had a lot of friends and a lot going for her. She seemed to have been a trendsetter."

"Yeah, everyone followed her lead down the rabbit hole," Duncan replied.

"What do we know about her personal life?" Kate began. "Was she dating someone? Where did she work? You know, it'd probably be a good idea to get the Floyds to give us more on their daughter. I'm thinking, if this girl was so popular in high school, that probably carried her a long way with the locals—from a job standpoint and friends. We know right now that our victims all knew her on some level. But who was her influencer?"

"Who was pulling her strings," Quinn added.

Kate nodded. "Yep."

SLOCUM PARKED HIS FORD TRUCK AND LOCKED IT BEFORE heading inside the hospital. He noticed a nurse behind the check-in desk, but it appeared the rest of the lobby was empty. She held a warm smiled as she spotted him enter. "Deputy Slocum, how are you? What can we do for you?"

"Chief left something here and I was on my way home and told him I'd stop in to see if I can find it."

"Oh. What did he misplace?"

"Just a note pad or something when they brought that girl in earlier today."

'Oh, right. Well, you go on and take a look around. Won't bother me."

"Appreciate that." He tipped his hat and walked along the corridor, but not before turning back to notice the nurse had resumed her duties. He pushed open the door to Lori's room. "Ms. Stewart? It's Deputy Slocum. Mind if I come in?" He stepped just inside the door while awaiting her reply.

"Sure," a quiet voice sounded. "Come in."

He walked to her bed, which was cast in the soft glow of an overhead light while the rest of the room was bathed in darkness. She appeared pale, strands of blonde hair resting on her cheeks. The gaunt expression of an addict feeling the effects of withdrawal.

"You need some water or something? Ice chips?" Slocum reached over to the side of her bed where a pitcher sat. "Isn't that what they give people in the hospital?"

A faint smile appeared briefly on her lips. "Just some water, thank you."

He poured a small amount in the plastic cup and inserted the straw before handing it to her. "They say you're going home tomorrow."

"That's what they say."

"Well, I think that's good news, don't you?"

She turned her sights toward him. "That depends on who and what you got to go home to. I ain't got much of neither. Especially now with..." She trailed off.

"I am sorry to hear about Kevin. I didn't know him personally, but I hear he was good people, 'cept for, you know..."

"Yeah, I know. Thanks anyway, Deputy."

He tucked his thumbs into the belt loops of his jeans, having returned to his civilian clothes before leaving the station. He wasn't the type to be well put-together, but Slocum didn't care much about what others thought and therefore didn't make much of an effort in his appearance. Not anymore. The former army private who'd completed half his tour in Afghanistan before returning home from injury only cared about one thing. This town. And the people in it. "You need anything? A ride home tomorrow or something?"

"No, thank you. My momma's coming to get me. Though I don't expect she'll want me at her place for too long. I wore out my welcome there long ago."

"I hear them feds asked you a lot of questions."

"I reckon they did. Not that I had much in the way of answers. Just told them where Kevin usually got his drugs from is mostly all they wanted to know. Guess they figure they can find out who's poisoning them or some shit, I don't know." She began to tear up again. "I just want them to find the monster that killed Kevin."

"They said he took the same drugs as you and, well, I guess he was already in pretty bad shape before someone got to him."

"That don't make it right. They could've saved him, like they saved me." She wiped away a stray tear. "Don't make no sense. None of this makes no damn sense at all."

"I know it don't." He looked toward the door and returned his attention to Lori. "Look, I know there ain't a chance in hell you're gonna get any kind of decent sleep. Your symptoms are gonna get a hell of a lot worse." He rummaged in his pocket and held out his hand. "You should take this to get you through till morning."

She eyed him and then the pill he held. Lori swallowed hard and her eyes blinked. "What? Where'd you...?"

"Don't matter. Let's just say I know what you're going through. I'm just trying to help." He placed the pill in her hand.

She moved it between her thumb and forefinger, eyeing Slocum and the drug, appearing to struggle to make sense of what he'd just done. But it didn't seem all that important in the face of her addiction. She knew the craving would worsen and the idea that it would all go away was tempting like no other.

"Here." He handed her the water. "It'll take the edge off. Best hurry, though, before one of the nurses comes in."

Lori plunked the pill in her mouth and washed it down with a large gulp of water.

Slocum grabbed the remote control. "Mind if I see what's on the TV?" He sat down in the chair next to her.

She studied him as he made himself comfortable. "Thank you, but you don't need to keep me company. I'll be okay. Just need some rest is all."

"Oh, I don't mind. Really. I got nothing to go home to anyway, 'cept my dog."

"Are we done here now?" Dumont asked. "They agreed to your outrageous requirement. They should be allowed to go back to their own home."

"I think it would be a mistake, Chief," Nick began. "They have no ties here. I believe they could be a flight risk."

"You know what." Chief's eyes darkened with anger. "These folks have cooperated with everything you've asked of them. Now I see no reason as to why they can't go on back home until we get results back."

"Chief, I would agree with Scarborough," Agent Ness stood. "The Floyds are our only lead in this investigation. No one can seem to find this Horton guy. And until we can prove they're not involved, I think letting them go home would be a misstep."

The chief paced the room, his long legs making short order of the task. "I don't like this. Not one bit. You people come down here and..."

"Chief, you asked for our help and that's exactly what we've offered," Nick replied. "How about this? How about we keep your man posted at their house to keep an eye on them. I realize none of you think any of this was necessary, but until we can clear Mr. and

Mrs. Floyd, I'm afraid I can't agree to letting them go on their own. I can, however, agree to have Lazaro or Slocum keep watch for the night. At the very least, we should have analysis back on the prescription pills; swab might even come back if Ness can work his magic."

Chief looked at Lazaro. "I can call Slocum back. Have him keep watch. You got Peggy and all to consider."

"I don't mind doing it, Chief. She'll understand," Lazaro replied. "No point in dragging him back here. I can handle it."

"Well, I know you can, son, it's just..."

"Chief, I can do it," Lazaro interrupted.

He pressed his lips together until they turned white. "I know you been looking to get out of Slocum's shadow, so if you want to do this, I can't say as I'll stop you."

"Much appreciated. I'll be just fine and I surely don't expect no trouble from the Floyds in any case." He looked at them. "Right?"

"No, sir. You won't get no trouble from us old folk," John replied.

"Then it's settled." Nick looked at Agent Ness. "This good with you?"

He nodded. "I'd better head out and start schmoozing with the white coats. See if I can't light a fire under their asses for me—again. Y'all have a good night and try to keep a lid on things until I get back tomorrow. Hopefully with some answers."

"You two doing all right back there?" Lazaro glanced into the rear-view mirror at the Floyds, who were still handcuffed in the back of his patrol car. "I'm sorry about the cuffs. I'll take them off when we get to your house."

"You know we ain't done nothing wrong, don't you, son?" John asked.

"This whole thing is all kinds of messed up, Mr. Floyd, and right now I just want to keep everyone safe. Nothing like this has ever happened in this town and I'm scratching my head trying to figure out why it has now."

"We all are," Lynn replied. "Listen, we ain't had nothing to eat for hours. You think you could take us to the KFC drive-through for some supper? I got the diabetes, you know. My blood sugar's dropping like a plane from the sky."

"I reckon I can, seeings how you been so cooperative and such. I'll have to make a detour, but I can do that. Wouldn't mind a bite to eat myself. Been one hell of a long day." Lazaro turned his car around and headed north, back into town where the KFC was located, along with the only other fast food restaurant in Crown Pointe, a McDonalds.

As he continued to drive and reached the edge of downtown, Lazaro passed the hospital. He did a double-take. "What the...?"

"What's wrong, son?" John Floyd asked.

"Uh, nothing. Nothing, I guess. I see the KFC up ahead. Y'all know what you want?" He pulled into the drive-through that was empty as it approached 8pm. On a Friday night, the place would be hopping with teenagers and such, mostly looking for some fun, but some looking for trouble. But tonight, it was dead.

Lazaro relayed the order and on receipt of the food, pulled away again. "Hope y'all don't mind, but I'd prefer if we wait till we get back to your place to dig in. Chief would put my head in a noose if he knew we was eating in the cruiser." He continued the drive back and again passed by the hospital. This time, he slowed down.

"Everything all right?" Lynn asked.

Lazaro didn't reply, only peered into the parking lot of the small hospital where he knew the young woman, Lori, had been taken to. And there it was still. "What the hell you doing there?" he whispered.

"What's that?"

Lazaro turned back to John. "Huh? Oh, nothing. Best get back before the food gets cold."

～

Eric Slocum turned when he heard the sound of Lori gagging. He switched off the television and quickly stood. "How you doing, sweetheart?"

Her eyes widened as she peered at him. "What did you give me?"

"What's that? It's hard to understand what you're saying."

"Why?"

He shook his head. "Sorry, but I can't hear you properly. You'll have to speak up."

She clutched at her chest as sweat poured down her face, dripping on the hospital gown that clung to her perspiring body. "You did this. Kevin?"

Slocum walked toward the door and opened it just enough to peek into the hall. No one was around. He closed it and returned to her side. "Just so you know, I'm real sorry about this. I didn't want it to come to this, but you said some things you shouldn't have and it could bring down a hellfire on me. Now, I probably fixed things on my end, but I just can't rely on anyone else not to blow it for me. Again, I'm real sorry. You seem like a nice girl."

He pulled a pillow out from beneath her head and bunched it in his hands. "God, forgive me." Slocum placed the pillow on her face and pushed down as Lori squirmed beneath.

Her arms flailed and slapped his hands a few times, leaving marks.

"Don't make this harder than it has to be. I don't want to break nothing." He pushed down again.

Her legs were the first to slow. No longer were they kicking under the covers. Then her hands lowered, no longer tugging at his arms. Soon, she stopped moving altogether.

"Like I said, I'm real sorry, Lori. Your boyfriend shouldn't have told you nothing. Never mind. You'd have been dead soon enough anyways. You're too weak to fight off the addiction. Anyone could see that."

Slocum returned the pillow underneath her head and started toward the door. Upon opening it once again, he noticed there was still no one in the hall. He stepped out and headed toward the back of the building and to the stairs that led to the first floor and into the parking lot.

Reaching the stairs, he walked down the single flight and pushed open the door leading to the lot outside. And under cover of darkness, Deputy Eric Slocum slipped into his truck and drove away.

19

Inside the station, the BAU team continued to parse every piece of evidence they could find on the victim's cell phone. The request for additional phone records had been made and now they waited to see if the other victims whose cell phones had not been recovered received calls from this victim or placed calls to the same numbers.

"Here's that number again." Kate pointed to the phone's screen as she spoke to Duncan.

"We need to get those records and hope to find a match," Duncan replied. "This number has got to be the dealer."

"And if we find it on the other records, we'll be that much closer," Kate replied.

"Finding out who that number belongs to is the first priority," Nick said.

"We're waiting on that information too." Kate looked to Walsh. "When do you think your guy can have that info for us?"

"He knows it's important. He'll get it as quickly as he can." Walsh checked the time. "I wouldn't mind stopping by the Floyds to see if Lazaro is okay. I don't know. The kid seems a little soft to me."

"There's not much else we can do tonight. Not until we get the records," Fisher added. "While you're there, see if you can find a phone, a burner, or anything, belonging to the Floyds. That'll speed this little exercise along."

"Nothing turned up when Duncan and I were there earlier, but that doesn't mean they don't have one," Kate said.

Nick stood from the table. "Walsh, you and I can stop by on the way back to the motel. I think the rest of you should go and get some sleep. We'll want an early start in the morning."

Nick drove the SUV while Levi Walsh sat in the passenger seat. It approached midnight and the roads were deadly silent. "Not much seems to happen around here past ten pm."

"I think the people are heeding the warning and staying holed up in their homes. They're all afraid," Walsh replied.

"They should be."

"You don't think the Floyds are the killers, do you?" Walsh asked.

"It certainly is possible, but my gut tells me no. Reid and Quinn have tossed around a few theories. They don't always pan out."

"Do you think she goes along with Quinn's ideas because he's her boss and she's still an apprentice?"

"Maybe. Reid's strong-willed and pig-headed, but in this instance, I do think she's deferring to him until she has proof otherwise. Don't get me wrong, he could still come out on the right side of this. We don't know what we don't know," Nick said.

"Well, hell, if we had proof otherwise, we wouldn't be here right now. We'd be back at Quantico and case closed."

Nick smiled. "You're right about that. However, we can agree the Floyds are involved to some extent I just don't know how much. The drug dealing? Sure. People get desperate. And these people probably felt they had nothing to lose. I think the phone records will reveal a contact. Someone who ties all the victims together. Someone who is also tied to Jenny Floyd." Nick turned down the drive. "Let's see how our deputy is doing." He rolled to a stop and cut the engine. Inside, the curtain pulled back and Lazaro's face appeared in the window.

Lazaro stepped outside with his hand on his holster. He peered into the darkness until Nick and Walsh came into view. "What's going on? Everything okay? Please don't tell me someone else has been killed."

"No. Nothing's changed," Nick began. "We sent the team back to the motel to get some shut eye and we're heading back there too, but wanted to see how you were doing."

"All quiet here. The Floyds have gone up to bed. I'm just sitting on the chair, ready in case something happens. Come on in, if you want."

They followed him back inside the house, which was dark except for the living room where he waited.

Lazaro scratched his head. "Oh, you know there was something. Well, not really something, but..."

"What is it?" Walsh asked.

"I noticed Eric over there at the hospital on my way back here a little while ago."

"Why were you near the hospital? Isn't that opposite of here?" Nick added.

"Yes, but Mr. and Mrs. Floyd was hungry and asked me to stop at the KFC and, you know, I didn't want them to starve, so I drove there. Anyway, I spotted his truck there. Was wondering if he'd had a word with the young woman, Lori."

"Don't know. I don't think anyone's heard from him. Did he know her personally?" Walsh asked.

"Maybe. It's a small town. Don't think he ever said as much, but it's possible."

"I don't think it's cause for concern. Like you said, he probably knows her and was just checking to see how she was doing," Nick said. "We can ask him in the morning." He surveyed the house. "Listen, if you happen to see anything relating to the Floyds' daughter, Jenny, maybe you could document it? And a cell phone, too."

"You want me to snoop around while they're asleep?"

"I'm inclined to believe the Floyds are innocent of the murders, but my inclination isn't nearly enough," Nick said. "Just keep an eye out for anything that might help in the investigation."

"Sure thing, Agent Scarborough."

"We'll leave you to it, then." Nick headed toward the door. "I keep my phone by my side at all times. You see something, call me."

THE BEACON OF LIGHT, THE NEON GREEN "VACANCY" SIGN, lit up the parking lot as the agents returned to the motel. The four of them stepped out of the SUV with Kate and Quinn making their way to the sidewalk fronting Kate's room. Fisher and Duncan were about to head in opposite directions.

"We'll be back at it in the morning," Fisher began. "Good work today, everyone. Get some rest." He continued to his room.

"Night, guys." Duncan headed to her room.

Kate was left standing alone with Quinn as they both approached her room.

"You know, I think I should tell you something," Quinn began.

"Yeah? What's that?" She inserted the key into the lock.

"I requested your case files. Hendrickson and Shalot."

Kate turned stone-faced. "I thought I said I wasn't ready to get into that with you. Why would you go behind my back?"

"I'm sorry, Kate. I just thought, well, I guess it doesn't matter now, but I wanted to learn more about you."

"About me? And you think digging into my past without my consent was the way to do that? You know, I've been nothing but upfront with you."

"I know you have. And that's why I'm telling you this now. What you went through—on both occasions—I just find it fascinating that you're standing here in front of me now."

"Fascinating?" She smirked. "It's called surviving. And what else would you expect from someone whose life was in danger? Shrink up and wait to die?" She pushed open the door. "I guess you don't know me as well as you think you do." Kate started inside, but Quinn pressed his hand on her door to hold it open.

"What I did was shitty and I'll be the first to admit that. Scarborough saw the files on my desk and warned me that if you found out, you'd be pissed."

She turned to him. "I'm not pissed."

"But you're disappointed, aren't you?"

"Quinn, I'm not your mother. Disappointment is reserved for parents who use it against their children to induce guilt. But I will tell you that you won't find anything more about me in those files than you would if you just talked to me. I'm so much more than what's in those archives."

"I know you are. I can see that. I have, up until now, underestimated you. And I guess that's really what I'm sorry for. Please forgive me. I'd rather, when you're ready, hear what happened from you directly. Not from some cop's interpretation of what happened. And certainly not from Shalot's testimony."

Kate turned her gaze as headlights caught her attention. "Looks like the boss is back." She eyed Quinn's hand, which still rested on the door of her room.

Nick emerged from the vehicle along with Walsh. He approached the two. "What's going on?"

"Nothing. Just saying goodnight." Quinn pulled his hand off the door. "Everything okay at the Floyds' place?"

Walsh joined them. "Right as rain. We asked Lazaro to have a look around. See if anything of interest catches his eye regarding Jenny Floyd. Otherwise, that's about it." He raised an index finger. "Although he did mention spotting Slocum's personal vehicle, a truck, at the hospital."

"Really?" Kate began. "That's interesting. Does he have a relationship with Lori? Figured he would've mentioned that."

"Your guess is as good as mine." Nick eyed Quinn. "Goodnight. See you in a few hours." He turned to Walsh and nodded.

"Right. See you all in the morning." Walsh continued to his room.

Kate walked inside, quickly followed by Nick. The door closed, leaving Quinn standing alone.

Walsh was several feet away but stopped and turned to him. With a keen eye, he began, "Be careful."

Quinn peered back at him, silently acknowledging his thinly veiled warning. He unlocked his door and walked inside.

ANNA HOLMFIRTH WAS THE NURSE WHO RAN THE SKELETON crew graveyard shift at the hospital. The job was usually quiet, except now there was a killer among them and Anna feared for her safety as much as anyone. Word had reached her too, that the Floyds were essentially under house arrest, but that didn't put her mind at ease; not one bit. Anna made the rounds at the start of her shift. It was a small hospital, only two floors, and there weren't many patients at the moment. She made her way along the first floor. Just four patients checked in and it was quick and painless. Waking them up to take their vitals was the worst of it. Anna started up the stairs and toward the second floor. She preferred taking the stairs to help keep her in shape. The chart she held in her hands indicated a young woman by the name of Lori Stewart had been brought in earlier in the day for a drug overdose. Not surprising. There were usually a handful of OD patients in the hospital at any given time. And she'd heard this girl was somehow related to the latest murder victim, which left her feeling even more anxious.

She gently pushed open the door of the dark room and walked inside, her penlight illuminating the way. Her brow creased upon reaching Lori's bedside. The monitors were dark, but no alarm had sounded to denote a problem. Anna flipped on the overhead light and looked at the woman. "Oh my God." She grabbed Lori's wrist and checked for a pulse. "Oh no. No, no." She placed two fingers on her neck. Still no pulse. With her penlight, in one last vain attempt to confirm what she already knew, she shined the light into Lori's eyes. No reaction. The woman was gone.

Anna pressed the emergency button, but it would do no good. Lori Stewart had been gone too long.

~

THE CHIEF'S CELL PHONE RANG NEXT TO HIS BED AS HE LAY

sleeping. He roused and reached for his reading glasses to identify the caller. "Chief Tate here."

"I'm sorry to wake you, Chief. It's Doc. Our OD patient from earlier? She's gone. Lori Stewart passed away between the hours of 10pm and midnight tonight."

He sat up in bed. "What? How?"

"Right now, it appears as though she died from asphyxiation. Possibly having choked on her own vomit. We'll need to do an autopsy to confirm, but that's my suspicion. I know she was part of your investigation and I thought it best to get in touch with you first."

"Good Lord. Why weren't resuscitation measures used?"

"I wish I could answer that for you, Chief. It appears the patient's monitors weren't in operation."

At this, the chief grew suspicious. "What do you mean, they weren't working? What the hell happened?"

"I—I don't know yet. We're looking into it. The battery might have died. I just can't say with any certainty yet."

"I tell you what, Doc, you'd better get certain real quick, cause if this starts to smell of homicide, we got an even bigger problem on our hands."

"I understand, Chief."

"I'm coming down. Best get the feds down there too." He ended the call.

"What's going on?" His wife turned to him. "Henry, is everything all right?"

"I wish to hell I knew." The chief quickly dressed. "I'm going down to the hospital. Just go on back to sleep. There's nothing you can do." He leaned over to kiss her. "I'll call you later. I want you to stay put and keep the doors locked."

He walked downstairs and into his office where he retrieved the sidearm he kept locked in a case at the top of a closet. His children were teenagers now and had been trained on using guns; nevertheless, he kept it under lock and key at all times.

With a coffee in his hand, Chief stepped out into the chilly midnight air. The sun was still hours from rising and it seemed he'd only just found sleep, but he knew something bad had happened to Lori Stewart. On the one hand, he felt this vindicated the Floyds, but on the other, it meant someone was still out there killing the people he was supposed to protect. He walked to his Tahoe, stepped inside, and made the call. "Agent Scarborough, it's Chief Tate. Can you meet me at the hospital?"

"What's going on?" Nick was roused from his sleep.

"Our OD victim is dead. And the doc can't tell me what happened. We best get down there and find out."

"Okay. Yeah. I'll be right down." Nick ended the call and turned to Kate, who'd been awakened by the conversation. "That was the chief. Lori Stewart is dead and the doctor doesn't know what happened."

"How could he not know?" Kate rolled out of bed and pulled on her shirt. "Should we wake the others?"

"Let's get Walsh for now. We might need the others to head up a search. I have a bad feeling about this. Walsh was with me when we stopped by the Floyds' house earlier tonight to check in on Lazaro."

"A search for who? And what's it got to do with Walsh?" She pulled on her pants.

"Lazaro said he saw Slocum's personal vehicle at the hospital. At the time, it didn't seem important, but in light of this...Kate, what if all this time, we've overlooked the obvious? What if all of us were wrong?"

THE AGENTS ENTERED THE HOSPITAL AND SPOTTED CHIEF Tate in the lobby. Nick headed straight for him. "Any new information from the doc?"

"I think we'd better head on back." The chief turned on his heel and headed into the corridor. "They've moved her already. Doc's waiting for us."

Inside, Nick, Kate, and Walsh entered the same room where the other victims had been held.

"Thank you for coming down so quickly." The doctor offered his hand.

"Doctor Powell." Nick returned the greeting. "What can you tell us? What happened to her?" He peered at the lifeless body of Lori Stewart.

"I've been talking to the chief, but he wanted to wait until y'all arrived before we got too far along. I had the opportunity to review the charts and speak to the nurses. Including the nurse on the previous shift. She was the last one to see Ms. Stewart alive." He turned to the young woman. Her lips were purple, her skin already greying. "As I've just relayed to the chief, I believe this is a case where the monitors were turned off—intentionally. We checked every other possible scenario. Now why that alone didn't raise an alarm, I can't say just yet. But what I can tell you is that on further examination, it appears asphyxiation was the cause of death."

"And the doc doesn't think it was vomit. You know, from the overdose," Chief added.

"That was my initial opinion. However, it appears her oxygen supply was cut off."

"She was suffocated?" Kate asked.

The doctor aimed his pinky finger at Lori's hands. "It appears there could be skin under her nails as well."

"Like she was struggling," Walsh added.

"Yes. Like she was fighting off an attacker."

"Lock this place down. Now," Nick said. "I want everyone on shift and those on the earlier shift in the lobby ASAP. Doctors, nurses, orderlies. Everyone. I want to know who was the last person to see her and," Nick paused for a moment, "Chief, we need to get Eric Slocum down here too."

"Why?"

Walsh stepped in. "Because Lazaro saw his truck here a few hours ago."

20

A dark cloud hung over the team's collective head as the idea took root that they'd missed a crucial piece of the puzzle. While no one had come out with a direct accusation, the fact that Eric Slocum had been at the hospital only hours earlier was far too coincidental. What might happen in the coming hours would confirm or rebuff their suspicions.

Walsh was already on the phone to Fisher as he stood in the lobby of the small hospital. "Scarborough, Reid, and I are gathering the staff for questioning."

"Do we know if the hospital has surveillance?" Fisher asked.

"We're looking into that now. How do you want to handle this? Technically, we have no proof Slocum's our guy unless he was captured on camera entering and leaving Lori Stewart's room at her time of death."

Fisher paused for a moment on the other end of the line. "I understand where Scarborough's coming from, but until you speak with the staff on the earlier shift, I don't want to jump the gun. How's the chief handling this?"

"Honestly, I think he's in a state of shock. But I also think he wants answers as much as we do. We won't get any more resistance from him. Not after this."

"Get me Slocum's home address. Duncan, Quinn, and I will run out there now. If he's there, we'll bring him in for questioning."

"And if he's not?" Walsh asked.

"Then it'll be all hands on deck to find him." Fisher ended the call, returning his phone to the bedside table. He gazed through the window where a streetlamp shone between the two drawn curtains.

"What's happened?"

He glanced over his shoulder. "Lori Stewart is dead. They think Eric Slocum might've had something to do with it." Fisher turned and placed his hand on Eva's cheek. "You should go back to your room and get dressed before I wake up Quinn."

Eva rolled on her side and sat up. "You know, if Scarborough and Reid don't have to hide their relationship, I don't know why we do."

"You know why." Fisher stood. "I'll meet you outside in twenty."

WALSH RETURNED HIS PHONE TO HIS POCKET AND HEADED toward Scarborough and Reid, who were with the chief at the nurse's station. "I just got off the phone with Fisher. He wants Slocum's address. They're going to drive out to his house and bring him down, assuming he's there."

Chief Tate placed his hands on his hips. "I'm sorry. I just can't get my head around this. My own deputy?"

"We just want to ask him why he was here," Nick replied. "No one's being charged with anything right now."

Walsh turned to the growing crowd of hospital staff. "What about these guys? Are we ready to talk to them?"

"We are." Nick turned to them. "I appreciate those of you who've returned from your earlier shift. I know it's late and I know you're all very concerned about what's been happening around here. We need an account from everyone present as to their whereabouts from 10pm to midnight."

Murmurs sounded among the people.

"First of all, is there closed-circuit television in use?" Nick asked.

A doctor stepped forward. "I'm the attending," Dr. Rhys began. "Unfortunately, the only surveillance the hospital has in use is on the exterior. Nothing inside the hospital."

"Okay. I'll need to see those tapes and the register for visitors tonight," Nick continued.

"I did see Deputy Slocum here earlier. He said Chief Tate misplaced something and he came out to find it. I'm sorry, but I didn't pay attention after that. I don't know when he left, or if he found what he was looking for," the nurse said. "I left shortly after that and Anna came on shift." She looked to her colleague.

Anna appeared shaken. "I don't know when he left. I—I didn't realize he was here. I should've looked at the register."

"That's on me," the nurse continued. "I didn't ask him to sign in. I didn't think there was reason to."

The chief raised his hands. "No one's done anything wrong here. We're just trying to gather the facts at the moment."

"The chief's right," Nick added. "I don't want to keep you all from doing your jobs. You have other patients who need your attention. And I'm sure the rest of you have families to tend to. However, we'd appreciate a brief statement from each of you before you get back to your duties. My agents are ready to listen." Nick looked to Anna Holmfirth. "I'd like to have a word with you, ma'am. Dr. Rhys, would you track down Dr. Powell? And I'd like to get those tapes ASAP."

Dr. Rhys nodded. "Of course."

SSA CAMERON FISHER WAS BEHIND THE WHEEL AS HE pulled onto the driveway of Eric Slocum's house. His headlights shone brightly on the small home nestled against the trees. The sun was still hours from rising.

"His truck isn't in the driveway. That's not a good sign," Quinn noted from the passenger seat. He stepped out onto the concrete driveway that was riddled with cracks and weeds, and opened the rear door for Duncan.

Fisher jumped out and joined the others. "It's the middle of the night. Bars are closed. If he's not here, then I think we'll have our answer as to his culpability." He walked to the small covered porch and knocked on the door. The house appeared dark inside. No lights shining through the curtains. No answer either. "Let's try this again." He knocked harder this time.

"Damn it," Quinn said. "He's not here."

"If that doesn't point the finger of guilt at him, I don't know what will," Duncan said. "The only woman who could talk is dead. And the last person who likely saw her alive is nowhere to be found. Looks like we missed the boat on this one. Even you, Quinn."

Quinn eyed her with contempt. "I'm not the only one on this team, but I've got big shoulders, so however you want to spin this, Duncan, you go right ahead."

"That's enough." Fisher stepped between them. "We're all tired and we all deserve a share of the blame. What we need to do now is to find him."

Quinn stepped back and took in a breath. "If the deputy did kill her and the others, what's to say the Floyds won't be next?"

Fisher nodded. "Get Lazaro on the line and make sure he's okay. We'll hit there next, but I want to split up first and have a look around here. I want to be sure Slocum isn't hiding out here somewhere." He started around to the side of the house.

Quinn grabbed his phone as he and Duncan made their way to the other side of the house. "Well, that's not good. No answer from Lazaro."

"Let's have a quick look around here and get going then," Duncan replied. "Hey, I'm sorry about what I said. None of this is your fault."

"Don't worry about it," Quinn replied. "Fisher's right. We're all tired."

He and Duncan searched the exterior and along the tree line. No sign of anyone.

"We're wasting our time. Slocum's obviously smarter than we've given him credit for. There's no chance he stuck around waiting for us to show up." Duncan spotted Fisher in the backyard and started toward him. "He's not here. Quinn didn't get an answer from Lazaro either. He and the Floyds could be in danger."

Fisher nodded. "Yeah. Okay. Let's go."

As they entered the SUV, Fisher backed out of the driveway and raced down the dark and quiet street. "If that Lazaro kid is dead too...damn it. We should've seen this coming."

"Nothing pointed to Deputy Slocum. We couldn't possibly have known," Duncan replied.

"This entire investigation, we've been trying to play catch-up," Quinn said. "Trying to get ahead of the killer and all we were really doing was falling behind."

Fisher peered into the rearview mirror. "Duncan, when we get to the station, let's cross-reference the numbers on the victim's cell phone with Slocum's phone. If we can make that connection, we'll be golden."

"I'll call Reid and give her the news." Quinn reached for his phone. "And let them know we're heading out to check on Lazaro and the Floyds. I think it's time we find out if our deputy has any ties to the Floyds." He returned his attention to his phone when Kate answered. "It's Quinn. How's things going over there?"

"Scarborough's talking with the nurses on shift at the time Slocum was here. No luck on your end, I assume?"

"He's not at his house. We're on our way to check up on the Floyds and Lazaro. There's a chance Slocum went to see them."

"Why would he do that if he just killed someone?" Kate asked.

"I don't know if he did, but at this point, we have to assume he has no place else to turn. And, given that our victims share a connection to Jenny Floyd, it's not outside the realm of possibilities that Eric Slocum does too. If he's our dealer, he might also be our killer. Listen, Reid, can you get with the chief and ask him to give us anything he can on his deputy?"

"Yeah. I can do that." Kate ended the call and approached Chief Tate. "No luck at Slocum's house. He wasn't there. Quinn and the others are on their way to check in on the Floyds and Deputy Lazaro."

"You look like you want to ask me something, Agent Reid. Shoot."

"Quinn believes Slocum might have known the Floyds' daughter, Jenny. He's asked that I request Slocum's files. Anything you have on him."

"I won't disagree with the theory, but I can tell you with some degree of certainty that I don't believe he knew Jenny at all. And all his files are going to show you is that he's been an excellent deputy here at Crown Pointe for several years."

Nick and Walsh appeared when Walsh began, "What's the good word?"

"Just got off the phone with Quinn. They're heading to the Floyds. No luck at Slocum's place. He asked that I get some background on him, though."

"It appears that your agents believe my deputy had some sort of history with Jenny Floyd. Something I honestly can't confirm or deny. He keeps to himself mostly about matters of that nature," the chief said.

"Probably should've had our guys search Slocum's house before they left. But I know they're concerned for the Floyds and Lazaro, and of course, they're hoping to find him there," Walsh said. "The staff here doesn't have anything for us and all we have on the tapes was that Slocum entered through the front doors at around 8pm."

"Right. Would've been nice if they'd had cameras around the back. Nothing showing when he left," Nick replied.

"Reid and I can run out to Slocum's house and see what we can find. It's time to divide and conquer before the deputy slips through our fingers." He started toward the exit but stopped and turned. "Well?"

Nick looked at Kate. "Go. Let me know what you find."

Kate hurried to catch up with Walsh. "You don't waste time, do you, Levi?"

"No, ma'am, I do not."

"You don't mind if I call you Levi, do you?"

He stopped and turned to her. "You can call me anything you like, Reid. You've earned the right."

"And feel free to call me Kate. I don't mind."

"Okay, Reid."

He pushed outside and hurried to the car, opening the driver's side door. "Better get there quickly. We have no idea what the others will find when they reach the Floyds' place." He stepped inside and started the engine, waiting for Kate to buckle in. "Let's roll."

～

FISHER ROLLED TO A STOP SEVERAL FEET BEHIND LAZARO's patrol car. He killed the lights and cut the engine. "On the plus side, I don't see Slocum's truck."

"Unless he's already been here and gone." Duncan stepped out of the SUV and brandished her weapon.

Fisher opened his door and stepped out. "Always the optimist."

Quinn reached the two of them while Fisher signaled the direction each would take. Duncan veered right and Quinn veered left, leaving Fisher to approach the situation head-on.

He continued toward the door and tried the handle. Locked. The curtains were drawn in the front window and in the darkness, Fisher struggled to see his own hand in front of him. Surveying the area, he headed toward Duncan, who checked the right side of the home. "Front door's locked. Let's look for another way in."

Both agents had a wealth of field experience. Duncan had been a field agent in Denver and worked in Violent Crimes. She also had extensive local law enforcement experience in Chicago, her home town. While Fisher, a New York field office veteran, had nearly fifteen years under his belt. Five with the BAU and ten with the NYFO before that. He even had a stint with the NYPD fresh out of college.

Both were prepared to encounter the worst as they reached the back of the home. A Dutch-style door led from the kitchen to the rear yard and would be an easy way in. What concerned them both was the fact that they saw nothing happening inside. No movement. Meaning Lazaro could be hurt, or worse.

Within moments, Quinn appeared. "Nothing so far?" he whispered.

Fisher pointed to the door and tried the handle. Finally, something had broken their way. "Here's to small miracles." The door opened. "Lazaro better be okay in there because the chief will skin him alive for leaving this door unlocked."

Inside, the home was completely dark. They felt their way around, waiting for their eyes to adjust to the scant light. A digital clock on the coffee maker and another on the DVD player led them into the living room.

"Shit!" Quinn stumbled over something but managed to keep his tone to a whisper. "Lazaro? Is that you?"

"Hey, what the hell's going on?" Lazaro was slumped in the chair, rousing from the kick to his boot.

"Thank God, you're okay," Duncan replied.

"What's going on?" Lazaro's voice raised an octave.

"Shhh!" Fisher helped him from the chair and led him to the front door where they all made their way outside. "Listen, Slocum's gone. We thought he might've tried to come here."

"What do you mean, he's gone? Did you check his house?" Lazaro seemed only partially awake.

"Of course we did. No answer. We came here because we thought he'd try to harm you or the Floyds," Duncan replied. "And then we tried to call you, but you didn't answer."

Lazaro retrieved his phone and spotted the missed call. "Damn it. I'm sorry. I must've fallen asleep. It was on silent too."

"We don't have time to dick around," Fisher said. "Do you know where Slocum might've gone?"

"I don't understand. Why are you looking for him?"

Quinn stepped in. "We think he might've killed the woman

who was admitted to the hospital earlier, Lori Stewart, the one who OD'd."

"No. No, sir. You got it wrong. There has to be another explanation. Eric would never hurt no one," Lazaro said.

"You said yourself you saw his truck there earlier tonight," Fisher added.

"Yeah? So?"

"So we got a call from the chief saying the girl was dead and he suspected foul play. We need to find Slocum to talk to him. Maybe he didn't do anything to her, but his sudden disappearance doesn't speak well to his innocence," Quinn replied.

Lazaro pushed his hand through his hair. The younger of the two deputies looked up to Slocum. Admired him, even. "Hell, I don't know. He ain't got no girlfriend that I know of. No family left here in town, just his dog, Gunner."

"Any family in Kentucky at all?" Fisher asked.

"Parents live in Lexington, I believe. Chief would know for sure." Lazaro appeared dumbfounded. "I'll be damned. You sure he's a suspect?"

"It must be hard to hear this, but it seems more likely than we could've ever suspected," Duncan replied. "It's possible he's gone —fled town."

"Wait," Lazaro raised a hand. "I think there could be one place. I don't know, but maybe."

"Where?" Duncan pressed on.

"The mines."

"The place where we found the first three victims?" Fisher asked.

"No. That'd been shut down for years. No, I'm talking about the big mines. Where the real jobs was at till they got shut down in the nineties. There's a road still there that goes up to the top of the hill. I know he liked to go there sometimes. Said it helped him to think. Cleared his head and all."

"How far is this place?" Quinn asked.

"Twenty minutes from here, I reckon. Should we go?"

"I'm afraid you'll need to stay here with the Floyds. Can't risk leaving them alone. Right now, we have no idea if they're a target or not. But as soon as it gets light, bring them back to the station." Fisher looked to Duncan. "Maybe you should stay here. If Slocum comes..."

"Got it. No problem."

THE SUN WAS STILL BELOW THE HORIZON, BUT A GREY LIGHT emerged in the pre-dawn hour as Walsh and Kate arrived at Slocum's house.

"Thank God for exigent circumstances. No way we could've waited for a warrant on this one. How do we plan on entering?" Kate asked.

Walsh smashed a decorative window pane in the center of the door and reached through to turn the handle. "Like this."

Kate grinned. "You remind me of someone I used to work with a long time ago."

"Oh yeah? Who's that?"

"Just a cop. A good cop."

"I like him already." Walsh entered the home and found a light switch. "And God said, 'let there be light.'" He turned to Kate. "And there was light. Come on. Let's see what we can find on our Deputy Slocum. See if we're even remotely on the right track here, like Quinn thinks."

"You don't agree?" she asked.

"I didn't say that. I know the man's good at his job, but sometimes it feels like we're going on a wild goose chase. No offense. Profiling is no easy gig. Hell, none of our jobs are easy, but this is as much a guessing game as anything. An educated guessing game, but one nonetheless."

"You're right. I've been wrong before and I have no doubt I'll be wrong again. I guess we just have to pray that being wrong doesn't cost lives."

"Amen to that, Reid. I suppose if we're going to find anything, it'll probably be in the bedroom. Unless you see some sort of office or a filing cabinet or something of that nature around here."

"I'll take a quick look around and join you in a minute." Kate walked toward the coffee table. A few magazines were spread across it. "He likes motorcycles." A side table next to the sofa had mail stacked on it. She sifted through it, but it was only utility bills, an offer from a credit card company, and a postcard advertising a free dental exam for new patients.

What puzzled Kate most of all was that if Slocum was the killer, and finding the dead body of a person he likely visited was a pretty good indicator, why try to point the finger at the Floyds when he found the drugs in their home? What had they done to him? Or was it just that the opportunity presented itself and he had no choice but to take advantage and attempt to frame them? Perhaps in hopes of casting eyes away from him.

She walked into the kitchen. "At least he's clean." No dishes in the sink. Nothing left on the counter, except for a toaster and coffee maker. She opened the drawers in search of the junk drawer. Everyone had one of those, right? Or was it just her? "Ha, I knew there'd be one." She pulled it out and emptied its contents onto the counter. After sifting through it for a minute, she realized it was, in fact, just junk.

"Come on, Slocum. There's a reason you're gone. What is it? What did you do?" She turned and faced the refrigerator. "Holy shit." Kate stared at the pictures held on the fridge with magnets. "Hey, Levi? You might want to come in here. In the kitchen."

She heard his footsteps draw near and he soon appeared.

"What is it?"

She pointed to the fridge. "He knew her. He knew Jenny Floyd."

Walsh eyed the photo. "And it looks like they were more than friends."

21

The discovery of a relationship between Eric Slocum and Jenny Floyd meant the likelihood that Slocum was the killer had grown exponentially. However, the extent of the relationship was still in question. It still raised concerns as to why Slocum would want to frame the Floyds if that was the case.

Kate removed the photos from the refrigerator. "There has to be more evidence in here. Did you see a laptop or computer in the bedroom?"

"No," Walsh replied. "It stands to reason, though that if he is, in fact, the killer, he's gone and so is any evidence we might find on a computer. But the fact remains, this girl died over a year ago. Why kill now? There had to have been a catalyst of some sort."

"I think the only way we're going to get more intel on him is to request phone records," Kate said.

"We don't have time. That will take days. Hell, we're still waiting on the victims' records. Slocum's gone. And I, for one, am not comfortable with the idea that he's missing and might yet kill again."

"The Floyds must not have known about the relationship. It would've come up when they were being questioned yesterday," Kate continued. "Why keep it a secret? She was an adult. Out of high school. No reason to hide it."

"What do we know about Slocum's past?" Walsh paced the kitchen. "He's not married. Doesn't have any kids. Oh, and didn't he have a dog? Where's the dog? He's been a deputy in Crown Pointe for what, five years or so?"

"Seems like the Floyds would've been happy to have their daughter dating someone in law enforcement. Is it possible Jenny eventually rejected him? Broke up with him before she fell in with the wrong crowd?" Kate asked.

"Are you saying that could have been his motive and that maybe she didn't die of an overdose, at least, not one she induced herself? Look at Lori Stewart. I imagine once the labs come back, they'll show the synthetic drug in her system."

"She was admitted because of an OD. That would stand to reason drugs of some sort would still be in her system."

"Hear me out," Walsh continued. "Is it possible he gave her more of the drugs, waited until she began showing signs of another overdose, then smothered the life out of her?"

"At this point, I'd say anything's possible. But right now, this is all conjecture until we can get Slocum into custody and grill him. We have to find him first." Kate retrieved her cell. "I'll contact Quinn. See how things played out at the Floyds." She waited for him to pick up the line. "It's Reid. We're at Slocum's place. It appears he knew and possibly had a relationship with Jenny Floyd. What's going on there? Are the Floyds okay?"

"They're safe. We left Duncan with Lazaro to keep watch. So he did know Jenny." Quinn paused for a moment. "Lazaro said we might find Slocum holed up on an old mining ground. A big one that closed in the nineties. Claims he went there to clear his head on occasion. But I didn't expect to find out they'd had a relationship. We thought it could be someone seeking revenge. It's starting to look like Slocum's been our guy all along. What'd you find that pointed to a relationship?"

"Pictures on his refrigerator, cozy pictures," Kate replied. "They look to be a few years old. Hard to say. But he must've come back here after the hospital because there's no laptop. No way he doesn't own one. It was like he knew he had to leave fast. Are you on your way to this mine?"

"Fisher and I are. Scarborough is still with Chief Tate. I don't know what's happening on their end. What's your plan, Reid?"

"Sounds like you all have the mine covered. I think Walsh and I should catch up with Scarborough. There's more to this Slocum and Jenny Floyd story than we know. If he isn't at the mine, maybe we can garner more information once we speak to the chief."

"Okay. Keep me posted and I'll do the same," Quinn replied.

Kate ended the call. "The Floyds are safe. Quinn and Fisher are on their way to an old mining operation. Apparently, Lazaro says Slocum would go there sometimes to clear his head. They're going to check it out, but Duncan's staying with Lazaro just in case."

Walsh headed toward the front door. "They may be spinning their wheels. But I guess we follow any lead we can get at this point to find him."

THE SUN BROKE OVER THE HORIZON AND THE DAY WAS ONLY just beginning. So was the manhunt for a potential killer who was also a beloved law enforcement officer. The paradoxical nature of the investigation would have to be analyzed another time, as was often the case in Quinn's line of work. Reid's conduct so far confirmed he had made the right decision, something that still plagued him no matter how many times he'd assured her that she had earned her position. And it seemed the rest of the team was coming around. The rapport was obvious, even with Walsh, a man who wasn't easily won over.

But it remained to be seen if Scarborough would gel with the rest. He had taken the lead, which was his job, but which also left Fisher to wonder where his place was. Scarborough had seniority, but Fisher had taken a place as a leader in the brief absence of now Unit Chief Cole.

"I don't know about you, but I think that could be the place up ahead." Fisher drove along the narrow lane, rife with overgrown shrubbery.

The stripped hillside was an obvious indication they were in the right place. It was clear this had once been a large operation that had brought prosperity to the region. Now both were gone; the operation and prosperity.

"Looks like the place, although he'd be unwise to come here," Quinn replied. "Of course, it might not be a question of rational thought in this instance. If he is here, he could be battling grief, guilt, and a host of other emotions that would suggest a desire to be captured. Right now, we don't know what his motives are."

"I see a parking lot just ahead. They left a job-site trailer here. When did you say they shut this place down?" Fisher asked.

"According to Lazaro, it was in the nineties."

"That's a long time for a place this size to sit abandoned. You'd have thought someone would've come in and bought the land, repurposed it or something."

"You see any other vehicles?" Quinn asked.

"Not yet. It'd be nice to have some backup right about now. The two of us covering the area is going to take some time."

"I'm not sure we'll need to waste much of it here," Quinn

began. "Slocum wouldn't have walked. I say we drive on the roads we can access and if we don't see any signs of life, my suggestion would be to pull the plug and head back to the station. After what Reid and Walsh found, Chief Tate might offer up information that's a little more worthwhile."

"Nevertheless, we can't overlook it," Fisher added.

"Then let's have a look around. I'll check out the trailer." Quinn unbuckled his seatbelt. "If you want to take a drive up, I'll be okay here for a few minutes."

"Probably best to split up and cover more ground anyway," Fisher replied.

Quinn stepped out of the vehicle and headed toward the small trailer.

Fisher rolled down his window and leaned out. "Watch your back, Quinn."

"I got this one." He continued along the path that led to the trailer and checked the handle before Fisher pulled away. With a smile on his face, he turned to the SUV with a thumbs-up." Quinn drew his gun and walked inside.

Fisher pulled away and headed up the hill to look for Slocum's truck.

Inside the trailer, it appeared that it had been abandoned for some time, though there were signs of habitation. Perhaps it had been used by the homeless or was a hideout for teenagers. Quinn spotted used needles and blankets strewn about.

He wondered, though, had Slocum's family been affected by the mine's closure? Had his father been a miner? These were things that could attribute to his current state of mind. Things Quinn needed answers to in order to form a conclusive profile. Although, in light of the current situation, was that really necessary? It seemed clearer by the moment that Slocum was the man responsible for the deaths of those people. The question lingered, why?

What Quinn needed was evidence Slocum had recently been here. Or evidence of where he might now be. Both seemed elusive, but he would press on while his colleague explored the grounds.

KATE HELD THE PHOTOS OF ERIC SLOCUM AND JENNY FLOYD in her lap as Walsh drove back to the station. "The Floyds should be there by now. Lazaro and Duncan were ordered to bring them in at first light. I'd sure like to talk to them about Jenny and Eric Slocum."

"I have a feeling that revelation will come as somewhat of a surprise." Walsh cast his eyes to Kate before returning his attention to the road. "What I'd really like to get my hands on are the DNA results on the Floyds."

"We'd have a definitive answer on their culpability and it could shed light on Slocum's involvement."

"I do know one thing," Walsh continued. "Our odds of finding him are dwindling by the second. I hope the Floyds can tell us something useful. Otherwise, we're up shit creek."

"I've been up that creek so many times, the smell doesn't bother me anymore," Kate replied.

Walsh revealed a smile. "I like you, Kate."

She peered out onto the road ahead. "Glad to hear it, Levi."

Within minutes, Walsh pulled into the parking lot at the station and cut the engine. "I don't see Lazaro's patrol car here."

"It must be that other shoe we've been waiting on to drop." Kate stepped out and headed toward the door.

"You're back." Nick headed toward them. "Duncan's on her way with the Floyds and the kid."

"Good," Walsh replied. "We've got some pictures to show you. Kate?"

She retrieved the photos and placed them on a nearby desk. Nick peered at her with confusion at the fact that Walsh had called her by her first name, but this wasn't the time to get into the complexities of inter-office relationships. "After searching Eric Slocum's house, we found these pictures on the refrigerator."

"You found them," Walsh replied.

Kate glossed over his comment. "These clearly show a relationship between Jenny Floyd and the deputy."

"What we don't know, however, is the extent of that relationship," Walsh added. "We were hoping the chief or her parents could shed some light on that."

Chief Tate meandered toward them. "Well, I had no idea he knew her. Of course, this was obviously some time ago, but if they were serious, Slocum kept it well hidden."

"Any chance we can pull Jenny Floyd's case file?" Kate asked. "Maybe there's something there."

"As it relates to Slocum?" the chief pressed on. "I can tell you for a fact there isn't."

"What about cause of death?" Walsh said. "What if the same chemical compositions found in the other victims matches Jenny Floyd's? You said she died of an overdose."

The chief cocked his head. "Now you think Slocum was the one who gave her the pills?"

"We're just looking for answers here, Chief," Nick said. "I realize how upset you must feel, but we need anything we can get our hands on that will help us find Slocum and ask him these questions ourselves."

In that moment, Duncan entered with Lazaro trailing behind alongside Lynn and John Floyd.

"Any luck finding him?" Lazaro cast a hopeful eye at the team but the answer came in the form of their silence. "What about the mine? The one I told Agent Quinn about?"

"How'd you find me?" Sterling Jensen, who'd fled his temporary shelter at Devil's Den, now stood in an apartment's living room, staring down the barrel of a nine-millimeter Beretta. The man holding the gun appeared frantic and unsteady. Given that this particular person was a law man, luck was not on Jensen's side today.

"You saw me that night, didn't you? You saw what I did."

Jensen held up his hands. "Deputy, I didn't see nothing. I can assure you, that's exactly what I told that cop the other day."

"Liar!" He waved the gun.

"I swear I didn't say nothing to nobody. I couldn't care less about them addicts. Get rid of them, I say. More power to you, my friend."

"I'm not your friend. Now sit down!" Slocum stepped toward the man in the tank top until he obeyed. "It wasn't supposed to happen like this. I just wanted them to pay for what they did to her. They destroyed my Jenny. But that Walcott boy—I didn't mean." His eyes reddened. "Then that girl pulled through and she ruined everything. She wasn't supposed to survive."

"I'm telling you, sir, I want no part of this, you hear? I'll keep my mouth shut. I know how to do that, that much I can tell you. No one will ever know you was here."

"Don't think it matters now. I wanted every last one of them to pay and there's still one more. I can't stop now. What'd be the point? I'm going to prison. Might as well finish the job."

Jensen scratched his nose. "You looking for someone? Cause maybe I can help you find them. I know things about the people around here. I can help you. Let me help you."

Slocum closed his eyes. "Just stop. I can't listen to you no more."

"Who you looking for, son?" he pressed on.

"I told her they were bad news. Those folks she was hanging around. She didn't believe me. Said I was just being jealous. Well, I wasn't being jealous. I knew she was starting on the Oxy. I knew it, and I tried to help her before she got too far gone. But she didn't want no part of me after a while. Said I was putting too much pressure on her. I thought about telling her parents. But she made me promise not to tell no one we were together. I never could figure out why, though."

Jensen continued to listen. "Like I said, you want to finish the job, I can help you."

Slocum eyed the man once again. "Why didn't you tell them it was me at Devil's Den? I know you saw me cause I saw you too."

"I don't know. I didn't want no trouble, I reckon. Still don't."

Slocum raised his gun toward Jensen's head. "I came here to shut you up permanently. Hell, maybe there's no point now. Those feds aren't stupid. They're gonna figure out what I did at the hospital." He seemed to reconsider Jensen's proposal. "I'll tell you what. You tell me where I can find the man I'm looking for, and I'll let you live. But you best get the hell out of Crown Pointe afterwards."

"I will. I swear, I will. I'll never say nothing to nobody."

"I need to find Billy Horton. He's the one responsible for all this. He took her away from me and let her die. I could've saved her."

"I'll help you find him. But we'll need to go now. If, like you say, you—did something at the hospital, they'll all be looking for you," Jensen replied.

"You know where he is—Horton?"

"I believe I do. He's the one that runs the show, don't he?"

Slocum nodded.

Jensen stood with his arms still raised. "I just need to make a call. Can I do that?"

Slocum waved his gun again. "Go on, then. But don't you say one damn word about me being here."

"I ain't that dumb, Deputy." He walked toward the kitchen where he reached for a cell phone. "I'm just gonna call a friend. He'll know where we can find Horton."

"You do that." Slocum stood only steps away from him while he made the call.

When Jensen hung up, he peered at Slocum. "Says Billy is at the grocer's. Today's soda pop day."

"I can't go down there. Where's he going after that?"

"Back down to Devil's Den, like everyone else."

"Then we'll go there and wait. They won't come back there looking for me."

QUINN WAS IN THE BACK OFFICE OF THE ABANDONED JOB-SITE trailer when he heard the door. He raised his gun and stepped carefully toward the front. "FBI. Who's there?" He continued forward.

"Don't shoot. Don't shoot." A young man held his arms high in the air.

"Who are you? What are you doing here?" The kid eyed a cabinet that was feet from where he stood. Quinn spotted the gaze. "What are you looking at?"

"Nothing. I ain't looking at nothing. I shouldn't be here."

"Damn right, you shouldn't. But since you are, why don't you tell me who the hell you are?"

"Billy Horton, sir."

22

Two members of the BAU team still searched the abandoned mining operation roughly ten miles away. Meanwhile, as the morning turned to afternoon, the rest had gathered at the station house, piecing together Slocum's motives. And still, no word on a location of the Crown Pointe deputy, the man who they now believed was the killer.

Handling the Floyds was the current and pressing problem. What part had they played in this horrific scenario? They'd lost their daughter—their only child—to drugs. And now they sat here, under suspicion of dealing drugs themselves. Perhaps even the very same synthetic, tainted drugs found in all the victims.

Deputy Lazaro leaned back in his desk chair, legs crossed and eyeing the two people no one could have ever suspected of committing a crime. "Lives are at stake, here, Mr. and Mrs. Floyd. You need to be honest with us. The drugs Slocum found in your house—did they belong to you? Were you selling the synthetic drugs to the people in this town?"

"I swear to you on the Bible that we did not sell bad drugs to anyone," Lynn replied.

"Ain't you got nothing better to do than to harass a couple of old folks who ain't done nothing wrong?" John said.

Lazaro shot upright and slammed his fist down on his desk. "Damnit!"

Everyone in the station jumped to attention at the disruption.

"Don't you see what the hell is happening here? Don't you people give a damn about anyone in this town?" Lazaro stood with his hands planted on his hips. "Despite what you might think, I ain't stupid. I see what goes on around here. And it makes me sick!"

The chief approached him. "That's enough now, Shane. This isn't helping anyone, and I think you know that."

"They know something, Chief, they just won't say! People are dying, the rest are scared out of their minds, and they don't give a good God damn!"

John stood from his chair, casting a deliberate gaze at the deputy. "You think we don't care what's happening here, boy?"

"No, sir, I do not!"

Lynn reached for John's arm. "Sit down, John."

He pulled it away. "No, ma'am! I will not sit here and be accused of killing nobody, you hear?"

"John, we're not accusing you of nothing, all right?" the chief replied.

"The hell you're not." He peered at Lazaro again. "Boy, you got any idea what it's like to lose a child? You got any damn clue what that feels like?"

Lazaro recoiled. "No, sir."

"That's right you don't. Well, let me tell you something. It feels like someone took a 357 Magnum and blew a hole straight through your damn heart. And ain't nothing ever gonna fill that hole."

Kate eyed Nick as they stood near the coffee maker at the back.

He shook his head, seemingly knowing what she was about to do, but as with most things, Kate was going to handle this the way she thought was best.

"John, I don't think Deputy Lazaro means any disrespect at the loss of your daughter. None of us do. And I don't think any of us can understand what it is you and your wife have gone through over this past year." Kate placed her hand on his shoulder. "I think we're all just really worried about the idea that Deputy Slocum could have something to do with the recent deaths. It's frightening to think someone you thought you knew, someone you thought you could trust, was capable of such a thing."

Lazaro returned to his seat.

"There's no denying what Slocum found in your house, but we are still considering the possibility that he could've planted the drugs in an effort to shift the focus of the investigation toward you and your wife."

John Floyd seemed to calm down as Kate came to his defense.

"That said, there are things that struck me as unusual when Agent Quinn and I visited you and Mrs. Floyd in your home the other night. John, it's vital we understand to what extent you and your wife are involved in selling drugs." Before he could object, she pressed on. "Please. There's no time to argue. Whether Slocum planted the bad drugs or not, we have cause to believe you're somehow involved in drug trafficking. There is ample evidence at your home that points to the fact. We can't afford to waste any more time, John. And there's a big difference between dealing drugs and murder."

Walsh ambled toward Nick with a knowing smile. "She is good."

"Tell me about it."

"We needed the money," Lynn replied. "That's what it boiled down to."

~

QUINN TRAINED HIS WEAPON ON THE YOUNG MAN WHO couldn't have been much older than twenty. "Well, Billy Horton. I've heard a lot about you. What is it that you're doing here? Are you supposed to meet someone?"

"Uh, no, sir." He again eyed the cabinet behind Quinn.

"You obviously came here for something. Is it in there?" Quinn tossed a glance toward the cabinet.

The kid remained silent.

"Look, I'm taking you in regardless. So if you want to make it easier on yourself then why don't you tell me what's in the cabinet?"

Horton shook his head. "I don't wanna."

"You understand that we're here because a killer is roaming free? And that someone in this town is passing around deadly drugs? Some people think it's you. If I take a look in that cabinet, am I going to find said drugs?"

"Don't matter what you find 'cause nothing in here belongs to me," Horton replied.

"You do not want to play this game, Billy, because you will lose." Quinn turned steadfast. He aimed his weapon at the cabinet and fired on the padlock. The lock sparked and the metal door flew open. "I guess I'll have to see for myself." He approached the cabinet and peered inside. Bags of pills, weed, and heroin rested on a shelf. "Well, well. This much dope will get you, what, maybe twenty to thirty years? And if they're a match with the forensics from the murder victims...?"

"Okay. Okay. I keep my stash here, but I ain't no killer."

Quinn stepped away from the cabinet. "Where did you get the drugs?"

"I got a dealer. He's part of an operation looking to get a foothold in Crown Pointe."

Perhaps Quinn wasn't as far off the mark as the team thought he was.

"But I swear, these drugs is safe. I mean, it's heroin, mostly, some Oxy. But none of it got that Fentanyl or Propofol in it. I ain't stupid. I seen too many people go down 'cause of that shit."

"Who are you selling to?"

"Just the local tweakers. Look, I know people's been dying 'cause of the bad shit going around. That ain't me. I swear it ain't me," Horton replied.

"They're being beaten to death too, in case you weren't aware of that." Quinn's attention was diverted by the sound of a car approaching outside. "Looks like the cavalry's arrived. You can tell your story to the chief." He approached Horton, and with his weapon still aimed at the kid, opened the trailer door and walked outside.

Fisher stepped out of the vehicle, "Who've we got here? You make a new friend, Quinn? I was heading back down when I saw this piece of shit truck here. Figured you might need some help. Truck belong to you, kid?"

"This is the elusive Billy Horton. He came to pick up his stash he keeps inside," Quinn replied.

"Nice to meet you, Billy. So you're the one selling the bad dope?" Fisher asked.

"No. I ain't responsible for none of what's happened 'round here."

"We'll find out soon enough. Let's load up and get him back to the station," Quinn replied.

"Guess our visit wasn't a total bust," Fisher said. "Get in the car, kid."

~

DEPUTY ERIC SLOCUM FORCED JENSEN INTO THE DRIVER'S seat of his car. There was no chance he'd make it far in his truck, and Jensen was practically a ghost in this town. No one would be looking for his vehicle. Everyone would be looking for Slocum's truck. It was only a matter of time before the state police would be on the hunt along with the feds and his own department. It was surreal. This whole cocked-up plan was falling in around his ears.

The way he saw it, he was doing the town a favor and yet no one else would see it that way. But more importantly, he was doing it for Jenny, a woman whom he loved more than anything. She had been ripped from this world by the likes of Billy Horton, a loser, a tweaker, who dropped out of high school and started selling whatever he could for a buck.

"Horton better be there, like you say." Slocum held his gun at Jensen's head. "Drive."

Jensen turned the engine and reversed out of the parking lot of the apartment complex.

Slocum had been a cop for a long time, arrested all sorts from minor to major offenses. He knew when someone was buying time and when they were being true. And right now, he got the distinct feeling Jensen was buying time.

It became abundantly clear to Slocum his chances of surviving the day were slim to none. He'd killed that young woman in the hospital. The nurse had seen him there. How long before they tied him to the other murders? No one would see reason as to why he'd done it. No one would understand.

"I don't mean to pry, but can I ask you something?" Jensen cautiously eyed Slocum before returning his attention to the road. "You the one give them addicts the bad drugs? Just trying to figure why. Seems you could've made a killing—I mean, a lot of money, dealing. Just like everyone else."

"How long you been in this town?" Slocum asked. "Cause I been here my whole life, born and raised. And I'll tell you what, it's a travesty what's happened here. My folks left. I told them it was getting too rough. But I stayed and tried to fight the good fight. Unfortunately, I see now my efforts amounted to exactly nothing. I didn't change nothing."

"You said you was doing this cause you lost someone?"

"I lost the best girl a guy could ask for," Slocum replied.

"I'm sorry for that. I truly am," Jensen continued.

"Just shut up and keep driving. You'd better hope that son of a bitch, Horton, is there too."

Jensen turned down the dirt road that led to the abandoned shaft and the dilapidated trailers that had become known as the Devil's Den.

"We should've burned down this place a long time ago," Slocum said. He recalled the day he found Jenny. She'd been inside one of these shitholes. A 911 call had come in. Emergency Services was dispatched and he was the only one on duty, so it was his turn to come out. They'd all been called out to Devil's Den plenty of times, but that day was different.

He had rushed toward the trailer where the paramedics worked on her. They tried to save her, but she'd been gone for too long. Seems the assholes with her waited too long to call for help because they were too wasted to use the phone. When he walked inside and saw it was Jenny, he had to play it off like he didn't know her, like he didn't love her.

"It's Jenny Floyd, isn't it?" one of the paramedics had asked him. "I seen her around a lot with these trouble makers. Damn shame. Thought she was gonna go places. Like she might actually make it out of this town and make something of herself."

"I didn't know her personally," Slocum recalled saying. "Of course, everyone knows her. Damn shame is right. Let's get her loaded up and clean this shit up." As he walked back outside on that horrible day, it was all he could do to contain his swelling grief. It was that day he took it upon himself to make right the wrongs that'd been done to her. It took a while to muster the courage, to get the drugs, and more importantly, to figure out how he could do it without getting caught. Guess he messed up on that count.

And now, as he returned to the place where his heart had been broken, he recalled the first of his victims and the feeling of vindication. A feeling that would carry him through the rest of the killings.

Jensen stopped the car and pulled the key from the ignition. "What do you want me to do now?"

"Get out." Slocum again aimed his weapon at him.

They stepped outside and the sun shone down on Jensen's balding head. He seemed to curse the clear day, wishing for a winter storm that might hinder this deputy's plans. Not today.

"I don't see no other cars." Slocum checked the area. "Looks like our boy isn't here."

"He will be. My guy promised me Horton would be coming here 'cause they all know he's got a new stash today. They'll all be wanting some of it."

With the heat on, Horton might get spooked, but Slocum had to take that chance. "Best get inside then, and wait for him."

~

AGENT NESS RUSHED THROUGH THE DOOR OF THE STATION house. "We got the phone records. The other victims' and Deputy Slocum's."

"Thank God for small miracles." Walsh approached him. "You look at them yet?"

"Not in detail. I wanted to get down here as soon as I could."

"Okay then, let's divvy them up." Walsh handed out the files. "We can search the victims' records and cross-reference any calls made to Slocum. He might be on the run, but we have to establish his connection to the victims. We have to be certain he's our guy."

"What about any calls between the deputy and Jenny Floyd?" Kate asked. "Do these records go back that far?"

"As a matter of fact, I was able to pull Jenny Floyd's phone records from before her death." Ness eyed the Floyds with a hint of remorse.

"This is exactly what we need to determine a history and whether Slocum had been planning this for a long time or just snapped," Nick replied.

The agents began their review into the phone records when Quinn and Fisher pushed through the door with a kid no one knew.

Nick caught sight of them. "Who's this? No Slocum?"

"No luck," Quinn replied. "Unless you count this kid." He tossed the drugs onto a desk. "And these. This must be what it feels like to be DEA."

"You must be Billy Horton. We've been looking for you," Walsh replied.

"I think this kid might know where we can find Slocum," Quinn pressed on. "But he's reluctant to talk to us."

"And, of course, he claims to know nothing about the drugs."

Fisher eyed the files the team reviewed. "Please tell me those are the phone records."

"Ness just got his hands on them. They're from the victims as well as Jenny Floyd. Should give us a history on Slocum and if he was dealing," Kate replied.

"Deputy Eric Slocum? A dealer?" Billy Horton asked with a snicker. "Not a fucking chance. I'd know about it if he was." He eyed the Floyds. "Just like I know what they was up to. Trying to poach my business and all."

"You're a disgrace!" Lynn Floyd spat at Horton.

"Oh, *I'm* the disgrace?" He wiped off the spittle that landed on his cheek. "Well, what the hell does that make you two old fucks? Just 'cause you got the good stuff from some shit doctor doling out scripts don't make you no different than me."

"We was doing it for the money. That's all. For survival!" Lynn replied.

"Duh! What the fuck you think I was doing it for? My health?" Horton said. "Do I gotta sit here and listen to this shit or what? Y'all gonna charge me with something?"

Quinn grabbed him and easily shoved the scrawny kid into a nearby chair. "How about I get my DEA buddy down here and he'll own your ass."

Kate hadn't seen or heard Quinn speak to a suspect, or whatever this guy was, in such a manner. Oh, he'd seen her do it plenty of times, something she'd come to regret. But it appeared he, too, had a darker side. There was more to Noah Quinn than she thought.

In that moment, Chief Tate emerged from his office. "Sounds like we're all starting to lose our cool here a little bit. Maybe the agents in the room need to step out and take a breath."

"Thank you, Chief," Horton began. "Everyone around here has lost their damn minds!"

Chief Tate continued his approach and stopped just inches from Horton, towering over the kid. "Boy, we ain't friends, we ain't even acquaintances. So you best keep that tongue of yours inside your head 'cause I got no problem turning a blind eye if someone was to sock you in the mouth."

Horton folded his arms, defending whatever dignity he clung onto.

"Now I came out here 'cause I had a chance to review, in greater detail, these photos y'all brought me. Seems this one," he held up one of the them, "was taken in Jenny Floyd's bedroom." He handed the image to Lynn Floyd. "Am I correct on that assumption, Mrs. Floyd?"

She peered at the image. "Yes. This is Jenny's room."

"And this one here." He held up the other image. "This one here appears to have been taken inside Eric's car, in front of the Floyds' home. Am I correct on that count too?" He again handed the image to Lynn Floyd.

"Yes, sir, that appears to be our house in the background."

"Meaning Eric had been to your house on at least these two occasions. That being said, Mrs. Floyd, I'm not entirely sure you're being truthful with us about your knowledge of a relationship between my deputy and your daughter."

John examined his wife. "Did you know about them, Lynnie? Why didn't you say nothing?"

"She never came out and told me directly, but I knew she was seeing him. It was a long time ago. I guess it didn't seem to matter none after she died. I didn't know how serious it was or if it was serious at all. Like I said, she never said nothing about it."

"Why didn't you question her at the time?" Nick asked.

"I was planning to. But then I didn't see him around no more and figured she'd broke it off for whatever reason. By that point, she'd been pretty heavy into the drugs and I was more concerned about that than the deputy and her maybe being boyfriend and girlfriend," Lynn replied.

"So you knew about the relationship. How does that help us now?" Kate asked.

The chief turned again to Mrs. Floyd. "Cause I think she might've called on ol' Eric to help when she knew Jenny was going downhill. And like any grieving mother, afterwards, maybe she called upon his help again when she couldn't pull herself out of that grief, a grief, I'm sure Eric must've shared."

23

It was her husband, John, who was perhaps stunned most of all by the chief's allegations. Had she asked the deputy for help to avenge their daughter's death? It didn't seem possible. This kind, hard working woman he'd been married to for almost thirty years. No. He couldn't believe it. Maybe she'd turned to the deputy for a shoulder to cry on, but pigs weren't flying just yet. There must've been an explanation of what the chief was suggesting.

"Lynnie, is this true?" John began. "You been keeping company with that deputy and not telling me?" His round belly heaved and fell with each word he strained to speak. "Did you know what he was doing? Did you know and choose not to stop him?"

"We refused to see what was happening to her, John. She withered away before our eyes and we did nothing to help her. We denied there was a problem at all. Well, I just couldn't do it no more after that. I let her down and I wanted to make it right." She peered at the eyes of judgment that surrounded her. "When one of you loses a child, you can tell me what you'd have done to make it right."

"When exactly did you and Eric come together?" the chief asked.

"I seen him at the funeral. Like I said, she'd broke it off some time before she died. But I know he kept looking after her. He tried to help her when we failed to."

"He was at the funeral. What happened then, Mrs. Floyd?" Kate pressed on.

"I asked him, after everyone left and John was walking to the car. I asked him if he still loved her. He said yes. Then I asked him if he could do something to help make things right. He didn't ask what, just nodded and walked away."

"But that was a year ago," Quinn said. "Why did it take so long to put a plan into action? I assume it was your plan."

"There weren't no plan. Not really. It just sorta came together, I reckon. Me and John needed money. I needed doctors' help in getting prescriptions. That took time. And I used John's disability to help with that. We agreed that we had to do something to keep from losing our house. Losing everything. And after losing our daughter, we just couldn't bear the thought of having to move from the only place our daughter knew as home."

"But you didn't say nothing about the deputy." John turned his sights to the chief. "I know what we did was wrong, scheming to get the Oxy. I thought it was just so we could bring in the money we needed."

"John didn't know nothing about what I was doing with Eric Slocum. And, to be honest, I didn't really know what he was doing. He just kept saying for me not to worry about it. Even when we were brought in cause he found them pills. I kept my mouth shut about our arrangement. He said he'd take care of things. I believed him. John had no part in any of this."

"How did you two get the synthetic drugs? And how were they distributed?" Nick asked. "Who else was involved in the plan?"

"I got the Oxy from the doctors. Traveled to Florida sometimes to get them. Ohio sometimes too. Course it started getting harder lately, but that's where I'd go. I'd keep some to sell for money, for John and me. The rest I gave to Eric. I don't know what exactly he did with them, but once people started dying—folks I knew had been Jenny's friends. Although 'friends' ain't what I'd call them. I'd call them junkies—I figured it was best not to ask."

Fisher eyed the woman, pushing the toothpick in his mouth from one side to the other, appearing to consider all she'd presented. "Walsh, you and Reid searched Slocum's place. Did you find any evidence he was tampering with the drugs?"

"No, we didn't," Kate replied. "If he did, he had to have been doing it somewhere else."

Lazaro, who'd been silent, astonished by the revelation, looked at Kate. "There's no way he would've known what to do. How to do that. I can't make heads nor tails from this. There's something else we're not seeing."

Billy Horton cleared his throat. "I might know something about that, but you know, I can't say for sure, unless... Well, I mean, if I can help you folks somehow..."

"You best continue on with that sentence, then, boy," the chief replied. "You want any chance of not spending the bulk of your adult life in some hell hole where no one's gonna protect you, best you speak up now."

"I might've told him about someone—once."

"You said he wasn't dealing. Who was this someone?" Chief asked.

"He wasn't. Not that I knew anyhow. Slocum threatened to

arrest me about six months ago. Pulled me over and caught me with a kilo of heroin."

"A kilo?" Chief clenched his fists. "And he let you go?"

Horton nodded. "Said he'd let me slide so long as I put him in touch with my supplier for Oxy. Figured he just wanted to make the bust. And if it kept me out of trouble, I didn't see no problem with it. I was planning on going somewheres else for the goods. Didn't matter to me if my supplier got pinched. No way he'd trace it back to me."

"You all know that, according to my DEA buddy," Ness interrupted, "a special compound was discovered in the pill found in Steven Schiller's car the other day. And it matched the chemicals found in the victims. What's been killing off the people around here was the use of that compound. Not just Fentanyl-laced pills."

"Is it possible Slocum knew about the dangerous chemicals and knew how to turn what he had into the deadly synthetics?" Nick asked.

"A year had passed since Slocum decided he was going to take care of whatever it was that needed taking care of. Learning how to form the compound, getting a supplier in place. These could've been the reasons it took time to get everything lined up," Kate added.

"And this was happening right under my nose." Lazaro's face masked in resentment. "Son of a bitch was my partner."

"It wasn't just happening under your nose. I'm the chief. He did this under my watch."

"There's enough blame to go around here," Nick said. "We can sort that out later. Right now, Slocum's still out there."

"He has to know we're onto him by now," Kate said. "I think it's time we call in the state police. Get some road blocks in place."

"Reid's right." Duncan emerged from the break room that had been set up as a command center. "I'm wasting my time going through these records. We know who Slocum is now. And we need to nip this in the bud before someone else dies. Chief, do you have a state police contact?"

"Probably gonna need to get the commissioner in on this." He headed toward his office. "I'll make the call now."

SLOCUM PACED THE SMALL TRAILER. HE REMOVED THE BALL cap from his head and pulled off his jacket, overheated by nerves. Concern over the arrival of Billy Horton, or lack thereof, had consumed him. Two hours had passed and still nothing. The afternoon sun was at its peak and time was wasting. He was unraveling and so was his plan. "You best hope Horton shows up or I'll make sure there's nothing left of you, you hear me?"

"I can make the call again and figure out what's taking him so long. It's possible the cops got him. I mean, after the hospital and all the shit that's gone down around here. You know, they're probably on high alert and just waiting for somebody to fuck up on something. Maybe Billy Horton did. And maybe they got him."

Slocum marched toward the haggard, middle-aged man. "Or maybe you planned it this way. You call the chief and tell him? Huh? Was that who you called?"

"If I'd done that, he'd be here by now. I ain't trying to fuck with you, Slocum. I swear it."

Slocum appeared to reconsider his situation. "I don't reckon I can just sit here. Something went south. Horton ain't coming. There's only one other place I can think of he might be. The old mining operation. Dumb ass kept his stash there thinking no one would turn up to steal it. Could be holed up there trying to ride out the heat."

"It's on the way out of town. Might be a good idea to high-tail it on out of Crown Pointe. We can go wherever you want."

"They ain't going to stop looking for me. It's too late for me to get out of town. Chief's a smart man. He'll be making the necessary provisions."

"No. They won't stop looking, like you say, but we can buy you some time. We can ride it out, too. Kill two birds, you know what I'm saying? And when the worst of it passes, we make a beeline for the border. I can help you get out of Kentucky."

"Why you doing this?" Slocum asked.

"'Cause you got a gun on me, and I don't fancy dying today."

THE CHIEF SURFACED FROM HIS OFFICE. "COMMISSIONER Hawthorne wants confirmation from Ness's boss. Just to be sure the feds are in on this full-bore, especially as we have zero concrete proof Slocum is our man. Doesn't like the idea of a manhunt against one of our own."

"I'll make the call to ASAC Garza now." Ness retrieved his phone and walked outside.

"He gets the all-clear and Hawthorne will put a team in place and coordinate the plan." Chief sighed. "I guess a part of me is hoping we're all wrong about this. But that's not very plausible now, is it?"

Lynn Floyd stood up, her shoulders pushed back. She straightened her blouse over her full figure and held the chief's gaze. "I did what I did for my Jenny. I ain't sorry none of them people died. They got what they deserved, and deep down, I think you know that. I am sorry, though, that Eric got in too deep. His only fault was loving my little girl. And this is where it got him."

The chief stepped closer to her, his reedy frame hunched

down. "People 'round here got problems. Lots of them. Some of them turn to the drugs because they think there ain't no way out. So you tell me one thing, Mrs. Floyd, whose problem is that? You turned your back on them people, enabled their addictions 'cause you were acting like judge, jury, and executioner. Well, I'll tell you one thing, I hope God shows you mercy 'cause you sure as hell didn't show it to none of them kids you helped kill."

"I didn't help..." But before Lynn could continue, Ness returned inside.

"ASAC Garza's making the call now to the commissioner. I also just got the DNA results back on the Floyds' swab."

In that moment, all eyes landed on him, desperate for the news. Contempt masked his face as he continued. "John's DNA didn't match anything found on the victims or the wooden shard Reid found in the shed." He turned to Lynn Floyd. "However, your DNA was a match to that found on Joanne Waverly."

"It was you." Stunned, Kate reeled at the evidence. "You were the one who tried to clean her up. You wanted to give her a shred of dignity in her death because you felt guilty." She eyed Quinn because they were right. Someone was helping Slocum, cleaning up after him. And it was her.

"Sweet Jesus." Lazaro retrieved his handcuffs. "Mrs. Floyd, you're under arrest for the murder of Miss Joanne Waverly." He placed the cuffs on her hands.

"I didn't kill her," Lynn pleaded.

"Your DNA was found on the victim. We have no physical proof Eric Slocum killed her. Just yours," Kate said.

"Take her back to the holding cell," the chief said.

"No. No. Please don't. She's all I got left. She didn't mean to do it," John pleaded. "Lynnie, why?"

"I didn't kill her. I swear it. I just—I'm sorry, John."

Lazaro pulled her through the station toward the only holding cell in the back.

Walsh turned away. "For God's sake. What the hell kind of shit show is this?"

"I need some air." Kate stepped outside into the afternoon air that turned cooler as the day dragged on. She peered upward and closed her eyes. Goosebumps raised on her skin as the air passed through her.

"Hey. You okay?" Quinn drew near and stood next to her. "Here's some water." He handed her a Dixie cup from the cooler inside. "Walsh sure hit the nail on the head, didn't he?"

"It's sad. A mother looking for revenge. A man in love seeking the same." Kate turned to him. "This isn't what I thought it was going to be."

"I don't think it's what any of us thought it would be," Quinn replied.

"You were right, though," she continued.

"I think we were both right about some things. Not about others. But that's the deal, isn't it? That's how we get better at our jobs."

"We still need Eric Slocum—and his DNA to prove he killed them all. It'll be easy to prove Lynn Floyd didn't do the deed, considering her size and age. We have to find Slocum to finish this."

Quinn stared out into the wooded land across from the station house. "I can assure you, we're not going to take a step back just because the state police are getting involved. We need to trace Slocum's steps. We need to get inside his head. And you and I are the ones to do it."

"And the others?" Kate asked.

"They all have their own areas of expertise. We'll come

together with our ideas and take it from there. Just like any other investigation."

She turned to Quinn with a bleak but curious gaze. "What would you have done if it was your child? If you'd seen your own kid sliding down the slippery slope of drug abuse."

"I honestly don't know, although I don't think murder would come to mind. What would you do, Reid? If you had a child and that child died."

A memory flashed in her mind of a time when she listened to the doctor tell her the pregnancy had to be terminated and that she would never be able to conceive again. "Well, see, that's the thing. I don't have to worry about that." Kate tossed the paper cup into the trash can and walked back inside.

Nick spotted her return and made his way toward her. "You okay?" He eyed the door as Quinn returned as well.

"I'm Fine. What's the plan?"

STERLING JENSEN HAD STEPPED OUTSIDE WITH A LARGE blanket that was tossed over the back of the sofa in the trailer. He laid it out across the back seat of his car. Pulling upright again, he examined the area. No cops—not yet anyway. Maybe this plan of his could work. It was the only way he thought he might actually survive this insane situation in which he found himself. Being held hostage by a cop was something new to him. And this was a crazy cop at that. A man with nothing left to lose who didn't seem to care who he might take down with him.

A final look around and he returned inside where Slocum stood, looming over him. It seemed that a man with a gun appeared much larger than he might otherwise. And right now,

Slocum looked like a giant. "I think we're ready. We should prob- ably skedaddle."

Slocum followed him outside. He slipped onto the back seat while Jensen entered the driver's seat and started the engine.

"I sure hope you don't try anything stupid." Slocum revealed the gun in between the seats, just enough to show the man he was still in charge.

"I haven't done nothing stupid so far and I sure as shit don't aim to start." He pulled away from the trailer before making it to the road ahead. "Should take us half hour, I reckon, to get there."

"Just take your time and don't draw no attention to yourself."

Jensen peered into the rearview. "I understand." He eyed the road ahead and accelerated enough to hit the speed limit. "I won't go a mile over the limit." He wished he had said something that day when the cops came. He wouldn't be in this situation now if he had. Of course, he couldn't know Slocum was a crazy son of a bitch. A fleeting thought shot through his mind, one he couldn't possibly act upon unless he wanted to end up dead. But it had occurred to him to drive right to the police station. It sure would save a lot of grief on his part. Maybe he was just too selfish and wasn't ready to die just yet. Not that he had much to live for. He hadn't worked in years. Drank too much. And his recreational use of heroin was becoming something more than that, a fact he only just now seemed to realize.

But in the end, he wasn't ready to die. And maybe this was his wake-up call, if he was lucky enough to survive the day. He would get his act together. Maybe even get the hell out of this God forsaken place. The town that the rest of the country forgot. He snickered.

"What's so funny?" Slocum asked from the back.

"Nothing. Nothing about this is at all funny."

"Then how 'bout you shut it and just keep driving."

"Will do." Whatever thoughts of bringing Slocum to justice at the expense of his own life had vanished as quickly as they had surfaced. He wasn't willing to die for this town. It gave him nothing and, in fact, only took away. He owed no one nothing in Crown Pointe. So when this was over, he was gone. One way or another.

~

"We ready to do this?" Walsh eyed his team.

"As ready as we'll ever be." Fisher turned to the chief. "Is that them coming up the road?"

A convoy of cop cars—state police—with sirens blaring, rolled into the parking lot.

"They aren't messing around," Walsh said. "So the plan is to split up and team up with these guys?"

"That's the plan," Nick replied.

A man with bars on the shoulders of his uniform entered the station. "Afternoon. I'm Captain Lowell. Guess we got us a good old-fashioned manhunt underway, is that right?"

"That is right." Nick offered his hand. "BAU, Senior Unit Agent Scarborough." He introduced the team. "Agents Reid, Walsh, Fisher, and Duncan. And this is Agent Quinn. We've been assisting Chief Tate with this investigation for the better part of a week. And we finally got a breakthrough."

"I figured that was why we were called out, Agent Scarborough. Pleasure to meet you and your team. I guess I'll start by saying my team and I know these roads better than most. Except maybe the chief here. So I'd like to take point on setting up the road blocks."

"I have no problem with that. In the meantime, we'll need to search the town and hope Deputy Slocum hasn't already made his way clear of it," Nick said.

"I don't much like knowing this is all because of one of our own. So you'd better believe my team will find this son of a bitch. Although I can't guarantee no one's gonna get hurt in the process."

Nick seemed to catch on to the captain's meaning. So did everyone else. "This has been a tough situation for everyone involved. Do what you need to do. But the deputy's been a part of this police department for a long time. And I think the chief would like every precaution considered when it comes to taking in Slocum."

"Well, I can surely understand that perspective. So we'll do what we can. But I won't let this law man take down any of my own. Or yours, if they're with me."

Nick patted the captain's back. "I wouldn't want it any other way."

24

Jensen's old Ford Taurus rumbled down the road toward the shuttered mining operation. With his eyes peeled for the police, his nerves stood on end. "My angina's gonna act up at this rate," he whispered.

"What'd you say?"

He peered into the rearview mirror at Slocum, whose head just peeked out over the blanket. "Nothing." And that was when he saw them. "Oh shit. You best get down."

"What's going on?"

Jensen shifted his gaze between the mirrors and the road ahead. "Son of a bitch. I can't believe we just missed them."

"Missed who? You best tell me what the fuck is happening right now." Slocum raised the gun into view.

"It's the cops. Two patrol cars, state police, just rolled up at the intersection. Looks like they're blocking the road. Holy shit. We made it through just in time."

"Just keep going. We gotta be getting close."

"We are. Five more minutes, I reckon. And we might just be in the clear."

"If they're blocking off roads," Slocum began, "chances are better than fair they'll turn up at the mines."

"Not necessarily. Once you get inside, there's only one way out and that's the road we're on now. This don't lead nowhere else, 'cept the mines. No reason for them to come back in here."

As the patrol cars shrank in the rearview, Jensen forged ahead on the road where the pavement was about to end and the pea-sized gravel path started. It was used to keep the dust down when vehicles rolled over it. Good thing too, because the dust would plume into the air like a fire in the sky. And that would surely draw unwanted attention.

Slocum poked his head between the seats as they approached the job-site trailer. "That's Horton's truck. Son of a bitch is here. Pull up next to him."

"Whatever you say, boss." Jensen stopped his car next to an old pick-up. "You want me to check it out?"

"Christ, you must take me for a fool." Slocum stepped out of the back seat and pulled open Jensen's door. "You're coming with me."

They approached the steps of the trailer and Jensen was the first to reach the door.

"You want me to open it?"

"Yes. Slowly." With his gun in Jensen's back, Slocum waited.

"Don't look like no one's here." Jensen walked inside and noticed the cabinet. "Not anymore, anyway."

"Shit. His stash is gone," Slocum said.

"And so is Horton," Jenson replied.

"Why the hell is his truck still here?"

"Well, I think we both know the answer to that. What say we make our way up the hill a tad farther and see if we can find some shelter? Best not stick around here much longer. Besides, most of this place is overrun with grasses and weeds and shit. Some trees even. Might be best to hole up around there."

Slocum considered the suggestion. "You know I could've killed you back at Devil's Den?"

"I do know that, sir." As if Jensen was attempting to take him someplace more secluded in an effort to kill him. "I'm just looking for a place to keep hidden is all. We can't turn around and head back. Not with the roads blocked off."

"Well, I guess I'll just have to trust you."

"You are the one with the gun, Deputy. I'll do as you please."

NICK RETURNED HIS WEAPON TO HIS HOLSTER AND STOOD IN front of the team as they waited for the go-ahead. "Captain Lowell's guys are getting into place as we speak. Road blocks will be installed on every route going out of Crown Pointe. Those officers who've remained will be teaming up with you all. They know the roads around here like the backs of their hands. So you will, no doubt, be in the best possible situation to find and capture Eric Slocum."

"Luckily, I just completed my firing range renewal hours," Walsh said to Kate. "Been a while since I had to consider the possibility of opening fire on a suspect."

"It's old hat for me." Kate chuckled.

Walsh nudged her arm and smiled.

"So if there are no questions," Nick continued, "I'll ask you all to get with your teams and head out. The sooner we get out there, the better the chances are of bringing him in."

"I'll catch up with you later," Kate said. "Good luck out there, Levi."

"Back at you, Kate." He headed toward Duncan, who would partner up with Deputy Lazaro.

Quinn walked toward her. "You ready to do this?"

"Yes I am. Who's coming with us?"

"I am." A young man in his late twenties, broad shouldered and pushing six feet two inches, appeared. "Officer Shelby. I grew up around here. I know every nook and cranny of this town. So if Slocum's here, we'll be the ones to find him."

"Let's hit the road," Quinn said.

Kate eyed Nick as she set off.

"Good luck." His voice was only a whisper, although he knew she understood what he'd said. He wanted to go with her, but it was best she went with Quinn.

"You ready to head out, boss?" Fisher approached him. "This is Sergeant Lee. Sarg, this is the boss, Agent Scarborough."

"Pleasure, Agent Scarborough. We should get out there."

A final check to see that Walsh and Duncan had paired up with Lazaro, and Nick was ready to go. "Lead the way, Sergeant."

Outside, the teams pulled out of the parking lot.

"What's our plan of action, Shelby?" Quinn asked from the passenger seat.

"With the BOLO issued, we're waiting on any calls of sightings. Short of that happening, our best bet, if y'all are in agreement, is to tackle his known hangouts."

"We've been that route for the past several hours," Kate said. "If he's still in town, should we consider a different approach?"

"Any suggestions, Reid?" Quinn asked. "Going door to door?"

"That might be a waste of resources." Kate peered through the rear passenger window. "However, given what we know of Slocum, he might feel desperation sinking in. He might consider going to see Jenny Floyd."

"You want to go to the gravesite?" Quinn nodded as though

thinking hard on the matter before responding, "Unless anyone else has any better ideas, what have we got to lose?"

"You'll get no objections from me," Shelby said. "We'll head straight there and see what we can find." He continued along the road, veering right at the intersection. "It's not far. Should be there in five minutes." He turned to Quinn. "Can I ask you something?"

"Go ahead."

"Y'all are supposed to be experts in what, like understanding crazy people, right?"

"That's a tad simplistic and not entirely accurate, but go on." Quinn replied.

"Well, I guess I don't understand how y'all didn't realize this Deputy Slocum was the one who was doing the killing. The BAU, that's Behavioral Analysis Unit, right?"

"Uh-huh." Quinn appeared offended by the officer's comments but held his tongue.

"Seems kinda obvious he would've been the one. I mean, no offense, just seems like the chief, at least, should've picked up on that fact."

"How long have you been with the state police, Shelby?" Kate interjected.

"About three years."

"And in those three years, you ever miss something? Ever have a theory about a case that turned out not to be correct?"

"Well, sure—I..."

"Sometimes, no matter how hard we work to put together an accurate profile, it just doesn't always pan out. And in this particular case, Deputy Slocum was extremely close to Chief Tate. It's a tight-knit department. And Slocum had kept his relationship with Jenny Floyd a secret, for whatever reason. So I have to tell you that you're out of line. When you've been around as many psychotic killers who've sliced open their victims or mutilated them in some way, as we have, you tend to see a pattern. Well, Slocum didn't fit the pattern. And so here we are."

"I'm sorry, ma'am. Of course y'all are doing the job best you can. I mean no disrespect."

"None taken," Quinn said. "Things just don't always pan out the way you think they will. You'll figure that out soon enough."

The officer was quiet for the remainder of the drive, which wasn't long in any case. "This is it up ahead. The cemetery. It ain't very big. We can probably find her ourselves. Unless you want to talk to the caretaker?"

"If he's here, we'll spot him." Quinn stepped out of the car after the officer stopped.

Kate joined him. "Sorry for the diatribe."

"Don't be. Kid doesn't know much right now. He'll learn." Quinn eyed the grounds. "Let's have a look around and get the hell out of here if we don't see him. Graveyards give me the heebie jeebies."

"Really?" Kate smiled. "I never would've guessed Superman's weakness was graveyards."

"I'm no Superman. And I have plenty of weaknesses." Quinn started in toward the grounds. "You coming, Shelby?"

The young officer jogged to catch up. "Sorry about what I said back there. I really didn't mean anything by it."

"Don't worry about it. Let's just find Slocum," Quinn replied.

FISHER CAST HIS GAZE BETWEEN NICK AND SERGEANT LEE as he drove. "Why are we going back to Slocum's house?"

"I don't want to overlook anything. Now that we know he's still out there, I want to be sure he hasn't left anything behind that might indicate his whereabouts now," Nick replied.

"Okay. I just hope we aren't wasting time."

"Look, Fisher, I know we've all gotten off to a little bit of a rocky start, but I hope that someday you'll come to trust me."

"I'm sorry, man. You're right. I guess I'm used to calling the shots, for the most part. Cole wasn't as hands-on as you are. And I need to make the adjustment. This is your team. I respect that."

"I can't imagine the shit storm you all deal with on a daily basis," Lee said. "Can't say I envy you one bit."

Fisher laughed. "No sir. Envy would not be the right word. Feel sorry for? Maybe. No, but we deal with some scary shit. No joke. This is probably one of the least horrific cases we've been on. Wouldn't you say, Scarborough?"

"I'd have to agree with you. The shit we've seen would curl your toes, Sergeant Lee." Nick peered around the corner. "This is his place."

"Copy that." Lee pulled onto the driveway and cut the engine. "Doesn't look like he's here. Don't see a car or anything."

"I wouldn't expect he'd be here. Just hoping for a clue." Nick stepped out of the car and headed toward the front door. He noticed the broken pane of glass. "Looks like our teammates already took care of getting access for us. That's too bad. I hear this is your area of expertise, Fisher."

"Who told you that?"

"I asked around. I know more about you all than you realize. Besides, not a lot of BAU agents start off with juvey records for B&E."

Fisher laughed. "You did do your homework. What can I say? It was the eighties in the Bronx."

Nick stepped inside, followed by Sergeant Lee, and finally, Fisher walked through before closing the door behind him.

"Okay, boss. What are we looking for?" Fisher asked.

Nick walked into the kitchen. "Reid and Walsh took the

photos, so if Slocum had returned after that, he'd know that we figured out his relationship with Jenny Floyd."

"Meaning?" Fisher pressed on.

"Meaning, he might believe his choices were limited. And that he might start to feel cornered."

"Um, excuse me, Agent Scarborough." Sergeant Lee approached from the living room. "I think I might've found something." He glanced toward the small bathroom adjacent to the living room.

They followed him back.

"Don't know if your people saw this or not. Or maybe Slocum had returned briefly, but it looks like he had some sort of operation here. You said he was pushing drugs."

"That's right," Nick began. "This looks like where he was making up his own compound."

Fisher picked up a prescription bottle from behind the bathroom door. "What's this?" He held it up and examined it. "It's an Oxy script in Lynn Floyd's name. No way Walsh and Reid didn't see this. And all this shit on the counter. No. It looks staged to me," Fisher added. "Come on. You know Reid better than any of us. You said she's got some sort of weird sixth sense about her. I've already seen a glimpse of it. And Walsh, yeah, no way they'd have missed this."

"What's the explanation?" Lee asked.

"Who would've come here after the fact? After we started connecting the dots?" Nick asked.

"Horton? You think Billy Horton might've come here, set this up, and then drove to the mine to collect his stockpile?" Fisher asked.

"To what end?" Nick added.

"Maybe he knows more about what's happening than he's letting on. Looking to frame Slocum for something else too."

Nick considered Fisher's comment. "Maybe we should go back to the station and have a word with Horton. Like you said, he might know more than he's sharing right now and just sitting back letting us chase our tails." He turned to Lee. "That work for you?"

"Yes, sir."

~

WALSH PEERED THROUGH THE WINDSHIELD OF THE PATROL car. "You'd think they'd tear this shit down, you know? All these shitty trailers. Just attracting junkies."

"I know y'all are from D.C. and so you don't know how things go around here in Kentucky," Lazaro began. "This problem, this epidemic of drug abuse, opioids and shit. It ain't getting any better. And I don't reckon it will until the jobs come back. It's the rural areas, these small towns that used to thrive. They're suffering the most. So when you say just tear the shit down, that don't change nothing. They'll just find someplace else to go. We need help here."

"No. You're right. I apologize. I don't mean to be insensitive. I'm not from here, and as an outsider, I only see the outside of things. Maybe if we saw the people here for what they are, maybe then the people responsible in D.C. will do something to help."

"We need to say that in our report when this is all over," Duncan replied.

"We'd surely appreciate that, ma'am. Any help we can get." Lazaro pulled near one of the trailers. "Let's find someone to talk to. See if anyone around here has seen Slocum today."

~

KATE STOOD OVER THE GRAVE OF JENNY FLOYD. "SOMEONE was here recently. These flowers look pretty fresh."

"Could've been her parents," Quinn replied. "I don't see any fresh footprints and these flowers look to be a couple days old, at least."

Kate placed her hands on her hips and surveyed the cemetery. "Scarborough and Fisher are at Slocum's house—again. Walsh and Duncan are heading out to Devil's Den."

"Guess the only place left is the mines." Officer Shelby approached. "No one's been back there yet, right?"

"I was earlier. That's where I found Horton. Lazaro did say Slocum went there sometimes, but I don't know. I'd say we can head out that way, but let's take our time. Look for signs of him along the way," Quinn replied. "I'm starting to think he's long gone. And I'm running out of ideas."

"We're looking for a cop. He knows what to do to keep hidden or slip away undetected. There's no chance he's still in his own car," Kate said. "Crown Pointe isn't that big a place. With the hours we've spent piecing this together, and the delay in setting up road blocks, we might have missed our window."

"We'll check the mines again after hitting some of the side streets and wherever else Shelby thinks we should go since he's familiar with the place," Quinn said. "But let's be prepared to issue a statewide BOLO. If we have to widen this search, then that's what we have to do. I won't lose him."

THE TWO LEAD BAU AGENTS ALONG WITH THEIR ESCORT, Sergeant Lee, returned to the station. Daylight was slipping away and the prospect of reaching the night without having found their killer would virtually seal the fate of the investigation. Slocum would be in the wind.

Inside, Billy Horton had his feet up on a desk and his cuffed hands in his lap. John Floyd was stretched out on a chair, arms folded across his wide belly, and dozing away. Lynn Floyd had already been placed in holding. And the only person who stayed onsite was Chief Tate. A man who, it seemed, was still coming to terms with the fact that one of his own was responsible for the horrific murders in his town.

"Didn't expect y'all to be back so soon." Chief stood from behind Lazaro's desk. "I see you've come back empty handed."

"Not entirely." Fisher placed the homemade compound tools onto the desk.

"What the hell you got there?" he asked.

"A mortar and pestle, syringes, and a silicone mold. The tools necessary to make your own drug compound."

"Where did this come from?" Chief asked.

"Eric Slocum's," Nick replied. "But what we don't know is whether these were there when Walsh and Reid searched his place. Because my guess is, if all this was just sitting in the bathroom where Lee found it, our people would have seen it."

"And if it wasn't?" the chief continued.

"Then someone put it there for a reason." Nick turned to Billy Horton. "And I think you might be that person."

25

The grey Ford Taurus traveled up the dirt road of the abandoned mining operation while the sun set below the hills.

"I worked here for a time." The steering wheel shuddered in Jensen's hands as he tried to steady it. The shocks on his Taurus were already worn and the pitted roadway made the drive all the more difficult.

Slocum was only partially hidden in the foot well of the back seat. "I remember when everyone worked here. Was a long time ago. Lot's changed since then."

"Yes, it has." He continued to traverse the slopes that had grown steeper and more difficult to climb. "I reckon we can stop up here, just ahead. Plenty of cover to keep us out of sight till we can catch a break and make our way out of town. Besides, don't think this old girl will make it up any farther."

"Is that how you knew about this place? Cause you used to work here?" Slocum asked.

"Yes, sir. I know the mines well. Too well." He stopped the car and pulled the keys from the ignition. "You want to keep hold of these?"

Slocum reached for the keys and snatched them away. He pushed off the blanket and crawled outside and in a long stretch, he surveyed the area.

Jensen soon joined him. "How'd you end up in this shit mess anyway?"

"Like I told you, I tried to help someone. Things got out of hand is all."

"Sure. Yeah. I understand. And what about Billy Horton got you worked up enough to want to snuff him out?"

"Horton's the devil himself. Brought a lot of the trouble with him. If I'd known sooner..." Slocum trailed off and turned to Jensen. "Why the hell you go out to Devil's Den anyway? You don't seem like the rest of them out there."

"It's either there or the streets. Apartment ain't mine. It's a friend's. At least, I think we're friends. Hard to say nowadays. Stay there once in a while is all. Got no job." Jensen locked eyes with Slocum. "You don't look like a cold-blooded killer either, but there you go."

Slocum's eyes turned dark. "Best you don't forget that."

SHELBY DROVE THROUGH THE RESIDENTIAL STREETS OF THE town as they continued to search for any signs of Slocum.

When an apartment building appeared in the distance, Kate sat up and took notice. "Hang on. What kind of truck does Slocum drive again? Shelby, slow down."

Quinn flipped through the file on his lap. "2001 red F-150, extended cab."

"Pull in there. I think I see it."

Shelby drove into the parking lot and pulled up next to the truck. "You think he's here?" The kid, who was still pretty green, appeared nervous.

"Only one way to find out." Kate unlocked her door.

"Wait," Quinn said. "If he's inside one of these units, he's bound to be watching. And he's most likely armed. We get out low and slow with sidearms ready."

They emerged from the patrol car using its doors for cover. Kate crouched down and started toward the rear of the truck just a few feet away.

"Shelby, I want you to stick with me." Quinn headed for the building, using other cars and shrubbery to shield them from the view of the apartment windows facing the parking lot.

"How are we going to know which apartment he's in?" Shelby asked.

"If he's in one of these, he knows we're here and as soon as he spots Reid at his truck, he'll either try for the door and make a run for it, or he'll just start shooting."

"I don't like either one of those scenarios, Agent Quinn."

"Neither do I. Just stay close."

Kate jumped into the back of the truck, still low and staying out of view of the building. She crawled to the back window and looked inside. Light was scarce and it was tough to see, but in the back seat, something jutted out from under it. "Oh my God." A quick glance to her right and she saw Quinn and Shelby making their way to the first floor corridor. She was on her own. They were too far to call back without someone hearing.

Kate would have to take a chance and bust in through the window. What was in that back seat, she was certain, was the murder weapon. If Slocum was here, he'd make his presence known the instant the glass shattered. The others were in a safe spot at the moment. The risk to their safety would be minimal.

However, she stood the most to lose if he charged out after her. "He's not here. He wouldn't still be here." Kate convinced herself, and with the butt of her gun, smashed the sliding glass panel of the rear window.

"What the hell?" Quinn spun his head in Kate's direction. "Shit." His eyes scanned every door and window, waiting for someone to come out. Curtains pulled back in one of the windows and Quinn aimed his weapon. "It's not him."

Shelby nearly froze, but managed to keep close to Quinn. "What are we going to do?"

"We're going to get over there and protect her. Now!"

Keeping as much cover as possible, they rushed back to her.

"Reid! What the hell?" Quinn reached the tailgate.

"It's the bat. I see the bat!" She eyed him. "He's not here. We'd know it by now. Quinn, we need to get that bat. Help me get inside."

"Shelby, I need you to cover us. Can you do that?"

"Um, yes. Yes, I can. Go." He seemed to find his courage and started toward the front of the truck, gun raised, with his eyes on the building.

Quinn jumped inside and helped Kate clear the glass. "You got some damn nerve doing this, Reid."

"I had to. I saw it and you were too far away. Quinn, he's not here. He's gone. But the murder weapon isn't. This is what we needed and now we've got it. Slocum's our killer."

DEPUTY SLOCUM GOT THE FEELING THAT JENSEN WOULD TRY anything to escape. He was smarter than he'd given him credit for. "Might as well find a spot for shelter. We're gonna be here a while." Slocum made his way toward several boulders that were placed in such a manner as to almost form a cave beneath it. "Looks like as good a spot as any." He sat down and pointed the gun at Jensen. "Sit. You're making me nervous looking over me like that. You don't want me to be nervous."

"No, sir," Jensen moaned and his knees cracked as he sat down next to him.

Slocum wondered if he could survive the night here. He had almost the entire county's law enforcement after him now. Who the hell would think to come here? "Billy Horton."

"What's that?" Jensen asked.

"Nothing." Slocum turned quiet again, but his head was spinning. Horton wanted payback for the loss of customers. He knew that Slocum and Lynn Floyd were working together. The kid had more moles in town than a golf course. Someone said something to him. This was exactly the reason he needed to take care of Horton himself. He was the primary dealer. The man who worked with the cartels out of Lexington. Only these weren't the typical, movie-type cartels. No. These were local folks who worked with the doctors on prescriptions, then when that got too hot, they started buying from the syndicates in Louisville. There were plenty of Central and South American drug cartels in this country. But here in Kentucky, these were local boys doing a local service.

"WE DIDN'T WANT TO WASTE ANY MORE TIME RUNNING THIS back to the station." Kate spoke on her phone while Shelby continued driving toward the mine. "But this is the murder weapon. And it came from Slocum's truck. I'll text you the address and you can have the chief arrange for it to be towed back as evidence."

"And you're confident he's at the mines?" Nick asked.

"Not at all. But we can't overlook it. We've checked everywhere and now we know for certain he's not in his own vehicle. He could have help from someone at the apartment, or..."

"He could've taken someone hostage," Nick said.

"Yes."

"Okay. Go check it out. We're working on getting information out of this Horton kid. He knows more than he's letting on. Keep me posted. Walsh and Duncan are with Lazaro and I need to call them for an update. Kate, I'm not feeling good about this."

"Neither am I, but what choice do we have?"

"Be careful."

Kate ended the call. "Scarborough says they found evidence Slocum was forming his own compound. Found the materials at his house. They're back at the station questioning Horton. But I don't know what good that will do."

"He's the boss. He must have something planned," Quinn said. "Looks like these guys up ahead are all set."

The road block ahead was marked by two patrol cars angled across the lanes, effectively blocking any vehicle that tried to pass it.

"We should stop and have a word with them," Kate said. "They might've seen something."

"That's what the BOLO is for, Agent Reid." Shelby drove nearer to the cars. "Surely they would've called something in."

"Yes, but what I mean to say is I want to know if anyone has been through here. We know Slocum's got a new ride and he has friends here. Maybe one of them is looking to get him out of town."

Two officers stepped out of their cars and all met in the middle of the roadway.

"Evening," Quinn began. "Have you guys seen any activity around here?"

"Afraid not, Agent Quinn," one of the officers replied. "And with the sun on its way down, I'm starting to feel like the deputy is long gone."

"We're heading up to the mines again," Kate said. "We found his truck, but not him. So, we're going to run through here. It's possible, because of his affiliation with Horton, he might've decided to come looking for him here."

"That's a big place with plenty of spots to hide. But at this point, I don't see as you have much to lose," the officer added.

"Neither do we."

"We'll move out so you can pass."

The officers hopped back inside their patrol cars and pulled back.

The others returned to the car and stepped inside. Shelby keyed the ignition. "Everyone seems to be losing hope of finding him."

Kate closed her door. "I haven't given up just yet. Sometimes, you just get a feeling, you know?"

SLOCUM TOOK A LEAK IN FRONT OF A TREE THAT HAD GROWN in the previously mined area. That was when he spotted a minor puff of dirt rise in the air. "Hey." He quickly zipped his pants and returned to the makeshift cave. "Hey, I think someone's here."

"What?" Jensen stood and peeked over the boulders. "You sure, 'cause I don't see nothing."

"Over there." Slocum pointed. "See that cloud of dust. That could be a car. Shit." He scanned the area for another place to hide. "We have to get out of here before they find us."

"Deputy, now just keep your cool. That could be a car, but it could also just be a dust devil. Let's sit tight until we see any other signs of life around here." He needed to keep Slocum calm or risk him panicking and possibly shooting him. This was a desperate man and a brutal killer and Jensen couldn't forget that. There was nothing stopping Slocum from taking another life.

"Just keep your eyes peeled, then." Slocum held his gaze firmly in the distance. "Shit. How the hell would they know I was here?"

"They wouldn't. That's what I'm telling you. We don't know anyone's down there right now." Slocum was starting to lose his shit. Jensen had to work fast to keep him relaxed.

"How about I walk down a ways and get a better view?" He raised his hands in submission. "I promise I won't do nothing stupid. And if I've done anything today, it's to prove to you I ain't no liar."

Slocum waved his gun, giving the man permission to walk ahead. "You best not leave my sight."

"I won't." The out of shape, middle-aged man started back down the hill. He turned his head to make sure he kept eye contact with Slocum. A few steps farther. He couldn't see anyone. No car. No more dust. But as he made his way down a little more, he saw it. The tiniest amount of dust rising in the air. Like tires running over the crushed gravel driveway. This could be his chance.

He again turned his head back and raised his hands to show Slocum he was still okay and still in his view. But when he turned around again, Jensen reached into his pocket and turned on the cell phone. Slocum's phone had tumbled from his pocket in the back seat and he spotted it when he reached inside to get the blanket for them to sit on. The phone had been turned off. But he knew that by turning it on, the feds would track his GPS location. Jensen dropped the cell phone just off the path—it was on.

He turned and walked up the hill. With a shake of his head and a shrug of his shoulders, he signified no one was there. And on his return, he reiterated his theory. "I didn't see no one. It must've been a dust devil you saw. Best get back to the shelter. That sun will be behind the mountain soon. Once it gets dark out here, we won't be able to see nothing till morning."

Slocum was hesitant, as though the man hadn't fully convinced him that no one was out there. "You sure you didn't see nothing?"

"You can go look for yourself, but you'd be wasting your energies. No one will find you here. That's why we came. We just need to ride out the night and take a fresh look in the morning at a way to get you out of Crown Pointe."

"ANYONE GOT A FLASHLIGHT?" KATE SAID UPON ENTERING the trailer. "It's too dark in here." She found a light switch, but it didn't work. "Didn't think there'd still be power here, but it was worth a shot." She reached for her phone and turned on its flashlight function.

"Here, I got a light." The officer turned on his police-issued flashlight. "You might want to conserve your phone's battery."

"Thanks," Kate replied. "So this was where you said Billy Horton kept his drugs?"

"Yes. It was just dumb luck he came here when he did," Quinn began. "That cabinet there. Heroin and some pills."

"Did he expose his supplier?" Kate continued.

"No. That could be what Scarborough and Fisher are hoping to get from him. I don't know. Slocum's definitely not in here though. What do you want to do? It's getting too dark to drive through the mines. It'd be too dangerous, especially since we don't know our way around here." His phone buzzed in his pocket. "Hang on." He answered the line. "Quinn here."

Kate looked on as Quinn listened to whoever was on the other end of the line.

"Are you sure?" Quinn added.

At this, Kate perked up. "What is it?" she whispered to him.

"Okay. We'll find him. It's getting dark. We'll have to take precautions." Quinn nodded. "Thank you. Let me know when you're here. I'm not sure how good the signal will be as we make our way inside, so we might lose contact." He ended the call and peered at Kate. "That was Scarborough. Ness had Slocum's cell phone traced. Except that it appeared he had kept it off until about twenty minutes ago. They pinged it. He's here. Slocum's here."

"Where?" Kate asked.

"They can't pinpoint his location any closer than here at the mines. Scarborough wants us to track him down by any means necessary. We're going to have to get out there and find him."

"How are we going to do that without giving up our location?" Shelby asked. "He'll get spooked if he sees headlights."

"From my perspective," Kate began, "we have two options. Drive with no lights, risk running into God knows what, and hope he doesn't hear the car. Or take to foot—split up and try to track him down."

"I don't like the idea of splitting up," Quinn replied.

"This operation covers almost one hundred acres," Shelby began. "Rough terrain. Abandoned shafts that haven't been filled or closed properly. Not only will it take time, but it will be dangerous. And if we're on our own, the risk of one of us getting hurt is high. With no one around to help, it's a chance I'm not sure I'm willing to take."

"We have phones," Kate said.

"I'd be surprised if we keep a signal out there," Shelby continued. "I don't know, Agent Reid. I know we need to catch him. But if he's up there alone, what's the harm in waiting it out? He'll have to come down sooner or later. He won't survive up there."

"Kid has a point," Quinn said. "Unless Slocum took an ample

supply of water and food, he's going to have to come back down sooner or later."

"On the other hand, what if he gets injured or is already injured and he's in trouble up there right now? Why was his phone turned on?" Kate asked. "He could've tried to call a friend for help. You want to wait it out? He could be dead by tomorrow."

"Would that be so bad?" Shelby asked. "I'm sorry. I didn't mean it."

"It's okay. It's not like it didn't enter my mind too," Kate said. "We also have to consider the possibility he's not alone. That he already has help—or a hostage—who helped him get here. Right now, we just don't know."

"Damn it." Quinn heaved a deep sigh. "If he's got a hostage..."

"Then we go up there." Kate looked at the men. "Scarborough wants us to find him, right?"

"He does. And they're coming now to help, but it'll still be a good 30 minutes."

"Then there's our answer. When they show up, it'll be dark and I'll bet at the top of this hill, anyone could spot a car coming a mile away. If that happens, whoever's with him might not survive. We'll take to foot. And we'll track him down."

"So we're splitting up?" Shelby asked.

"We're splitting up. Unless you don't want to join us. You don't have to. I'm not your boss," Kate said.

"No. I want to."

"Okay, then. Let's pack some waters and head out."

26

The chief pressed his hand against the window sill and looked through, beyond the station's parking lot and into the woods ahead. The sun faded, leaving a faint hue of purple and orange in the winter sky. "It'll take us a good half hour to get to the mines. By that time, it'll be completely dark." He turned back toward the agents. "The mines are a dangerous place during the day, let alone at night. And yet you instructed your people to go out and find Slocum."

"We can't let our guard down. He has to be brought in—tonight. Scarborough made the right call," Ness replied.

Fisher's phone rang, and as he retrieved it, he noted the caller ID. "It's Walsh. I need to take this." He stepped into the corridor. "Where are you?"

"We took a ride out to the Devil's Den on Lazaro's advice in hopes of talking to someone who might've seen something. Lazaro thought we might find the guy he talked to a few days ago, but no luck there."

"Agent Ness just picked up a cell signal from Slocum's phone.

He's at the abandoned mining operation north of town. We were just putting a plan together to head out there. Quinn and Reid are already there, but they need backup. Just come back to the station, ASAP."

"We're on our way," Walsh ended the call.

Fisher returned to the others. "Walsh and Duncan are heading back with Lazaro. They didn't find anything, but I told them we're going out to the mines. We need everyone on board for this one."

The chief eyed Horton. "What do we want to do about this boy and the Floyds?"

Nick peered at the old man. "Get him out of here. Let him go."

"I'm afraid I can't do that. Regardless of his intentions, the man is still a drug dealer," Chief replied.

"His wife is behind bars for conspiracy to commit murder. John's not going anywhere, are you, John?" Nick asked.

"No, sir."

"Captain Lowell, can you keep Horton and Lynn Floyd company with Deputy Lazaro? I'd like the chief to come out there with us. He might be the only one Slocum will listen to."

"Consider it done, Agent Scarborough."

QUINN WALKED DOWN THE STEPS OF THE TRAILER AND joined Kate and Officer Shelby as they stood on the dirt lot."

"How's your cell battery?"

Kate peered into the growing darkness at the grounds of the operation before answering, "Seventy percent. I should be good for a while."

"Got about eighty here," Shelby replied. "I'm good. So long as we don't spend all night up there. I can promise you, though, I ain't going near one of them shafts. I wouldn't trust the company that left this place in such a condition."

"I don't want any of us to get hurt out there," Quinn said. "So let's just stick to the paths where the heavy equipment traveled. Should be a level enough surface. Just keep your weapon ready. We have no idea the condition Slocum will be in or his state of mind, let alone whoever might be with him."

"I'll go straight ahead," Kate began. "One of you head left and the other right. Unless anyone else has a better plan?"

"Nope. If anyone gets into trouble, get a message out by any means possible. Head back down, if absolutely necessary. We won't be out here alone for long. As soon as I get sight of the others, I'll do my best to get a call out to Scarborough and let him know our positions." Quinn checked his weapon and his phone. "Be safe." He headed right.

"Guess that leaves you to head left," Kate said. "Good luck, Shelby."

"Same to you, Agent Reid."

Kate drew in the cold night air and took a step forward. The road ahead was steep and appeared to be the main ingress and egress from the mines to the boundary of the operation. She started up the hill.

The dirt road was littered with rocks, weeds, and even metal pieces, probably from the earthmoving equipment that traversed this road for many years. And the slope of the hill began to burn her thighs. It had been too long since her last PT test and she could feel it now, regretting not visiting the gym more often.

She checked her phone. "Still a signal, good." Of course, the more she pressed the home screen button, the more battery power she would use, as well as illuminating the ever-darkening sky. But it put her at ease as if she wasn't completely alone, even though she was.

The occasional intermittent flash of light from the others suggested they weren't any farther ahead than she was and were likely only a few hundred feet on either side of her.

And then it occurred to her, for whatever reason, be it because she was alone, or that she was about to come face to face, once again, with a killer. But there it was. Seven years. It had been seven years since her life redirected to this path. The time seemed almost incomprehensible. And Nick had been at her side for virtually all of it, leading her, guiding her to her destiny. But this place—where she was now—this was her choice. It was her decision to join BAU. Yes, Nick had been there and it seemed a logical decision. But in truth, she'd wanted to be here because of Quinn. Because of his expertise. It seemed she was well on her way to becoming an expert in her own right—without Nick's help. It was an important distinction for Kate. He might have led her here, but the end game was hers and hers alone. She would one day be better than Quinn. It wasn't an affront on his character or his experience, it was just a fact that she knew in her heart.

She also knew he would try to use her. He'd already shown his hand in some respects. She wasn't a woman who would sit idly by and allow herself to be used. Perhaps he was doing it to better his own career or to grow in his own knowledge. The reason didn't matter. The action did. Kate liked Quinn. There was no question about that. But he was who he was and she knew that too. There would come a time when they would be confronted with that fact.

But until then, she would learn from him. And yes, perhaps give him the crumbs to keep him from getting too close to her truth. Nick was the only man who knew who she really was and he accepted her.

There was, however, a man she was beginning to view as an ally, besides Nick. A man who reminded her of someone she lost a long time ago. Levi Walsh would become that ally. Their bond would be unbreakable. She saw it as clearly as she saw what Quinn was. Although Nick would be her love, always, Walsh would be her friend, her confidant, her champion.

People always told Kate she had a keen intuition. Well, that intuition was telling her who she would become. And that person was going to be a force with which to be reckoned.

THE TEMPERATURE DROPPED AND THE LIGHT ALL BUT extinguished. How long would it be before Slocum realized his cell phone was gone? How much time did Jensen have left to live? The silence forced him to listen to the sound of his own heavy breathing. Years of smoking and drugs left him with a black chest full of toxins and a heart that labored with only a few steps. Perhaps this was to be the end of the man who had no life anyway. No love, no family. Simply living day to day, driven by his growing addictions.

He peered at Slocum, who sipped on what remained of the water. There were more supplies in his car, which was tucked away several hundred feet from their present location. It wasn't likely he would die of thirst. But then, that was the least of his concerns.

The cell phone battery wouldn't last forever. Had they picked up on the signal yet? How thick were these agents anyway? He'd handed Slocum to them on a silver platter, and yet they were still not here to take him.

"How long's it take for you to take a piss?" Slocum asked. "You thinking of trying something?"

Jensen zipped his fly and walked back over to the makeshift shelter. "No, sir. Just looking at the sky is all."

"Yeah, well, you're risking being seen, so just plant yourself here, all right?"

He squatted down, his knees crackling from the pressure, until his backside rested on the cold dirt.

"Damn it. I don't want to be stuck up here all night. It's getting cold." He turned to Jensen. "I'm going to get my jacket in the car. And yours too." He stood up. "You stay here. I'll do it, old man. I can hear your breathing from a mile away. You should consider exercising once in a while." Slocum started back down the road toward the car.

"Shit." The phone was down there too, and now Jensen wondered if he'd see it. It would only take him slipping his hand in his pants pocket to jog his memory that his phone was no longer there. Either way, he was screwed. So what were his options? Hope the feds picked up the signal and were on their way? Or take his chances, bad lungs and all, and high-tail it the hell out of there; risk falling down a shaft or a retention pond or any number of serious hazards the operation held within these grounds.

Jensen's chances for survival were diminishing by the second. He'd been so clever. Telling Slocum exactly what he'd wanted to hear. Manipulated him like a pro. But to what end? This? "Shit. I can't just sit here and wait." Jensen stood up again and spotted what he thought was a flash of light in the distance. "What the...?" But the problem was, he didn't know if it was Slocum or someone coming to save him from this disastrous predicament. With no weapon of any kind at his disposal, his options were few. Slocum had a gun, he was a much younger man, and he was a monstrous killer. The trifecta of being screwed. Maybe what he saw was Slocum himself, which would mean he'd found his cell phone.

It occurred to Jensen that he could still work his way out of this if that was the case, simply by assuming Slocum must've dropped the cell phone himself. It was plausible and Slocum just might buy it.

The light was gone. He waited. Still no Slocum. Jensen swallowed down the lump in his throat. For the first time in many years, he was truly afraid. Had he pulled it off, or had he only delayed the inevitable?

∾

KATE CROUCHED DOWN AT THE FLASH OF LIGHT AHEAD. IT disappeared as quickly as it had appeared. It could've been Shelby or Quinn; she couldn't be sure. Hell, if she was supposing, it could've also been Slocum. But that would be too easy. Her journey into the treacherous grounds had only begun minutes ago. That kind of luck rarely came her way. Still, she had to follow it, just to rule it out.

Kate veered to the right and followed the path where she spotted the brief light. In the dark, however, it was a difficult course to maintain. She needed light to guide her way. "Just for a minute." She retrieved her flashlight and aimed it in the direction for just a moment, then quickly dowsed it. Moving slowly, Kate was careful to avoid pitfalls or injury. Boulders, equipment, potholes. The potential for physical damage was extreme. She wondered if the rest of the team had arrived. And if so, were they also making their way onto the grounds? It might be a foolish action that could leave Slocum with no alternative but to fight. And with a hostage, friend or enemy, there was an additional life at stake.

A smaller dirt road, perhaps used by pickup trucks and such, revealed itself ahead of her. This was the path she would converge upon. This was where the light came from. And the farther she traveled down it, the less likely it became that this was the way of one of her own team. Quinn had headed much farther right. Now that the sun was down, her sense of direction almost vanished. It was unfortunate that that particular sense wasn't also heightened. In fact, she had a terrible sense of direction, but so long as she kept on this road, she felt it would lead her to her prey.

~

SLOCUM RETURNED AND HIS EXPRESSION STRUCK FEAR INTO Jensen's heart. He would have to think fast because he knew what was coming.

"Did you see that?" Slocum asked.

Jensen appeared oblivious. "See what?"

"Are you serious? You didn't see that fucking light in the distance? They're here. They found me." Slocum held the jackets in his arms and tossed them to the ground. "I also found this." He held his phone into view. "Now I distinctly remember turning this off. Funny how it's on now. Oh, and that the feds are climbing up this hill as I speak." He raised his gun, aiming it at Jensen's head.

"I don't know what to say. I guess you must've dropped it or something."

"And it mysteriously turned itself on?"

"Anything's possible. Look, Deputy, I been nothing but cooperative with you this whole time. I told you I ain't stupid and that would've been a stupid move on my part. You have to believe me. I mean, if I did find and turn on your phone, don't you think I would've called 911 or something instead of just leaving it somewhere?"

By the look on Slocum's face, he just might have swayed him. It was still too early to be sure, but the tide appeared to be shifting in his direction.

Slocum appeared to consider his explanation and Jensen

didn't want to squander the opportunity by allowing him to think on it further. Slocum still needed him to get him out and he had to use that fact to his advantage. "Look, if they are here, we'd best get a move on before they track us down." Something caught Jensen's eyes. He saw someone.

"What? You see something?" Slocum cocked his gun and turned on his heel.

"Stop! FBI!" Kate appeared before he could complete his turn. "Don't move, Deputy. Our entire team is here. It's over. Now put down your weapon."

Slocum lowered his arm. "Let me guess, it was the signal on my phone?" He shifted his gaze to Jensen only briefly. "Well, I tell you what, Agent Reid. Why the fuck don't you just shoot me then?"

27

Leaves spun in a whirlwind above the asphalt as the chief's Chevy Tahoe sped along the road leading to the mining operation. No street lamps illuminated their way, only the amber beam of the SUV's headlights that shone just a few feet in front of them.

Nick was in the passenger seat and peered at his cell phone. "I've got a weak signal and who knows if that will last the closer we get."

Fisher pulled up between the front seats as he sat in the back seat with Walsh and Duncan. "We picked up the signal from Slocum's phone. There has to be a tower somewhere near there."

"I'll tell you one thing's for sure," Chief Tate began. "If your team is up there scouring around for him, they're crossing some damn dangerous territory. That place ain't safe, which is why it's been fenced off for years."

"I see the roadblock," Nick continued.

The chief slowed to a stop, his headlights shining on the patrol cars ahead. Both officers walked toward the SUV, peering inside.

"Chief," the officer said. "Captain reached out to us. I hear our boy is up there in the mines?"

"You heard right. We're joining the others. You see anything yet?"

"No, sir. Been quiet since your FBI folks went up in there about an hour ago."

"I'll need you boys to keep your eyes peeled. If Slocum starts to feel cornered, he might do something stupid. And right now, we're inclined to believe he might've gotten some help getting up in there."

"We'll be ready, sir."

"Good enough. We best get on through and help those people track him down," the chief said.

The officer nodded and waved to his partner. Both returned to their vehicles and pulled back, allowing the chief's SUV through. They quickly closed the gap again.

Although Nick would never show it, he was concerned for his team, but mostly for Kate. From day one, he always worried about her safety. But if he ever hoped for their new team to accept both of them, accept that there was no favoritism, he had to remain impartial at any cost.

"I see the state patrol car up ahead and that must be Horton's truck at that trailer," Walsh said. "Chief, kill the lights."

With the headlights off, the chief pulled up behind the other car. "I suggest we create a plan of action and hop to it. Every minute that passes is another minute your team could be in danger."

Nick stepped out and looked beyond the chain link fence into the grounds of the operation. He checked his phone once again. "One bar." He turned to Fisher. "You?"

"Same."

"Me, too," Duncan said. "Better than nothing."

"Divide and conquer. It's the only solution." Walsh headed toward the fence, waiting for the others.

Nick regarded Fisher with concern. "We drive and we risk Slocum panicking."

"We walk, and we risk not only injury, but wasting time. Reid and Quinn and that kid trooper are up there now."

"What if we try to make contact? Send a text to our team?" Duncan asked.

"I'm on it." Fisher typed in a message to Reid and Quinn. "I'll tell them we're here and that they can pull back and wait for us."

It was Nick's call to make. And whatever he decided, he had better be right.

KATE AND SLOCUM LOCKED EYES. BOTH HAD WEAPONS AIMED at one another. Even in the dark, she could see the pain and anger in him. "I know you loved her—Jenny. I saw the pictures in your house."

"What the hell do you know? You come down from Washington with your fancy talk about profiling people and you still didn't know it was me."

"I know you didn't act alone. I know Lynn Floyd helped you. She cleaned up your mess because she believed what you two were doing was right, but still couldn't hide her guilt. So many young people. Kids. You not only poisoned them, but you took out your anger on them, too. I found the bat you used. It's time to stop, Eric before you hurt anyone else."

"What the hell does it matter now anyway? I didn't want to kill that girl from the hospital—Lori."

"I know. I don't think you wanted to kill any of them. But pain and revenge took hold of you. I understand the power of those emotions more than you might think."

Slocum laughed. "Yeah, sure you do."

"Why don't you let the man go." Kate briefly shifted her sights to the older man wearing only a tank top and jeans. "You don't need him anymore. You have me."

"Oh, so you gonna offer up a trade? What do you think this is, Agent Reid, some sort of negotiation? We ain't negotiating nothing," Slocum replied.

"Okay. But I should tell you, I'm not the only one out here. There are others approaching and more on the way, including Chief Tate. There's no way out for you, Eric."

"I figured as much. I don't want a way out either. What's the fucking point? This town's turned to shit. Anything good inside it just ends up getting eaten away by a damn cancer."

"I don't believe that," Kate pressed on. "I've seen good people here. I've talked to them. They lost loved ones, same as you. But it made them want to make things better, not worse."

"What's going to happen to Mrs. Floyd?" Slocum asked.

"She'll go to prison. There's no way around that. She helped you kill innocent people."

"Where's Billy Horton?" he asked.

"Last I heard, they brought him in to the station. They got him on possession."

Slocum laughed. "Possession. So he'll spend, what, a year or so behind bars and then he'll be set loose to do the same damn thing. Get people hooked on heroin and shit. He's the problem. And he's the only reason I'm still here."

"You were poisoning human beings. Then you beat the life out of them. I don't see how you're any different from Billy Horton, except he's not a brutal killer. You are." Kate kept an eye on the older man, hoping he wouldn't make any unnecessary moves.

"I was making them people pay for what they did to Jenny. For making her take the drugs too. Billy's the only one left. The only son of a bitch that hasn't been reckoned with yet."

"So you were just doing this to make things right? A reckoning for Jenny?" she asked.

"That's right."

"Well, you know I can't give you Billy Horton. So what do you want to do, Eric?"

Slocum turned the gun on himself and aimed it at his temple. His lips quivered and he swallowed hard.

Jensen stepped back in surprise.

Kate flinched at Jensen's movement and diverted her attention for a split second. Then the spark of light flashed before her eyes. The hot, burning sensation crawled inside her leg. Kate looked down as blood streamed along her thigh, seeping through her pants.

Slocum started to run and soon disappeared into the darkness.

"He's running!" Jensen lurched after him.

"No!" Kate raised her weapon and aimed it at the vanishing figure in the night. Another shot rang out along with a light trail that faded in the path.

A thud sounded.

"You got him." Jensen rushed to Kate's side. "We need to get you some help."

Kate wrapped her arm around him. "I need to see him. I have to know if he's dead. Here, turn this on."

Jensen turned on the flashlight and helped her hobble toward the sound of the thud. Her gun still aimed at the dark.

They came upon him just a short distance away.

"You got him, ma'am."

Slocum was on the ground, his head spilling blood, but his eyes were open.

"He's still alive." Kate grabbed her phone and called Nick.

"I think it's too late, ma'am." Jensen pointed at him. "He's gone now."

THE SOUND OF GUNFIRE BROUGHT QUINN TO ATTENTION. "Shit." He ran in the direction of the sound, though out here, the noise could've bounced around between the hills and mountains of tailings. His best shot was to head back toward the main in-road and up because that was Kate's path. As he ran, he aimed the flashlight to light his way. His legs pumped hard, but his speed was slowed on the rough terrain. "Come on. Come on, Reid. Just call me or something." He feared calling her, unsure if it was she who fired the shot or Eric Slocum. And if she was in trouble, the sound of her phone could make the man flinch and fire on her.

He couldn't be too far away, though. He heard voices in the distance and the faint sound of trotting through the mud and dirt and debris. "That's got to be Shelby."

Within moments, the two spotted one another, each shining a light in the other's eyes.

"It was Agent Reid. The shots came from up there." Quinn pointed toward the top of the hillside. He was out of breath with sweat pouring from his brow. "Let's go!"

THE ECHO OF THE SHOTS REACHED THE TEAM AT THE BOTTOM of the hill, just inside the mine's entrance.

"We don't have time to pussyfoot around. There's trouble and we have no idea if it's the good guys or the bad," Chief said. "Best get back inside the vehicle and drive up the hill."

"Yeah." Nick rushed back to the SUV. "Chief, I need you with me in case you need to talk Slocum down. Fisher, call for help. Get emergency services out here ASAP."

"We should go up there with you, Scarborough. You don't know what you'll be up against," Walsh said.

Nick eyed the rest of his team.

"He's right. Take Walsh and Duncan with you," Fisher replied. "I'll get help down here. Go!"

"MA'AM? WHAT CAN I DO?" JENSEN HELPED KATE TO THE ground as her legs grew unsteady.

"Just put pressure on the wound. Take off my jacket and wrap it around my leg. You have to be quick though, okay?"

"Okay." He helped her take off her jacket and rolled it up lengthwise. "I'm sorry, but I gotta lift your leg a little."

"It's okay. Just do it quickly." Kate grew dizzier by the second. "Where the hell are they?"

Jensen yelled. "Help! Help!" He wrapped her leg and pulled the jacket tightly into a knot.

"Ahhh!" Kate reeled back in pain.

"I'm so sorry, ma'am."

In that moment, a figure appeared and Jensen leaped up. "Who's there?"

"Agent Quinn and Trooper Shelby." Quinn emerged from the shadows with Shelby only steps behind.

"Oh my God, Reid!" He rushed to her side and examined her leg. "What the hell happened?"

"That crazy ass deputy shot her and took off. She took him down, though," Jensen said.

Quinn looked around for a quick exit. "We need to get you the hell out of here."

"I'm getting really dizzy," she said.

"I know." Quinn stood up. "I see headlights. That's gotta be them. That's gotta be Scarborough."

"Christ, they better drive faster." Shelby took over and applied pressure to her wound while Jensen stood back.

The SUV skidded to a stop on the road down about fifty feet from where Kate lay.

Quinn jogged to the car as Nick opened his door. "Reid's been shot. She needs help. Now!"

Nick pushed him out of the way and jumped from the SUV. "Kate!" He ran toward her.

"I'm okay. Slocum's dead."

"You're not okay." Nick slid his arms beneath her and lifted her up.

Walsh quickly approached. "Let me help."

The two carried her while Quinn opened the cargo area and laid down the third-row seat. "Set her down here. Careful!"

"Oh my God." Duncan eyed Reid. "You'll be okay. Fisher called for help."

"There's not enough room for everyone," Shelby said. "I'll stay here with you." He looked at the hostage.

"Name's Sterling Jensen. I'm okay. I'm not hurt."

"Y'all get her out of here," Shelby continued.

The chief tossed his keys to Scarborough. "Go. I need to see to my boy."

"We'll come back up for you." Nick examined Kate's leg. "You're not hurt anywhere else?"

"No."

"I'll drive. You stay back here with her." Quinn reached for the keys. "Walsh, jump in. We need to roll. Now!"

～

THE SMALL HOSPITAL WHERE KATE HAD VISITED THE YOUNG woman, Lori, less than forty-eight hours earlier, was now the place she was being wheeled into at this very moment.

"She's been shot. Right leg. It didn't hit her femoral artery. She'd be gone already," Nick said to the doctor.

"Let's get her back to surgery." He barked the order at the two nurses who flanked him.

Kate looked at Nick as they pulled her away. She smiled and disappeared beyond the doors.

The team waited for Nick in the lobby.

Walsh was the first to approach him and he placed his hand on Nick's shoulder. "She'll be all right. They'll take good care of her."

The anger balled in Nick's chest and climbed to the surface. "How the fuck did this happen? Where the hell were you, Quinn?"

"We split up and tried to find Slocum because he had a hostage. You said find him. And that's what we did." Quinn grew defensive.

"Hey, this isn't the time or the place," Fisher began. "Quinn and Reid made the call together. It was their best chance at finding Slocum. You know that."

"I know you want to lash out right now, but you got to keep your shit together. Kate needs you," Walsh pressed on.

Nick closed his eyes. "I'm sorry." He returned his attention to the team. "I won't second-guess any of you. You know what you're supposed to do and how to do it. I'm out of line."

"It's okay. We understand. But she'll pull through just fine," Duncan replied.

"Look, why don't you guys head back to the station house. Brief Ness and the rest of them. I'll stay here," Nick said.

"You sure?" Walsh asked.

"I'm sure."

THE CHIEF HAD ALREADY RETURNED ALONG WITH SHELBY and the hostage. It was then Billy Horton decided to speak up.

"I gotta say something here. I know Slocum's dead and all, but the shit that just went down. It's crazy as fuck."

"What are you trying to say, boy?" Chief Tate asked.

"I—I gave Eric the names of them people who were friends with Jenny Floyd. I didn't know what he wanted them for. I swear it. He just said it would keep me out of trouble."

"You seem to be offering up a lot of useful information." Ness turned to the chief. "Suppose he's looking for a way out of this."

"I suppose he is."

Ness turned back to Horton. "I'll tell you what, you tell us what you know. And I mean everything, including the name of your supplier. We might just be able to work something out, considering the fact that you gave him those names and essentially signed their death warrants. Whatever you can give might go a long way to keeping you from spending the rest of your life behind bars."

NICK STOOD NEXT TO KATE'S BED AND BRUSHED THE STRANDS of dark hair away from her face. "Hey. You're awake. How you feeling?"

"Okay. They must have me on some good painkillers."

"I'm sure they do." He examined her, lying in a hospital bed, as he'd done in the past. Only this time, she was his girl, not anyone else's. And it hurt much worse than before. "I'm sorry I wasn't there with you."

Kate held his gaze as steadily as she could. "I'm glad you weren't."

"What?"

"Nick, you can't be there for me every time. You have to let me be what I'm supposed to be. You're the one who taught me that, remember?"

"I do. Of course I do."

"How are the others?"

"Fine. Everyone's fine. They're all back at the station house."

"You should head back there too. Between Ness' office, the state police, and us? You're going to have to run interference and get everyone on the same page. I'll be fine now. Besides, I'm tired. I should sleep."

He nodded. "Yeah. Okay. If you're sure."

"I am."

He bent over to kiss her and placed his hand on her cheek. "I love you, Kate."

"I love you too."

THE TEAM WAITED IN THE CONFERENCE ROOM BACK AT Quantico, ready for a briefing and to close out the remainder of the Slocum investigation.

With Nick finally arriving, he sat down at the head of the table. "I just got off the phone with Ness. Slocum's DNA was a match to what was found on the bat as well as all of the victims. Except for Wyatt Cavanaugh, his death was caused by an overdose. According to Chief Tate, Lynn Floyd signed a confession for her involvement. She'll be charged with conspiracy to commit murder, but the drug charges were dropped for her cooperation."

"What about the husband?" Quinn asked.

"Possession with intent to sell. First offense. He probably won't serve any time. But it does appear he had no idea what his wife had done."

Duncan leaned back in her chair. "All those lives taken for revenge by people who you'd never believe had the proclivity for such things."

"And what about our boy Billy Horton?" Fisher asked.

"Turns out, Quinn and Reid weren't far off with the cartel connection," Nick gave a nod to Quinn. "He gave up his supplier in exchange for a plea deal, according to the DEA. But it's unlikely he'll serve any time for conspiracy to commit murder."

"Can't prove he knew what Slocum was going to do," Quinn added.

"No."

Kate hobbled in on her crutches.

"Hey! You're back." Walsh stood up to help her inside. "Didn't think you were coming in until next week."

"I didn't want to miss the meeting. I won't stay long." She eyed the rest of the team. "I just want to thank you all for what you did back in Crown Pointe. I mean, I could've, well, just—thanks." Kate was rarely at a loss for words, but it was difficult to express just how grateful she was to this new team of hers.

Duncan examined Kate's leg for a moment. "You know, I've never been shot before. You get my vote for Agent of the Month for taking that bullet."

"Well, this isn't the first time I've been shot," Kate said.

"It isn't?"

"No. He shot me once." She darted a look to Nick.

"One time! You shoot somebody one time and they never let you forget it."

And that was it. Whatever tensions remained among this team of six had simply vanished amid the laughter.

"You shot her? What the hell, Scarborough?" Duncan added.

"I do love telling people that," Kate said.

"I know you do," Nick replied. "Now, if you want to take a seat and join us, Agent Reid, I'll continue."

"I apologize for the interruption. Please, go on." Kate sat down and listened as Nick finished his summary of the investigation. She would be okay. Now she knew that these people accepted her —and Nick.

There were things Kate still needed to do. If she wanted to get inside Quinn's head, she would have to let him get inside hers. And the only way to do that was to bring down her walls. If he wanted to know about Hendrickson, she would give him every last juicy detail.

If it meant becoming a better agent, a better profiler—perhaps even better than Quinn, then she would do it. Nothing was going to stop her from being who she was destined to become.

THE END

ABOUT THE AUTHOR

Robin Mahle has published more than 30 novels in the mystery/thriller genre. She also writes historical fiction as <u>Christine Chase.</u>

It is Robin's fast-paced style of storytelling combined with tense action and thrilling twists that bring her readers back for more. So be sure sure to subscribe to her newsletter to keep up on all the latest releases, sales, and giveaways. Go to <u>robinmahle.com</u> and sign up today!

Robin lives in Coastal Virginia with her husband and two children.

If you enjoyed Ms. Mahle's work, please share your experience by leaving a review on <u>Amazon.</u>

ALSO BY ROBIN MAHLE

The Kate Reid FBI Thriller Series (17 books)

The Chef (stand-alone psych thriller)

The Man in My Attic (stand-alone psych thriller)

The Compound (standalone psych thriller)

The Remy Fontaine Fugitive Hunter Thrillers (4 books)

The Det. Rebecca Ellis Thrillers (5 books)

The Allison Hart PI Thrillers (5 Books)

The Lacy Merrick Thrillers (4 books)

**Sign up to receive Robin's Newsletter on her website robinmahle.com so you can stay up to date on her new releases, events, contests and even exclusive new material!

www.ingramcontent.com/pod-product-compliance
Lightning Source LLC
Chambersburg PA
CBHW062117170626
46813CB00002B/479